ELIZA HARWELL

Shelter

Book 1 in the Bridging Divides Series

Copyright © 2020 by Eliza Harwell

All rights reserved. No part of this publication may be reproduced, stored or transmitted in any form or by any means, electronic, mechanical, photocopying, recording, scanning, or otherwise without written permission from the publisher. It is illegal to copy this book, post it to a website, or distribute it by any other means without permission.

This novel is entirely a work of fiction. The names, characters and incidents portrayed in it are the work of the author's imagination. Any resemblance to actual persons, living or dead, events or localities is entirely coincidental.

Eliza Harwell asserts the moral right to be identified as the author of this work.

Second edition

ISBN: 978-1-7353415-0-7

This book was professionally typeset on Reedsy.
Find out more at reedsy.com

*In memory of my mother, Myra Harwell Young,
who always encouraged my love of reading and writing.*

*Big thanks to Kathryn Manning and Patty Leggett
who read, commented, and encouraged.*

Chapter 1

Casey walked through the shelter and surveyed the rooms: the multiple cats and dogs in all sizes, the African Grey parrot in its enormous cage, the tarantula, the two aquariums full of hamsters. This was both her happy place and the source of much of her stress.

That stress was exactly why she needed to go for a long run at the end of a busy workday. She sat on the bench by the front door and put on her sneakers, noting that all of the dogs were looking at her hopefully. She smiled at the big dogs apologetically and then walked over to let the three smallest dogs out of their play area. She couldn't find the leashes with the flags that read, "Ask about adopting me at the Pleasant Valley Animal Shelter!", so she put on the regular leashes and herded the dogs outside. The late afternoon sun greeted them, and she took a moment to enjoy the feel of it on her face before the dogs insisted that she get moving.

They headed toward the city park. There were many reasons to love living in Pleasant Valley, Tennessee, but one of the biggest reasons was the city park. It was on the western end of downtown, bordered on one side by a lazy river and several hundred acres of woodland on the other. The sidewalk led down to the ball fields and grassy areas, and a dirt path led up through the woods to a stunning view of emerald green, central Tennessee pastureland.

As she ascended the hill, she looked back over the town with love, enjoying the play of the sunlight against the white- and pastel-colored buildings. She had lived here for five years and loved it more with every additional year that passed: its gentle, friendly inhabitants who mostly seemed to know each other by name, big yards full of flowers, neat streets swept carefully by shop owners and residents, banners on every light pole announcing the upcoming carnival and fair. There was a lot of pride in this town, which she shared even though she was still a relative newcomer.

Once at the top of the hill, various paths led in different directions. She chose her favorite running route and began. One loop around would take her a mile and a half, so she would do a couple of laps to ensure both she and the dogs got plenty of exercise. As always, the first two minutes were the hardest as her breath got faster and it felt as if her lungs wouldn't be able to keep up. By the third minute, her body had relaxed into the run, her feet pounding against the pavement. The dogs mostly stayed right behind her, in a three-wide row, trying to stay out of one another's way while keeping up with her.

One of the sources of the stress that she needed to pound out during these runs was her concern about their fate. One dog had recently arrived, but the other two had been in the shelter for a couple of months or more. She prayed they'd soon be adopted into happy, deserving homes. Although she and the volunteers tried to make their life at the shelter as comfortable as possible, the fact remained that the animals were confined to a small space and mostly monotonous days. What they needed instead was lots of attention and love from a warm-hearted individual or a family with children who loved to play. Until they went into such homes, she couldn't take in any more dogs, either; the shelter was already stretched beyond its resources. And there were so many other dogs out there who needed shelter.

At the end of the run, she and the tired dogs sprawled out on a grassy patch. She gave them water and took them off their leashes so they could go smell flowers and grass to their hearts' content. Even though the late spring air was already hinting at the heat and humidity to come, the breeze was cool and light. She loved this time of day.

After sitting there for a few minutes, Casey heard another runner slow down as he came around the bend, accompanied by the jingling of a dog collar. "Oh, look: food!" she heard a male voice cry out as an imposing looking German Shepherd bounded toward her and the dogs.

Casey looked up in alarm but saw the smile on the man's face and followed his eyes to the German Shepherd, who was submitting to the three small dogs as they sniffed the larger dog's entire body.

"Once again Barney is the submissive one," the man said, shaking his head. "Good thing I don't have my masculinity wrapped up in my big, tough dog."

She laughed. "More of a car kind of a guy, are you?"

"Yes," he affirmed and put on a look of mock arrogance. "I drive a Lambo."

She laughed again and took a moment to enjoy looking at him. He was gorgeous, with dark hair that curled around his ears and neck, and dark eyes. He was tall and had a confident air, but he also had an easy smile.

She tried to imagine how she must look: strawberry blond hair pulled back in a ponytail, red-faced from the run, with stray hairs sticking to her sweaty neck and temples. At least she wasn't wearing the paint-stained Vanderbilt t-shirt she usually ran in, she thought gratefully. His own shorts and shirt were immaculate and obviously very high quality.

She motioned toward the dogs, who were clearly glad to have found one another. "Did you two have a good run?"

"Yeah, we did. This is a nice place. I couldn't decide if I should go here or by the river. I'm glad chose here." He said it simply, not flirtatiously, even as he smiled at her to indicate she was the reason for his gladness.

"Me, too." She smiled at him but then lowered her eyes, embarrassed at such a bold statement. She decided to cover it with a joke, nervously delivered. "I mean, me, too, I thought about going down by the river." He laughed. "But I haven't seen you before, and I think I know just about everyone in this town who likes to run. Are you new here, or visiting?"

"Is the town that small?"

"Even smaller."

He pointed toward the ground next to her. "May I join you?"

"Of course. I think the dogs will be busy for a while."

They both watched as he let Barney off the leash and the dogs tumbled around, with Barney again playing the submissive role.

"I'm Will, by the way. Will Ingalls."

"Casey Young. And yes, I know just about everything that goes on in this town. So either you're visiting family or you're here for the regional insurance agents' convention downtown." She looked at him doubtfully; he didn't look much like an insurance agent.

He laughed. "Neither one, but I am in town on business for a couple of days."

"Where are you from?"

"Nashville."

"Oh, not far away, then." The outskirts of Nashville were about a twenty-minute drive, and it only took about an hour to get all the way downtown.

"No," he affirmed. "So you're from here?"

"No, I'm from Nashville, too. I've only lived here for about five years."

"Just two for me. I'm a transplant like just about everyone else. I came there from St. Louis."

"Nashville is a nice city, as cities go." She couldn't help feeling a bit of native pride, but otherwise she was getting a little embarrassed at her inability to make more interesting conversation. What next: the weather, for crying out loud?

"Of course, all I ever do is work," he continued. "So I really only know what Nashville looks like from my office window or apartment window."

"I know the feeling." Pointing toward Barney, she asked, "Do you always bring your dog on business trips?"

"Yes. I can't leave him behind in an apartment." He winked at her and added, "Plus he helps me meet chicks."

He flashed her an adorable grin, and she realized how nice it felt to be in his company.

The subject of the dog steered them toward a good half an hour of conversation about all the pets they had had. He was clearly a dog person, didn't much like cats, found parakeets annoying, and was still upset with his mother, who had never allowed him to have a sugar glider. Casey, however, had had just about every pet in the book, with or without the permission of her parents. Now she had added barn animals to house pets.

Chapter 1

The conversation was funny and light, and at some point Casey noted that she had laughed more in that half hour than she had in the last month.

After a while, Barney sat down by Will, seemingly ready to head on his way, and Casey realized it was time to get the little dogs back as well.

"Listen," Will said. "I hope I'm not moving too fast. But I'm only in town through tomorrow afternoon, and I'd love to keep talking to you. Could I take you out for dinner tonight?"

The question surprised her, as did the sudden feeling of excitement that rushed through her body. She felt herself begin to blush and tried to cover her embarrassment with another joke. "Hmmm," she said, cocking her head to one side as she looked at him. "The rule book says that I should play hard to get and say I'm busy. But since the situation is time sensitive, do you mind if I ignore the rule book and just say yes?"

"Permission granted. And do you mind if I take your copy of the rule book and throw it in the river?"

She found herself laughing yet again.

"Can you suggest a restaurant?" he asked.

"There's a nice Italian place on the way out of town," she told him. It was really the best date restaurant the town had, owned by an elderly couple and their son who had immigrated from southern Italy some four decades ago.

"Great. What time should I pick you up?"

"Ooh, in your Lamborghini?"

He pretended to look embarrassed. "Oh, uh, it's in the shop. Yeah, it's in the shop. I'm slumming it this weekend."

"Hmmm, too bad. The car is really the only reason I said yes. But actually, given that we've just met, it's probably better to meet at the restaurant." She hated to put a damper on the flirtation, but really: safety was safety.

He clapped his hand over his mouth in an exaggerated gesture of surprise. "You know, you're right. I should have thought of that. You don't seem dangerous, but I really should watch out for myself a little better."

They walked back toward town and nailed down all the details. After parting from Will, she looked at her watch and realized she'd better get moving. She took the dogs back to the shelter, fed and watered everyone, and said goodnight, then headed home quickly so she would have as much time as possible to get dressed.

At home, she made herself a quick cup of tea and inventoried what she had learned or noticed about Will. He seemed to like her and enjoy talking with her. He laughed at all her jokes, even the not-so-funny, nervous ones. And he was a good listener. All of that boded well for the dinner conversation to come.

He liked animals at least enough to have a dog. He liked to run and be outside. So far that gave them more in common than she had found with most other men she had dated since moving to Pleasant Valley five years before. A dearth of eligible men was one of the tradeoffs for a life of freedom in the country, surrounded by nice people, following her dreams. But she had hoped that Mr. Right would find her eventually. For one brief, ridiculous moment, she let herself consider the question: what if he finally had?

As she sipped her tea, she surveyed her wardrobe, knowing that there was really only one choice: the "date dress" her mother had recently bought her. "For when you go out and have fun," Katherine had said, winking to keep things light but nevertheless conveying her usual concern: "Tick tock, kiddo."

The dress was teal silk, tightly fitted in the chest and waist and then flared out in an A-line down her hips to just above her knees. It was simple and chic, with a hint of cleavage at the top. "You don't want to give it all away at first glance like so many young women do today," Katherine had noted, pursing her lips.

Yes, that's where Casey was at 32: her mother buying her dating clothes. She realized she hadn't even been on a date in six or seven months. She wondered if that fact would be obvious to Will and reminded herself to guard against letting her nervous sense of humor take over the date.

She showered and dressed, then blew out her shoulder-length, naturally wavy hair. She glanced at her makeup bag, wondering if cobwebs were starting to form on the edges, and decided to keep it light, applying a little mascara and lip gloss. She put on some strappy high heels and petted her cat, Meow, before heading out the door.

Chapter 1

When she entered Gino's right at 8:00, Will stood and motioned her over to the table, a big smile spreading across his face. He was dressed in beautiful dark gray slacks and a sport coat, with a black button-down shirt open at the neck. Even though freshly shaved, he had a rugged look because of his longish curls and thick black eyebrows, and a long scar down his temple and cheek that made her think of sword-fighting pirates or jousting knights.

Will was taking her in, too, with a glint in his eyes that told her the dress worked, the blowout worked, and heavier makeup was not required. She couldn't help matching his big smile with one of her own, and she felt some of her nervousness dissolve.

After they ordered food and a bottle of wine, he leaned forward in his chair and looked at her. "So what's a good first date question? Let's start with the basics: what do you do?"

"I'm a vet."

"Oh really? What branch of the military did you serve in?" He smiled to let her know he was kidding.

"The Marines," she replied, deadpan. "No, I'm a vet-er-in-ar-i-an. I have a little practice down on Main Street."

"That makes sense after our conversation about pets."

"Yes, I've always had a thing for animals. Although liking them and providing medical care for them are two very different things."

"What do you mean?" he asked, and she liked that he asked. He wasn't just making conversation; he wanted to get to know her.

"Well, for instance, it was hard to learn how to handle them roughly and impersonally in order to examine them or give a shot. Sometimes they're in pain, and I have to hurt them even more." She shrugged. "It would look pretty unprofessional to burst into tears and beg them to forgive me, but believe me, I've almost done it a time or two."

"I can imagine. You should see how apologetic I am when I trim Barney's nails. And did you move here to open the practice?"

She told him a bit about her upbringing in Nashville. She didn't tell him the full extent of her family's wealth, how they had used it to suffocate her, how she had longed to make her own way in life. But he seemed to read between the lines: she was an only child, her parents had expectations, she had to get away.

"So you moved out here to be your own person?" he asked, but it was really more of a statement.

Casey liked that he understood. "Exactly. We're close in a lot of ways, but they would like me to live life a certain way and I needed independence. They didn't even give me an independent name. They named me after themselves: Katherine and Charles, K and C, Casey." She shook her head. "That's uncharacteristically cutesy of them, by the way. They must have been sipping a lot of martinis when they came up with that one!"

He laughed at the joke but then looked at her with sympathy. "I can imagine it. The perfect couple, the perfect home, the perfect status, and the one daughter who must be perfect, too."

She nodded. "Even worse, they had me late in life. So the perfect and long-awaited one daughter. But I was always different. I wanted a simple life, a country vet practice, an old house with too many animals. I liked to go hiking and buy clothes at the thrift store, and my mother wanted to dress me up like a Barbie doll, take me to cotillion, teach me tennis, all that stuff." What she left out of the story were the more serious ways they had expressed their disappointment in her and tried to interfere in her life. Instead she forced a light note into her voice and said, "We get along fine, but let's just say I needed some space."

Their food arrived: penne fra diavolo for her, steak for him. The wine was a robust chianti, and she was beginning to feel more than a little woozy from it and from his company. "What about you? What did your parents do to make you move from St. Louis all the way to Nashville?"

He hesitated, and a fleeting look of unhappiness crossed his face. "Well, my story is complicated, but basically I'm on my own in life. My mother left when I was young, and then my father died while I was in college. I have a brother, but we don't keep in touch." He softened the seriousness of these facts with a joke: "So lemons to lemonade: I can live where I want!"

She sensed that he would not want to hear words of pity or concern, especially from a near-stranger, so she didn't offer them. "Are you generally a lemons to lemonade kind of person?"

"Yeah, I guess I am. I try to look on the bright side. For example, I may have lost my father young, but he was a wonderful influence in my life and I am thankful for him." He looked down at his plate and cut a piece of steak. "And this date is a total disaster, but at least I'm getting to eat a delicious steak."

She laughed. He wanted to keep it light, and that was fine with her.

"Actually, this date is far from a disaster," he continued. "Already one of my better recent ones, I have to say."

"And have there been a lot of recent ones?" she asked. She couldn't help herself.

"Yes, actually," he said in an offhand way. "A guy's gotta try, right? But people are very superficial, don't you think? They've got a laundry list of things they're looking for: the right kind of this or that. But what about a connection? What about someone who understands something deeper that is inside you?" He added, jokingly, "Not to mention the fact that everyone seems to have daddy issues."

She had her own laundry list and felt the need to defend it. "But can't the laundry list get you closer to the connection? I mean, if you know you require someone with, say, a certain level of education, or a certain set of interests, then aren't you doing everybody a favor if you just go ahead and start with that?"

"Well, what are you looking for?" He had a teasing look on his face, but she also got the feeling that he really wanted to know.

She decided she would tease, too. "A connection, someone who understands something deeper inside me, someone who will help me resolve my daddy issues."

He grinned. "No, seriously."

"Well, I want someone who likes a simple life, who loves nature and animals. I don't really care what he does for a living as long as he's passionate about it and feels he is serving a purpose. He should be educated and curious and interested in lots of things, and always willing to learn more. He should be family oriented and able to balance his family and personal life with other priorities. He should be honest and kind but also fun and adventurous. And he should ...".

Will was staring at her, eyebrows raised.

"Dear God, I sound like someone who has thought way too much about this, don't I?" She could feel the blush creeping up her neck and settling into her ears and cheeks.

"No, I get it. We're of a certain age, aren't we, that has given us time to think about these things?"

She made a sound of protest. "Of a certain age? How old do you think I am?"

He laughed. "I don't have to have been on a lot of dates to know that that's a question I should never answer! But I'm thinking college, vet school, five years in Pleasant Valley. You have to be somewhere in range of my own age, which is 35."

"Fair enough. I'm 32."

"And haven't you been thinking about these things?"

"Clearly I have. You have a lot of time to think about these things when you're not dating because you live in a small town with no one to date. Unless you happen to run into a random jogger in the city park, that is."

He acknowledged the last statement with a nod. "Well, there may be more people to date in Nashville, but trust me: that does not guarantee success." He placed his utensils on his plate, wiped his mouth with his napkin, and leaned back, looking at her more seriously. "I'll be honest with you. I really do work all the time. So you see, my priorities are not very well balanced. I'm not sure how simple my life is, and I don't have a particular love of nature or animals. But I am curious, and I am passionate about what I do, and I do have a certain level of education. So can I enter the competition?"

Her eyes widened in surprise, and suddenly she wasn't sure what to say. He was so direct! She searched for words to cover her embarrassment, perhaps a nervous joke. Was there anything she could think of that would disqualify him? "As long as you're not a serial killer, I guess." An image of her father and her last serious boyfriend flashed in her mind, and she added, "Or a greedy real estate developer."

He didn't reply, just looked at her with an amused expression.

She took another bite of her food and swallowed. He still hadn't spoken. "So I'm a Marine Corps veteran," she said. "What do you do?"

He lifted his eyebrows. "Actually, I'm a greedy real estate developer."

She laughed, but understanding dawned as he continued to gaze at her in silence, eyebrows still raised.

"No, a real estate developer, really?" she asked.

He nodded.

She put on a look of utter dismay. "But please tell me you're not a *greedy* real estate developer."

He grimaced. "I'm afraid I am a little greedy."

She leaned forward and looked at him intently. "Well, guess what? I have daddy issues."

A barking sound boomed out of his mouth and across the restaurant. The other diners turned and looked at them, and they were both overcome with silly laughter.

"Did you just guffaw?" Casey finally asked, after her post-laughter giggles finally calmed down. "You know, I've heard the term, but I don't think I've ever actually experienced a guffaw."

"Yes, I think I did just guffaw." He shook his head. "Ah, daddy issues. History repeating itself."

She raised her wine glass toward him. "And a greedy real estate developer. Here's to relationships that are doomed from the beginning!"

He touched her glass with his own. "And to the fine art of guffawing."

His deep brown eyes lingered on hers, a smile crinkling up the skin in their corners. She felt the cursed blush rise yet again and needed to break his intense gaze, so she scanned the restaurant, wondering how many of the couples were working through the embarrassment of a first date. She sensed that Will felt strongly about her, and she was confused by this even though she felt rather strongly about him, too. How could this be, after only a couple of hours of knowing each other?

"Will you have dessert?" he asked. She was grateful that the question broke the intensity of the moment.

"Yes, they have very good cheesecake here."

He motioned to the server, and they ordered cheesecake and coffee.

"I'm putting some pieces together," he said. "A particular dislike of real estate development, parents named Katherine and Charles, the last name Young."

"Do you know them?"

"Of them only. We've never met. But I'm going to their fundraiser next weekend."

She felt a thrill: she would see him again, one short week from tonight. But she also felt worried now that he knew who she was, the family she came from. This knowledge attracted some men for the wrong reasons and put others off altogether. She searched his face for a few moments and felt relieved: he seemed completely unaffected.

"My mother forces me to go to all of her fundraisers so that I can meet eligible young men."

"Well, I like to think I'm eligible, so hopefully she'll at least let me talk to you that night."

"Oh, trust me, she'll be shoving you toward me from the moment you arrive. Metaphorically speaking, of course, in the politest way possible."

"I hope so."

She allowed herself to say, "Me, too," and tried to hold his gaze, which was back to a level of intensity that could only be described as smoldering.

After a moment, he continued the conversation. "So how else do you like to spend your time, besides running, hiking, loving nature and animals, and hating serial killers and real estate developers?"

"If we hadn't just thrown the rule book in the river, I might consult it now and tell you that I like shopping for lingerie and getting bikini waxes." He chuckled and rolled his eyes. "But without the book to help me, I will confess some very unsexy hobbies: I like to garden and I like to read."

"Ah, more common ground! I like to read, too. What do you read?"

"Mostly thrillers."

"Really? Me, too. Crime? Legal? Medical?"

"All of the above."

Chapter 1

"Same with me, but especially legal. Okay, I really think I'm in the competition now, right?"

She narrowed her eyes and peered at him as if to inspect his qualities. "First, can you clarify your greed level?"

"Slight to moderate. It's not so much greed for money, but more that I like to win."

She considered this. "Okay, you're in the competition. In fact, congratulations! Once again, due to the fact that I live in Pleasant Valley, you are now the only competitor."

He pumped a fist in the air. "Yes!"

"But fair warning," she added. "I will be watching the greed situation very closely."

"Okay," he conceded. "But remember what I said: I like to win." He winked at her and leaned back in his chair. She tried to relax back into hers as well and look more casual then she felt about the idea of being won by such an intriguing and attractive man.

Their cheesecake arrived: chocolate for her, strawberry for him. After the server moved away, he ate a spoonful. "Mmmm, berry good!"

She liked that he could be goofy.

"I have something to confess," he continued. "My secret dream when I was in college was to become a thriller author. I even wrote a thriller—a very, very, *very* bad thriller."

"What was the plot?"

"Well, it started with a man who met a country vet while he was out running one afternoon. She seemed nice enough, but it turned out she was deadly. Daddy issues, you see."

"Wow, great premise. Keep going. He didn't remind her of her father, did he?" She stuck out her tongue in disgust.

"Oh, no way. He was the very opposite: a gorgeous guy, unbelievably charming, greedy but down to earth." He flashed his cute, mock arrogant look once again.

"Both greedy and down to earth, huh? An unusual combination."

"He was an unusual guy." His tone grew dramatic. "But he was an innocent.

He thought he would walk her out to her car after their first date, and she turned on him."

"Surgical instruments from the vet clinic, right?"

"Nope. Death by cheesecake."

He pushed his plate away and took a sip of coffee. She could feel him watching her as she took another bite.

"You know, I've been on a lot of dates, as we have already established"—he flashed her that arrogant look again—"and I think you're the only woman who actually ate dessert. I like it!"

"Well, I say what's the point of running everyday if you're not going to let yourself enjoy some cheesecake when you have the chance?" She sipped her coffee. "So did they never eat dessert, or just not on the first date?"

"They *never* ate dessert. Can you believe that?" He lifted his hands in the air as if demanding an explanation from the universe.

"Wow, you have had a pretty dismal dating life." He held her gaze until she felt herself blush again. Until now, his eyes seemed to say. She felt the same way. This was the best first date she had ever been on. Being with him and talking to him felt as natural as sliding her hand into a perfectly-fitting glove.

She didn't want the night to end, but she was afraid she might lose control of her heart if she continued talking to him and looking at him and flirting with him. She needed to go home, have a cup of tea, and assess the situation before her feelings got completely out of hand.

So, after they finished their coffee, she forced herself to say, "Well, I have an early morning tomorrow, and I always like to get a good night's sleep."

"I guess I could say the same," he said agreeably. "Can I walk you to your car?"

"You're not afraid?"

"I have pepper spray. What about you?"

"Cheesecake." She patted her handbag, and he laughed.

As they walked out, he said, "I haven't told you the next part of my book." She enjoyed the feeling of the cool breeze against her skin, his arm occasionally brushing up against hers as they walked.

Chapter 1

"Oh, yes, do tell."

"Well, they went out on a second date, and then another, and then another."

Her stomach flip flopped. They really would go out again! "Even though he lived in Nashville and she lived out in the country?"

"Whoa, whoa, where's that coming from? I never said he lived in Nashville and she lived out in the country!" Just as she caught his meaning and began to feel embarrassed, he laughed. "Ha ha, gotcha. Yes, he lived in Nashville, and she lived out in the country. And yes, they saw each other again. It was a thriller with a happy ending, a romance really. That's why it was such a horrible, career-ending book."

"Well, maybe you should have been a romance writer."

"Problem is, I'm not a very romantic kind of guy."

"I'm not sure I believe that," she replied. They had reached her small SUV and turned toward each other. His eyes were dark and glittering in the moonlight, and she felt mesmerized as they stared into her own. How could anyone have such long lashes?

"I think *you* just might be able to bring out the very little bit of romance there is in me."

He smiled, and her eyes were drawn to his thick, full lips. He noticed and moved his own eyes down to her lips, then back up to her eyes.

"May I kiss you?" he asked softly, suddenly serious. She nodded, and he touched her lips lightly with his own. He placed his hand on the back of her head and pulled her toward him to deepen the kiss, and she felt a response throughout her entire body. It was the most romantic kiss she had ever experienced: slow, sensual, and full of promises. When he broke the embrace and moved back away from her, she was flooded with a sense of loss.

"Good night," he said simply, moving his hand to cup her cheek and caress it with his thumb.

She reached up and placed her hand over his, pressing its warmth into her face. "Good night." She forced herself to drop her hand and turn away from him, and he held her door open as she got in the car.

"One last thing: your phone number, please?" he asked. They did the you-call-me-and-I'll-record-your-number thing, which fortunately killed the romantic mood, allowing her an opportunity to get some control over her feelings. The phone was hard to manage because of her trembling hands.

He stood and waved as he watched her drive away. After she had traveled about a mile away from the restaurant, she opened the windows and let the breeze fill her car and blow through her hair. "Weeeeeeeeee!" she screamed into the night as she flew down the dark roads to her home. The world had always seemed mostly beautiful and good and full of possibilities to her. But now it was filled with a new kind of wonder. The breeze seemed lighter and fresher than ever before. The moonlight in the night sky was brighter than ever before. In just a few hours her life had completely changed. *She* had changed. She realized with both happiness and dismay: she was already on her way to falling in love with this man.

Chapter 2

Casey let herself sleep in until 6:30 the next morning, after a restless night. Her post-date assessment session had continued into her dreams, which overwhelmingly confirmed that she had already developed strong feelings for Will. The choice to get out of bed was an agonizing one. She didn't want to leave those dreams and get back to the real world just yet. But the cat and chickens and goats and rabbits were waiting. She slipped on some old clothes and boots and headed out.

Greeting and caring for the animals brought her out of her stupor. Then she made herself a strong pot of coffee, hoping to make up in liquid form for the lack of sleep. She looked out at the new day from her back porch, eyes skimming over the vegetables and herbs in the kitchen garden. They were sagging a bit after several days of heat with no rain. She made a mental note to get home early enough that night to give them a good soaking with the sprinklers.

Just as she began her second cup of coffee, her phone buzzed. A text. "Good morning. I can't stop thinking about you."

A jolt of electricity shot through her body, and she felt her lips stretch into a broad smile.

"That was the best first date of my life," he continued.

"Really? Pretty typical for me." Why this need to banter?

Smiley face. "Want to see if a second one lives up to the first?"

"Yes. Definitely." There: less banter, more concession.

"I'll be in touch. Gotta run."

"Have a good day." Should she add a heart? Yes, why not?

He hearted her back. Thank goodness.

She finished her coffee, allowing five additional minutes of daydreaming, and then it was time to get in the shower and go. She put a little extra effort into her appearance this morning. After all, he was still in town. Who knew what might happen: a chance encounter at a stoplight, a surprise run-in at the coffee shop? As she drove toward the clinic and shelter, the whole town seemed infused with his presence and the wonderful possibility that she might see him again.

"Morning, Jakob," she called to her vet tech when she had arrived at the clinic and entered the already-unlocked front door. Once again, he had beat her in, no doubt to finish up some of the previous day's paperwork.

"Morning, Doc," he called from the kitchenette. "Coffee or tea?"

"No, thanks, already had some."

He moved into the office, where she was putting down her things. "Uh oh, rough night?" He knew her habits by heart, even the amount and timing of her caffeine consumption.

"No, I just couldn't sleep." She felt the blush rise in her cheeks.

"Whoa, whoa, whoa, did you just blush?" Jakob leaped over to her, excitedly examining her cheekbones more closely. He often teased her about her wretched blushing, which made it impossible to hide any feelings of embarrassment from him or anybody else. "What, did you have someone over?"

The world-class gossip in him was giddy with excitement. Having a man over would be a tasty tidbit that he could share with his girlfriend, friends, and even random acquaintances he ran into at the grocery store.

"No, no, nothing like that," she assured him, hoping she sounded convincing. "But I did have a date, and it was a really good date, and it did disrupt my sleep a little bit."

"Who was it? Not Warren Hasby."

She made a face. "No way. He's finally given up." The local playboy wannabe had dogged her for a year, unable to believe that she wasn't interested. "I met someone while out running the little dogs yesterday. He's in town for a couple of days on business."

"And you went out on a date with him?" Jakob looked at her with eyebrows raised. "That sounds sketchy."

"No, he's okay. He's a nice guy. He brought his dog with him on a business trip. That should tell you something!"

Jakob nodded his head approvingly. "Yes, good sign. Tell me more!"

"Well, he's nice and funny and cute and sweet. We had a great time."

"Wait, is he more cute or more sexy?"

"Sexy. He has kind of a pirate look."

Jakob nodded again, impressed. "Will you see him again? Where's he from?"

"Nashville, and yes, I think so. He texted me this morning to ask if we could see each other again."

"A next-morning text?" Jakob gasped. "What time?"

"Seven thirty."

"Oh, he likes you! Even with Katie, I didn't text her until the following afternoon."

"Wow, that's a surprising amount of restraint for you!" Jakob had asked Katie to marry him within a week. Wisely, she had suggested they slow things down a bit. Jakob was wonderful, but even at 28 he had some growing up to do.

Casey looked at him affectionately: his red hair, his chubby cheeks, the big smile that was always plastered on his face and intensified when he was working with animals. She knew he craved gossip, but she also knew he wanted her to find someone who made her as happy as Katie made him.

"Yes," she conceded with a smile. "I think he likes me."

The phone rang. Bobbie May Rogers was worried about her dog, who seemed to have lost his appetite over the last couple of days. Could she bring him in for an early appointment? Of course, Casey told her; they could always find time for Mrs. Rogers in the day's schedule.

"Well, Jake-O, time to get to it," she said. She headed into the back to make sure the appointment rooms were set up, and Jakob returned to his paperwork. The professional in Casey claimed most of her attention, but she knew that thoughts of Will would hover in the back of her mind for the rest of the day. In fact, the thought of him put an extra bounce in her step. Will was here, in her town, close by. That knowledge thrilled her.

"Doc, come look," Jakob said later that morning when she had a break between appointments. He led her over to the computer. "There's an e-mail from the folks over in Clarksville. They've found a hoarding situation and are wondering if we could take some of the cats and dogs." She looked at the photos.

Oh dear, Casey thought. Hoarding situations were some of the saddest. They usually began in kindness: someone decided to take in animals in a desire to help strays or rescues and perhaps to relieve some loneliness. But then the impulse couldn't be turned off, and the individual took in more and more and more animals. Without money for spaying and neutering, kittens and puppies added to the little population over time until it reaching a breaking point. Then the person could no longer afford all the food and litter and couldn't keep up with the animals' needs. In the worst situations, the still living were locked up with carcasses, covered in feces, whining pitifully when the rescuers finally came.

Casey was dismayed. "We're full up. What can we do?"

They agreed that Jakob would call around to the people who had volunteered to foster animals in the past and see if they had room at home or any dog kennels the shelter could borrow. "I'll go clean out the back office a bit and see if I can make room for some cats in there," Jakob told her.

She nodded. "Tell Clarksville we're working on it and hopefully we can take up to eight animals." That seemed like such a small number considering there were more than 40 animals rescued. "We'll take some of the sickest ones," she added. If she couldn't make space for more of them, at least she could make time to provide medical care.

These kinds of challenges made her feel overwhelmed and depressed. She tried to remember that their shelter was doing what it could and that nobody could do it all. But still, it seemed they were always coming up short compared with the vast needs of all the animals out there in the world.

She thanked God, as she so often did, that the Ramseys had given her the land and building for her shelter. They owned the lot and some acreage behind the clinic, and they had allowed her to convert the unused office building on the lot into a shelter. She had been thinking lately to buy the lot and expand the shelter. Jakob was supposed to be looking into the availability of grants to help her, but there never seemed to be any extra time to do so. If we had been more proactive about it, she thought ruefully, we might have the space to take in more animals now.

Will was still hovering in her thoughts, but now the plight of these animals was in competition with him. Please let things work out, she prayed over and over again as she went about her work. They had the usual lineup that morning: checkups, shots, stern discussions about the need for good diets and fewer table scraps. Jackie the parrot kept saying, "Oh boy! Oh boy!" as patients and their families entered and "Goodbye! Goodbye!" as they left.

She had to leave early that day, so she left Jakob to continue addressing the hoarding situation, and set Bethany, the receptionist, with the tasks of cleaning up and closing the clinic and the shelter. She changed into jeans and a t-shirt and headed to Nashville to attend a protest outside of the Tennessee Development Commission. She had been attending it annually, as she served on the executive board of the organization that coordinated it in hopes of pressuring the TDC to be more cautious in permitting what had turned out to be rampant development throughout the state. The TDC was not mindful enough of how development—mostly of residential neighborhoods and big business parks—jeopardized the air, water, and wildlife of sensitive ecosystems. It also led to unsightly landscapes and traffic snags. Casey and the committee took this occasion every year to remind them.

The protest had swelled in numbers over the years, and this year they were expecting over 5,000 people. The committee's continued work was beginning to show some fruit. They had convinced the TDC to re-site a couple of major developments in the last year and helped write new policies for keeping more of local ecosystems intact even when a development project was approved. They had even convinced one of the largest residential developers to landscape their apartment complexes with native species and include pollinator gardens along their walkways.

She sped to Nashville to meet her friends but still ran late due to heavier than expected traffic.

"Hurry up, get in!" Samantha yelled from the driver's seat of her minivan as Casey pulled into the grocery store parking lot where they had agreed to meet. "We're late!"

Casey parked and hurried over to the vehicle. Peering inside, she saw that Jamila and Jen were already in the back. Casey got in the front passenger's side and smiled at everyone in turn. They were her best friends from college. She didn't think any of them particularly cared about development issues in the midst of their current busy lives. But she was able to force them to go to this event every year as a throwback to their more politically involved days—and with the promise of a drink and catch-up session afterward.

Samantha reached over to hug her, engulfing Casey in the combined fragrances of strong perfume and hair-care products. Samantha was wearing very sexy jeans, strappy stilettos, and a low-cut blouse, and she was decked out in jewelry and heavy makeup.

"Wow, Sam, you look amazing." Casey looked down at her own not so sexy jeans and t-shirt. "You do realize we're going to an outdoor protest, not a club, right?"

Samantha's tinkly laugh filled the minivan as she pulled out of the parking lot and headed for downtown. "Girl, it's been a long time since I've worn anything dressier than an old maternity shirt with spit-up stains all over it. This is a big deal for me!" Samantha had five children, which was always a source of surprise to Casey—and, it seemed, Samantha herself. She was the last person anyone would have expected to devote herself to wifehood, motherhood, and life in the suburbs.

Casey turned to face her friends in the backseat. Jamila, reserved and stately as always, gave her a wave and blew her a kiss from her fingertips. Even in jean shorts and a t-shirt, she looked more elegant than any of them. "Happy annual protest day, my friend!" Jamila said.

Jen leaned forward to pat Casey's shoulder. "More like annual stick-it-to-

Chapter 2

your-Dad day, right?" Jen was still wearing a business suit and high heels, which was like a second skin to her.

They all laughed. Casey's antipathy toward rampant development had begun in her love for nature and wide-open spaces but been honed over the years by a distaste for the work of the corporation her father had founded. CY Properties was one of the largest developers in the state and had drained countless wetlands and pulled down even more woodlots so that Charles Young could be a multimillionaire. It had been a topic of heated discussion between Casey and Charles, to say the least, for much of her lifetime.

"If only a protest could do any good with dear old Dad," Casey replied. "But since he won't listen, we have to go above his head to the TDC." She smiled at her friends. "Thanks for making time for this once again. I thought we could try that new fusion barbecue place everyone is talking about afterwards."

They murmured their assent, and Casey looked more closely at Jamila. "What's up with you, Jami? You look different somehow."

"Yeah, you do," Jen seconded.

Jamila hesitated, then smiled. "Well, I was going to wait and tell you at dinner, but why not? I'm pregnant!"

Samantha screamed and almost drove the vehicle off the road, and they all laughed. Jen put her hand on Jamila's. "Oh, congratulations, my friend."

"How far along?" Casey asked.

"Just three months. I've been waiting for that magic date, the end of the first trimester, to tell anyone, and y'all were to be the first." She smiled at her friends and shrugged her shoulders happily.

Jamila and her husband Anton had been trying to have a baby for four years, without success, even after trying everything possible at a world-class fertility clinic.

"I thought you weren't doing IVF anymore," Samantha said.

"We weren't. This happened naturally. It's a miracle!"

Jamila's big brown eyes were filled with joy, and Casey felt happiness and relief flood through her. She had seen Jamila go through years of pain and anger, although in the last year or so she had come to a place of acceptance and peace. And now, unexpectedly, it had happened!

"Guess what else?" Jamila said.

"It's twins?" Jen offered.

"Lord, no. But almost as crazy. We've made a decision: I'm going to quit and stay home once the baby is born."

"Oh, welcome to my world," Samantha chimed in. "Don't do it, Jami! It will suck the soul of you."

Jamila had fought for the right to a career as a public defender amid a traditional Jamaican family that actively discouraged her pursuing any route but marriage and motherhood.

"Did Mama Mary talk you into this?" Casey asked.

Jamila smiled and shook her head. "No, it's all me. After working so hard for this, I want to enjoy every second of it."

They chattered on about the pregnancy and what Jamila was doing to prepare for it, how her family had reacted.

"Well, this is big news!" Samantha finally said with a sigh. "Let's see: my big news is I'm still a soccer mom with a minivan, way too many kids, and a husband who would rather hunt than change a diaper. And Jen, you're still a workaholic with a boyfriend in California you never see, right? Any news there?"

"Nada," Jen replied.

"And Casey, still toiling away in a clinic and animal shelter in the freakin' sticks to prove that you can do it on your own instead of becoming the heiress, socialite, and corporate CEO in training that you were born to be, right? Any news there?"

Casey smiled. "Well, actually..."

They all leaned toward her in interest. Casey never had news.

"I've met someone."

Samantha screamed and almost ran off the road, and once again they all burst into laughter.

"I *think* I've met someone, that is," Casey added.

"You're already taking too long to tell this story," Jamila said. "Go, go."

Casey filled them in on meeting Will, their perfect date, the romantic banter, the kiss, and her sense that she was already falling in love. She was taken right back to their time in college together, sitting around their dorm suite, discussing every single detail of every boy, every party, every conflict, every life dream. They had laughed and cried and hugged together. She couldn't believe she was lucky enough to still have them as her best friends.

She also couldn't believe she finally had a "met someone" story to tell them. Since Casey was the last of them to find her way to love, they had been waiting very impatiently for this kind of news.

They ooh'ed and ah'ed in all the right places and agreed that Will did indeed sound wonderful.

"But the real estate development thing," Jen reminded her. "Can you handle it?"

"Who does he work for?" Samantha continued. "Is it one of the bad ones?"

Casey stared at them. "I didn't even ask. I guess I don't really know anything about it. Believe it or not, in the moment I didn't even really care."

"Geez, you are in love," Samantha joked, patting Casey's knee.

The conversation came to an end as they watched Samantha do a terrible job of parallel parking the van in a downtown spot. They got out, walked a few yards, and soon enough were in the middle of the protest, chanting with gusto as Casey looked for the other board members. She saw Randy and Latasha waving at her from the tall steps leading into the commission building and headed their way, friends in tow.

"Wow, great crowd!" Casey said, giving them both a hug when she reached the steps. They all said their hellos and then were joined by Shay, another executive board member of Save Wild Tennessee.

"Hey, Casey, you're late!" Shay said, blunt as always.

"Sorry, yeah, I didn't leave enough margin for traffic."

"We need you to help with petitions. Are you ladies here to yell, as always?" she asked Samantha, Jamila, and Jen.

"Yep, that's what I do best!" Jen replied. She was a girls' softball coach in her off hours.

"Okay, you join in over there by the megaphones."

"I'll go with her," Jamila said.

"I'll hang with Casey," Samantha said. "Meet some people, you know?"

"All right, you and Casey cover that sidewalk to the North," she instructed, pointing. "Lots of pedestrian traffic over there today and the occasional traffic jam. Hopefully you'll get a couple hundred signatures."

"No problem," Casey said, happy to obey orders. Shay could be bossy, but her heart was in the right place. Casey grabbed a handful of petitions and walked quickly to her new territory.

She glanced over the petition, which she had helped to create, asking the Tennessee Development Commission to lend particular scrutiny to a handful of development corporations that were clearing a more significant amount of acreage than others. The list included her father's corporation, CY Properties. It and most of the others had been on their list for years, but there was a new one: Coach Lifestyle Solutions.

She and Samantha worked together. Samantha channeled all of her need for conversation with adults instead of children into a winning ability to grab people's attention and engage them in a discussion of the issues. Then Casey approached to provide more information and answer questions. People were friendly and interested, for the most part, although they had more than a few car horn honks and heard one guy yell, "Burn the earth!" out of his car window between honks.

"Burn this, you turd!" Samantha yelled after him, and she and Casey broke into a fit of giggles.

They had been working the sidewalk for about twenty minutes when one of the local television reporters approached Casey for an interview. She recognized him from past events and was happy to comply. Samantha preened and made sure she was in the background as Casey answered the reporter's questions on tape.

"Is Save Wild Tennessee against development and the economic benefits it brings to the state?" he asked.

"It's not that we're against development," Casey said. "We're against the kind of insane development that is allowed to continue, uncontrolled, throughout the state. Birds are in decline, our forests are fragmented, our water sources are increasingly in jeopardy. The state government has got to think about more than the tax dollars it receives, and these real estate developers have got to think about more than the bottom line."

Samantha whooped at this and moved in a little closer to Casey, smiling at the camera and giving a thumbs up.

"Coach Lifestyle Solutions posted a statement online today protesting their inclusion on your petition. What would you say in response?"

"I haven't seen the statement itself, but I have seen a list of the properties they've developed since coming to Tennessee last year. They're eating up land, often valuable land in the center of a community, where people have enjoyed the woodlots, wetlands, parks, and other sites of natural beauty that have been there for generations. Then Coach clears a huge lawn, without concern for any natural features, and builds a sprawling complex of homes and buildings and walkways. As far as we can tell, they have resisted any attempts to encourage them to show concern for the environment. And the Tennessee Development Corporation lets them continue, unchecked."

"Coach claims to strive to provide ethical senior care in a state with a rising elderly population," the reporter continued. "Should they really be treated as Public Enemy #1?" Casey was surprised that he was following up so carefully, but she didn't mind the opportunity to explain the organization's position.

"Of course, a corporation can do good, but *how* it accomplishes that good is also important. A lot of manufacturers make good products that people need, for example, but they use slave labor. The end doesn't justify the means. I firmly believe that Coach Lifestyle Solutions cannot claim to be ethical if they're not ethical with regard to the environment as well."

That was the most she was willing to say, not having read their statement. In fact, she didn't yet know a great deal about Coach Lifestyle Solutions and its projects. Randy had simply presented her with numbers on a page and his recommendation that Coach be included in the petition. Casey, trusting his research, had added her consent to that of the other executive board members.

"Thank you!" she said to the reporter in a way that indicated she was finished commenting. Samantha gave one last pouty smile and waved to the camera, and then they turned away.

"Nice job," Samantha said, linking her arm through Casey's.

"You know how much I hate doing that kind of stuff," Casey replied, shaking her head and internally willing her heartbeat to return to normal speed.

"Yeah, but your hair looked great, all windblown and sexy. I'm sure you're going to convert a lot of men to your cause! Maybe a couple of broads, too."

"And I'm sure you'll have at least one stalker after your own sexy performance," Casey replied, laughing. They returned to their petition signing efforts, and soon enough they could hear the speeches and chanting come to an end.

It was a successful event, and the rest of the board seemed as pleased as Casey did. They assured Casey that they and the other directors could handle all the cleanup and removal of signs so that she could go out with her friends. And thus the day ended with delicious food and a whole lot of laughs, before Casey and the others headed their separate ways around 7:30. That was one big change from college: no more late nights. There were too many children, husbands, and animals to return to, and too many responsibilities to wake up to early the next day.

As she drove home, her mind kept traveling back to two things: the plight of the animals rescued from the hoarding situation and, of course, Will. She felt good about the steps they had taken to care for the animals, although the situation prompted larger worries in her head about the shelter and the need for expansion and a permanent home. In the short-term, she felt much more worried about Will. His jokes about being a greedy real estate developer the night before had seemed so funny and harmless. But who was he, really? How would he feel about the mission of SWT to control overdevelopment in the state? Did he work for the kind of corporation that ravaged the earth and was destroying Tennessee's remaining wild areas? And would she fall in love with him only to find that they were as much of a mismatch as she and her last boyfriend had been?

Her father had introduced her to George, an up-and-comer on the real estate scene, soon after she had graduated from college and entered veterinary school. She had fallen pretty hard for him, and very quickly, because he was charming, outgoing, and seemingly down to earth. He had made a point to share her interests, taking her hiking and skiing, running half marathons alongside her, joining in her volunteer work as a wildlife rehabilitator, staying up late to help her study for exams.

He was ten years older than she was but seemed youthful and idealistic. There had been some niggling doubts about his job and how he seemed to transform instantly into a slick corporate salesman when they were at his work events together. And she didn't like the way he ingratiated himself with her father and was always insisting that they get together with her parents. But she ignored those warning signs because she was so happy to be in love and have such a solicitous, charming boyfriend.

She hadn't been very lucky in love up to that point. Most of the men she had been introduced to were of a world very different from the one she wanted to inhabit. Her world had been so limited: prep school, a snooty college with students who had way too much money, and her parents' country club had comprised the bulk of her entire social world. With the exception of Samantha, Jamila, Jen, and a few other friends at college, the people she met were more like her parents and less like her. She had worried that she would never find true love, and George had rather easily swept her off her feet.

She still remembered using the spare key to enter his apartment and surprise him early on his birthday. He was in the bedroom, talking loudly. She tiptoed in and sat outside the room, waiting to pounce on him with a long kiss as soon as he walked out.

"Yeah, I've got her on the hook," he said and then paused. She realized he was talking on the phone.

"Yeah, Charles is working the deal, and it's going to be the making of me."

Pause.

"Well, it's the price you gotta pay, you know? At least she's hot. But I tell you, I can't pretend to like hiking and messing around with the stupid wildlife much longer."

He paused again and then laughed. "Right, yeah, once we're married I can just golf and leave her to it."

Pause.

"I'm asking her this weekend. She'll say yes for sure."

Pause.

"Definitely the way to Charles' heart. I would have found a way to get there eventually, but marrying his daughter will put me on the fast track."

Pause.

"Yeah, even sharks have their blind spot. Anyway, gotta run. I'm spending the morning with Sarah before I have to go play the good fiancé-to-be. Birthday dinner and all that."

Pause.

"You know Sarah. All she cares about is how much money I have to spend on her. She's willing to keep out of the way."

Pause.

"Yeah, all right, bro. Talk to you later."

Casey sat quietly, trembling violently, until George made his way into the room and saw her there. Then she simply got up and walked out, ignoring his attempts to call her back or explain. Thankfully she had never seen him again. He didn't work for her father for very long after that, although from what she understood he had simply moved on to another firm and was doing quite well. Someone like George would always end up on top.

Greed, pride, attraction to wealth and fame—these were the characteristics of her father's world and the men like George that it attracted. And that's why she wanted nothing to do with it. Her memories brought her back to her original question: Who was Will? Was he her father in the making, becoming greedier over the years? Was he another George, another empty charmer who cared about nothing but money, who would use her for his own ends?

None of these seemed likely. Will had come across as too nice, too decent. Or was she still the same vulnerable woman, too quick to believe in someone who was way too good to be true?

Once home, she had just enough time to water the garden as planned while she breathed in the fresh country air and enjoyed watching the animals. As she looked out over the neat rows of plants, listened to the noise of the goats coming back from the woods and settling into the barn, and watched the sunset, she tried to ground herself in who she was and who she wanted to

Chapter 2

be. A single date—not even such a wonderful one—could allow her to forget those things.

She checked her phone as she went back in. One text.

"Back in Nashville now. Hope you had a good day. See you Friday night at the fundraiser?"

She felt the rush of excitement go through her. It was somewhat muted by her determination to tread carefully, but it was still there.

"Yes!"

"See you then and there." With the heart.

Slow things down, Casey, she thought. She sent him back a thumbs up, no heart.

Chapter 3

The following Friday morning, Casey's benefactor Mr. Ramsey dropped by the clinic. The short, mild-mannered, septuagenarian dressed to the nines every day, his scent a wonderful, old-fashioned mixture of starched shirts and aftershave. Casey greeted him fondly. He had been good to her, not only in giving her the use of his property but also funneling patients her way and talking her up in the town. It could be hard to break into a small-town business community without the help of people like the Ramseys, and she was grateful to him and his wife. She liked that he dropped by once a week or so to chat with her and congratulate himself a little on what he had done for her and the community.

Today he looked serious, however. "Could I speak with you in private?" he whispered.

"Of course." They went into one of the exam rooms. "What's wrong, Mr. Ramsey?"

He sighed, and she waited patiently for him to begin. "I'm afraid I have some bad news." His eyes looked past hers to the wall behind her. "It's all come about rather suddenly, but I have decided to sell the lot."

She opened her mouth in shock, and he hurriedly added, "I worked really hard to arrange some extra time for you to move the shelter out of the building, but I'm afraid the new owner has only agreed to give you two months."

Chapter 3

Casey felt as if she had been struck by lightning. This news, just after the news that more animals urgently needed shelter? She couldn't believe it.

"How did this come about?" she finally asked.

He looked away from her and worked at straightening the bottles and jars on top of the cabinet. "I should have told you this was in process, but it's all happened so quickly. You know I'd love to keep you here. But Jeanne has had some medical bills this year, and we need to turn some assets into cash and get ourselves a little more financially stable." He moved over to look out the small window. "I just can't keep sitting on this lot."

"Well, would you let me buy it from you?" she asked, although she knew she wasn't financially set up for such a purchase right now.

He turned to her and smiled patronizingly, a father talking to his young daughter. "There's no way you could match what this developer is paying. He's turning the lot into a retirement home. Which will be good for this town!" He straightened up a little bit: he was disappointing one person, but for the good of the community. "I'm sorry, Casey, but we've signed the papers. There will be a public hearing sometime next week, but it's just a formality. The town council is already behind the project."

Casey's mind was reeling as she began sorting through her options. She promised herself that she would work something out. She smiled at Mr. Ramsey, who was looking at her pleadingly, hoping for absolution. "Thank you for coming in to tell me."

"Of course." He bowed his head slightly to acknowledge her thanks. "I've been happy to be helpful to you all these years, and of course to help the animals. But it was time for you to think of something more permanent. I'll use all my connections to help find you another space. I doubt anyone else will be willing to *donate* a space," he added, with a flash of pride at the reminder of his own generosity, "but I'm sure you can find a fair rental somewhere nearby."

"Thank you," she replied. "So who is this developer?"

"Coach Something or Other. An impressive young man named William Ingalls. He's a retirement home builder, as I said. Been growing his company big around here over the last year or so. Young guy, but successful."

She hardly heard anything after the name. Will? She felt immediate relief. She could talk to him tonight, explain the situation. Once he understood, he would change his mind. Maybe she could find a way to buy the property. He could at least give her more time to find a new location and move the shelter.

"Well, I need to go, my dear," Mr. Ramsey said, looking relieved to have completed an onerous duty.

"All right. Give my best to Mrs. Ramsey."

"Will do. And don't worry, Casey. Everything is going to turn out just fine."

She imagined Will telling her the same thing later than night and managed to muster a smile for Mr. Ramsey.

She made it through the day's work despite her worries and then left around 4:00 to head to Nashville for the dinner. Leaving early twice within one week was unusual for her, and she couldn't help feeling a little guilty for it.

"See you later, slacker!" Jakob called as she opened the front door. She smiled and stuck out her tongue at him, knowing he and Bethany would be out the door within five minutes of her leaving.

She felt nervous and was already beginning to rehearse, in her mind, the scene to come. She was determined to make Will understand her situation. He had to, for the sake of the precious animals under her care.

Soon she was zooming down the interstate into Nashville, through countryside that she had always found beautiful. There were low, rocky hills, green fields and pastures, the occasional river or creek. She rolled the windows down and enjoyed the fresh air. The abundance of life surrounding her cheered her up considerably, despite the situation Mr. Ramsey had dropped so unexpectedly in her lap earlier that day. She couldn't understand how any Tennessean would be willing to sacrifice this beauty to another neighborhood full of cookie cutter houses or another industrial park. There were already so many houses up for sale, so many empty industrial buildings. Why this need to push further and further into the little bit of nature that was still intact?

But she knew that men like her father felt differently. She dreaded seeing him tonight, as she always did, never knowing if he was going to be in a kind mood or a mood to pick at her relentlessly about what a disappointment her life had turned out to be.

Normally, she would also have dreaded attending another one of her mother's fundraising dinners. These dinners, in Katherine's opinion, were Casey's best chance to find a suitable husband, and her mother was more than happy to introduce Casey to a handful of pre-approved prospects. Casey wondered if Will had made his way into her mother's field of awareness yet. If so, he was sure to be at the top of the list. That made the thought of attending the dinner much more palatable, especially if she could secure a change of mind from him about buying the Ramseys' land.

She rapped on the front door of her parents' home a couple of times before walking in. "Mom? Dad?" she called.

Her father called out a hello from the living room. "There's my beautiful girl!" he said as she entered the room and bent down to kiss his cheek. Good, he was in a kind mood. "How was your drive?"

"Fine. Great, actually. It's such a beautiful day."

"Well, of course it is. God wouldn't dare send bad weather on the day of one of your mother's dinners."

"If only you were as cooperative," Katherine said as she entered the room. "Your father is refusing to wear the shoes I want him to wear," she said to Casey as she kissed her on both cheeks. "Can you imagine such willfulness?"

"I have to reclaim my manhood every once in a while," Charles said. "Even if only in the small ways."

"Well, I'm glad you're here, dear." Katherine handed Casey a glass of ice water. "Now, chop chop. I need you to get upstairs and start getting ready."

"Mom, I just got here! Let me settle in for a second. Don't we still have plenty of time?"

"Yes, but you need to take the time to look your best." Her eyes scanned her daughter's outfit and windblown hair. Katherine was the kind of woman who did not allow anyone to see her in the morning until her hair was perfect and her makeup on, and she had never worn a pair of jeans in her life. Her personal, family, and Southern honor were at stake, after all.

This had led to innumerable fights with Casey as she was growing up. "But times are different now, Mom; people are more casual," Casey had pleaded on numerous occasions.

"All the more reason to resist, Casey. Otherwise someday people will be wearing pajamas in public." How prescient that warning had turned out to be!

Casey didn't feel like arguing today, so she headed upstairs to make her mother happy. Her bedroom was still the same as it had been when she left for college at age eighteen: thick plum-colored carpet, a canopied bed with linens and pillows in various shades of pink, white wicker furniture, neatly framed photos on the wall. Her mother had never allowed the rock band posters, bold colors, and mess of her teenaged friends' rooms. Fortunately, Casey had always liked things neat herself, so that was one conflict they could avoid. Now she kept clothes, toiletries, and other necessities here for her weekend visits.

She opened her closet and rolled her eyes when she saw a couple of new dresses there. Katherine was always adding to the closet, despairing of Casey's ability to dress herself appropriately and worrying that she might be seen twice in the same dress. Casey had to admit, reluctantly, that her mom had really good taste and knew exactly what would fit her best. She could never bear to refuse the gifts once she had seen them. And tonight she was grateful: she had a lot on her mind, and it was a relief not to have to think about how she would look when she saw Will again.

She looked over the new ones. One was jade green, with intricate, asymmetrical strapping, appropriately modest but hinting at sexy. The other was black but with colorful hand-embroidered flowers. Katherine insisted on couture. There was also a new pair of black heels in the closet, higher than Casey usually wore but beautifully designed.

She decided on the green dress. She dressed slowly, feeling her usual languor at being home where everything was taken care of for her. She put extra care into curling her hair so that she wouldn't get any criticism or anxious glances from her mother, and she put on a bit more makeup than

Chapter 3

usual. The dress fit perfectly and made her feel beautiful. Even her mother gave her an approving glance as she descended the stairs to join her waiting parents in the foyer.

They arrived at the Frist Art Museum just before the arrival time. Katherine never came early to these events. Only an event that had not been planned well would need her oversight at this point, she argued, and her events were always planned well. She simply came in time to welcome guests as they arrived.

Both Charles and Casey would be deployed to make people feel welcome and warm about the cause they were there to support—in tonight's case, a renovated and expanded oncology wing at the hospital—and Casey knew the routine well. She had come to know many of the usual attendees pretty well over the years, so she mostly felt as if she were greeting old friends. The first-timers were often rather annoying, though: they tended to be wannabes there to impress, who couldn't care less about the cause du jour.

She saw Will immediately as he entered and felt her belly flip flop at the thought of being close to him again. Just at that moment he looked up and saw her, too, and smiled warmly. He moved toward her as quickly as possible, pausing only to shake hands with a couple of people along the way.

She tried to focus on her conversation with her parents' old friends, the Morrises. He owned a group of car dealerships that boasted his own name, and she was the brains behind the operation and the one who insisted on spending a lot of their money on philanthropy. Casey usually enjoyed the banter between them, but now she felt impatient with it, ready instead to immerse herself in the banter to come between herself and Will.

She realized she was hyper aware of her appearance, her posture, the look on her face, and everything else. Her body buzzed with anticipation as he drew closer, and she longed to have him there, to get past that first nerve-wracking moment of seeing him again. At last he was standing in front of her, that big smile on his face. He kissed her on the cheek and held her hand. "You look absolutely beautiful!" He didn't need to say it, though; his eyes had already told her.

She laughed, feeling so giddy that she didn't even mind she was blushing.

"You're not so bad yourself."

He looked down and brushed the lapel of his tux. "Ah, this old thing?"

Will noticed the Morrises and turned to introduce himself. As soon as possible, though, he pulled Casey toward an empty corner where they could be at least somewhat alone.

"Hi," he said.

"Hi," she answered.

"I'm really glad to see you again."

"I'm really glad to see *you* again."

"I understand your mother is quite the philanthropist. How many of these dinners have you had to endure?"

"Lots of them. And 'endure' is the right word. This is definitely not my scene."

"Nor mine. But, in my line of work, you get used to shaking a lot of hands, so I can bear it. I'm already enjoying *this* event much more than I normally would." His eyes searched hers.

"Oh, good, you two have met!" Katherine's voice, which managed to exude liquid warmth and a razor-edged tone of command at the same time, announced her presence before Casey could even see her. Then she was beside them.

"Mr. Ingalls, allow me to introduce myself: I am Mrs. Charles Young." Casey could see her giving Will a quick assessment and approving of what she saw.

"It's very nice to meet you, Mrs. Young."

"Katherine, please."

"Will."

"And I see you've met my daughter," Katherine cooed, looking at Casey with put-on motherly pride. Here we go, Casey thought. "Casey is our pride and joy, a very successful doctor of veterinary medicine and business owner. And Casey, did you know that Will is our guest of honor this evening?"

Casey put on her most over-the-top impressed look. "No, I did not know. Mr. Ingalls very modestly didn't mention it. For what are we honoring you tonight?"

Chapter 3

He was trying not to laugh.

"Will's business efforts have had tremendous success, and he is setting a wonderful example of generosity for other donors to follow."

Will smiled at Casey and, when her mother wasn't looking, winked at her. Now Casey tried not to laugh.

"Will, I'm glad to meet you at last," Katherine said, "and I know Charles will want to say hello as well. We'll find you later. For now, I'll leave you two young people to get better acquainted."

Casey looked at Will, eyebrows raised, as Katherine walked away. "I'm surprised she didn't go ahead and set a wedding date!"

"Oh, it wasn't that bad," he said, laughing. "And she's a very skilled mind reader. I *was* hoping to be left alone to get better acquainted."

Casey realized this was her best chance to talk to him about the shelter.

"Actually, Will, me, too. There's something I need to talk to you about."

He noted the serious tone of her voice and looked at her questioningly, moving in more closely. Even though his face had been in her mind all week, she had forgotten its nuances: the dark eyes, the heavy brows, the angular chin, the scar down his cheek that made him look a little dangerous. She lost herself for a moment in enjoying the sight of him before the seriousness of her situation jolted her back to reality. "It's business."

He raised his eyebrows in surprise. "What kind of business?"

"I hear you're buying the Ramsey lot in Pleasant Valley, and that's where my animal shelter is." She sighed and decided to plunge right in. "I was relieved when I heard you were the developer because I hope I can talk you out of the deal."

"Talk me out of the deal?"

"Yes, now that you know me and understand my animal shelter is hanging in the balance, hopefully you'll back out of the deal."

He stared at her for a long moment and then used a measured tone to ask, "Why would I do that?"

Her anxiety heightened. Was this not going to be so easy after all? "Those animals depend on that space. I depend on that space to help them. There's nowhere else for them, and there's absolutely no way I can find a solution in only two months."

"But, Casey, I've given my word. Business is business."

One of her father's favorite expressions. So Will really was the greedy real estate developer after all. This was the problem with men like him: it all came down to the contract, the dollar. Anything could be sacrificed to all-important business.

She didn't even try to keep the disdain out of her voice. "Business may be business, but lives are lives."

The pleasure in his eyes at seeing her again was now replaced by a look that she could only interpret as wariness. He hesitated before continuing and then said, in a determinedly gentle tone, "If lives are so important, then why would you put them in such a precarious situation? Ramsey could have sold the lot at any time."

Was he making this her fault? She felt a stab of guilt at the truth of his words but at the same time refused to accept that she was primarily responsible for this situation. What she should have done didn't have any effect on the immediate situation, and he was the only one who could solve her problem.

She tucked her guilt down under the anger that was beginning to course through her. "Well, but you swooped in and took advantage of his desperate circumstances, didn't you?"

"What are you talking about?"

"His wife's medical bills. How did you find out? Do you do research to find vulnerable landowners who can be talked into selling their property to alleviate their financial hardship?"

His eyes narrowed in surprise. "He sought *us* out. Months ago. And not because of medical bills but because he and his wife want to sell up, buy an RV, and travel around the country. I think someone's been massaging the truth because he didn't want to disappoint you." She saw a flash of anger in his dark eyes. "But thanks for giving me the benefit of the doubt."

That last comment stung. "Well, I think he could be talked out of the decision," she replied rather feebly.

"Casey, you can't run a business on charity!"

"An animal shelter is not a business—it *is* a charity!"

Chapter 3

"And that attitude is why so many charities fail. Did you think that you would have a free building in perpetuity?"

"Yes, I did." It was the truth. There were good people like Mr. Ramsey in the world who were willing to give generously because they already had so much. "Pleasant Valley is a small town where things happen face to face and where people are kind to each other. Until, apparently, real estate developers get involved. That's why I moved there—to get away from people like you and a world where only money matters."

He sighed heavily. "In other words, you ran off to a place where you could cling to your delusions about people until cold, hard reality became apparent. And cold, hard reality is that things change and legal contracts are more dependable than people, no matter how nice they may seem."

"Yes, and money is more important than anything else, right?"

"Money is important," he answered evenly. "Maybe someone who has had it all her life doesn't understand that. But when you've been poor like I have, trust me, you understand it just fine."

She had no idea what he was talking about, which reminded her that she knew almost nothing about him. She had built her feelings for him on a fantasy, and her fury at him was matched only by her fury at herself for letting this happen yet again.

"So being poor sometime in the past gives you license to think only about yourself for the rest of your life?" she asked.

He swiped his hand through his hair, frustrated. "Yes, I think about myself. I don't ever want to go back to where I came from. So I live a little, try to enjoy what I've got. I also save and invest so that I won't ever have to be hungry again and so that the family I'll have someday won't ever have to be hungry either. Is that so wrong?"

She didn't know how to answer that. It was and it wasn't, in her opinion.

"But how can I expect someone like you to understand that?" he continued. Now he sounded condescending. Apparently she was nothing more than a spoiled rich girl in his eyes.

"Now thanks for giving *me* the benefit of the doubt," she spat out.

"I apologize. I shouldn't have said that." He paused as if expecting an apology in return and looked disappointed when she said nothing. "Anyway, none of that matters here. The main thing for you to understand is that I don't renege on contracts. I did nothing wrong in making this deal, and I won't back out." He looked at her and his eyes softened. "However, I can work out some extra time. I'll look into it and get back to you."

"Please don't bother. I'll figure it out on my own." She sounded sulky, which probably reinforced his image of her as a spoiled rich girl. At that moment, however, she wanted nothing from him.

His eyes were hard again. "Suit yourself. Now, if you'll excuse me." He walked past her without another word.

She tried not to watch Will as the evening progressed and as she forced herself to greet other attendees and engage them in small talk. He moved easily and affably through the crowd, shaking hands and joking with people. But he seemed closed off. His smile wasn't the big, open smile he had used with her on their first date and earlier this evening.

She watched as her mother sidetracked Will, with Charles in tow. They spent a few minutes in conversation. Katherine nodded her head toward Casey, and the two men looked her way as well. She had enough time to see the coldness in Will's eyes before she turned away in a pathetic attempt to appear as if she hadn't noticed them. Then she decided to go hide in the women's lounge, where she pretended to apply mascara for a good 15 minutes before she had the courage and sense of calm to re-emerge.

When she did, Katherine was waiting for her with Plan B.

"Casey, I'd like you to meet Dr. Henry Carruthers, a new resident at the hospital who has just arrived from Hawaii, of all places! Henry, my daughter Casey is a doctor of veterinary medicine who owns a practice locally. She'll be able to answer all your questions about how to meet young people." Casey smiled and shook his hand, while he gave her a friendly look in return.

"Oh, I'm sorry," Katherine said. "I need to say a quick hello to one of our long-term supporters." She waltzed away, leaving Casey and Henry smiling a bit awkwardly at each other.

"You're lucky you've arrived during warm weather," Casey said. "How do you think you're going to like the winter?" There was nothing more boring than a comment about the weather. If she was lucky, that might be enough to run him off.

"I'm excited to see. My family once went on vacation to Montana during the winter when I was a kid, so I *think* I like winter weather. Not that I'll have time to do anything but work, of course." He shrugged as Casey nodded her head in understanding.

"Yeah, come to think of it, I don't know when I've taken time to enjoy the winter weather myself."

"Well, we're just a few decades away from retirement, right?" he joked. He already seemed much nicer than many of the men her mother had introduced her to over the years.

"So you're a vet, huh?" he continued. "I've always heard it's even harder to get into vet school than medical school, and believe me I had to work *hard* to get into medical school." And he was modest, too.

"Well, I've always thought that's because animals are worth so much more than people," she said with a smile to let him know she was kidding. Well, half kidding.

"Part of me really wants to agree with you on that, but don't tell that to the other hospital people here tonight. Or my patients. And especially not the donors."

"What kind of medicine do you practice?" she asked.

"Pediatric oncology."

"Yikes, the most heart-wrenching kind."

"That's the sense people have, but actually it's really rewarding. You can save a life or you can at least cheer up a kid and give them some hope. Either way, you feel like you're doing something wonderful."

She smiled at him and nodded. "I know they are very different situations, but that's exactly how I feel about working with animals."

"I bet. I mean, our patients are similar: they aren't usually angry or violent, they don't refuse to take their meds, and they don't ask too many questions. They're relatively easy. Now, if I were a geriatric oncologist, forget about it."

Casey was surprised to find that she was actually enjoying herself. Something about Henry's pleasant manner calmed her down, and she felt a bit of distance grow between her and her anger toward Will. They continued to make small talk for a few more minutes as they sipped at their wine and accepted the occasional bite from the trays of hors d'oeuvres coming around. As people Casey knew walked by, she greeted them and made sure to introduce them to Henry.

But she couldn't keep her eyes off of Will, especially during the times when he was standing just a few feet away from her. She still felt self-conscious, especially as she caught him glancing over at her and Henry from time to time. She also felt angry with herself for caring so much. Was she flirting a little bit more than she normally would with Henry, just in case Will noticed? Such behavior was beneath her. At last she lost sight of him, and it occurred to her that he might want to avoid her as much as she wanted to avoid him.

The evening was passing by rather quickly, and soon enough people began to move toward the room where dinner and the ceremonies would be held. "May I accompany you to dinner?" Henry asked a bit shyly.

"I would like that," Casey answered, smiling at him sincerely. "But I'm sure my mother has assigned you to the doctors' tables. I'll be stuck somewhere at the back, knowing her. You're the stars here tonight!"

"Well, too bad," he answered. "We haven't had much of a chance yet to talk about what I could do around here when I do have some time off. Would you mind if I called you to follow up?"

This was weird: she had met two interesting men in a matter of days. Of course, Henry didn't bowl her over as Will had done so immediately. But he was a nice, attractive man, and she would enjoy seeing him again. Maybe he could take her mind off of Will for a couple of hours.

"I'd like that," she said, finding that she meant it, at least a little bit. She pulled her card out of the pocket inside her clutch and handed it to him.

The dining area was beautifully decorated, as always. Casey was seated at a table in the back with some of the lesser donors. They were mostly people from the local community who had had a particular experience with cancer and wanted to help out this cause buying a ticket or two, but not potential big donors for her mother's future causes. Casey conversed easily with an older couple whose granddaughter had received successful treatment for leukemia at the hospital five years earlier.

After dinner was served, Dr. Evans, the hospital chief of staff, stood to greet the crowd and call their attention to the program. First, they would hear a few stories from former hospital patients now in remission thanks to the care they had received. As each speaker called out the names of particular doctors, the crowd applauded heartily. It made for a very moving half hour, and Casey felt overwhelmed with admiration for the hard work and commitment of the medical staff, and for the courage of the survivors and their families.

Then there was a series of short speeches by a couple of doctors and researchers explaining what the hospital was poised to do if it were able to renovate and expand the oncology wing: the cutting-edge research to be carried out, the additional patients to be treated, the support to be provided in order to attract the very best doctors in the world. They also shared horrifying cancer statistics from the region, making it clear that they planned to address Tennessee's growing cancer problem. It was a brilliant set of speeches to open up all the pocketbooks in the crowd.

But they saved the best speech for last. Dr. Evans introduced Mr. William Ingalls, a real estate developer who had already been moved to match all donations up to a maximum of $7.5 million. Mr. Ingalls had graciously accepted their invitation to speak about why he had made this momentous decision and what he hoped it would inspire among attendees tonight.

Casey felt the breath sucked right out of her as she watched him walk to the podium. How could such a young man have that kind of money to give to a cause he cared about? He had truly seemed open and down-to-earth on their first date, which surely was impossible in someone already so wealthy and successful. She thought back to his perplexing statement about once being poor. She longed to know more, but it occurred to her that she wouldn't have the opportunity to ask him because she wasn't likely to see him again.

The sadness that accompanied the thought competed with the anger she still felt. It was sadness about the loss of a fantasy, she reminded herself. Surely such sadness would dissipate quickly.

Will was confident and persuasive, obviously at ease in this environment and with such an audience. He spoke simply about how he had been blessed with a successful, growing business building retirement and assisted living facilities. He spoke of his desire to do more in a state and community that had embraced him so generously upon his arrival two years earlier. And he described his relationship to a kind man who had taken him in when he was a mere 12-year-old boy with no one else to turn to.

In matter-of-fact terms, he told the audience that he had been born into poverty and neglect, finally abandoned by his mother while still in middle school. Coach Ingalls had taken him in, then adopted him, and taught him to be a man rather than an angry, sullen kid. The audience members were on the edge of their seats as he continued to describe Coach Ingalls' long battle with lung cancer, which finally took him at the young age of 54, just after he had sent Will off to college.

Will looked out from the podium. It felt as if he were looking straight into Casey's eyes as he continued speaking, although that seemed unlikely in such a large room packed with so many people.

"Any goodness I have in me is thanks to God Almighty and Coach Ingalls. I have lived a selfish life in many ways, but Coach always tried to teach me to take care of others as he had taken care of me. I was unable to do anything to help him then, so I am determined to help others in his name now. I ask you to join me in digging deep and donating every bit you can to this very important effort, which is sure to save the lives of people like Coach Ingalls, people like the survivors you've heard from tonight, and people like you and me long into the future." He left the podium to thunderous applause.

For a moment Casey felt like a heel. This was the man she had accused of selfishness, of caring about money more than anything else? But a part of her insisted on clinging to those beliefs. Sure, Will was willing to be generous when he could get up in front of an audience full of illustrious people and receive their applause. But he couldn't help out a small-town vet and a handful of needy animals because there was no limelight to shine on him as he did so. She recalled his arrogance and aloofness when he had informed her that business was business. Who was he kidding?

Fortunately, she didn't run into Will again that night. He stuck around for

Chapter 3

a little while, and she could see him receiving the handshakes and thanks of many of the attendees.

Katherine was next to her as they watched Will leave. "I was really hoping you would hit it off with that Will Ingalls," she said with a sigh. "What an impressive young man he is!" How surprised she would be to know that Casey and Will had already kissed in a parking lot. Casey couldn't help smiling at the irony.

Katherine seemed mollified later when she saw Casey talking with Dr. Henry Carruthers again. He made polite conversation about the success of the dinner, the moving speech of Will, and his hopes for the future of the oncology unit. He also made it clear that he would like to see her again, and she tried to muster some enthusiasm. So what if talking to Henry seemed a little dull next to the excitement of talking to Will? He was nice and modest and sweet. And *not* a greedy real estate developer.

Chapter 4

The following Tuesday, Casey entered the town hall with a feeling of dread. It was a rainy and muggy morning that had left Casey feeling sweaty and annoyed. Of course, the task ahead of her contributed to that annoyance.

The town council had called a meeting to discuss the conversion of the tree-filled lot into a retirement home and assisted living campus, and it was her last chance to convince anyone that her shelter should remain. She would even make an offer to buy the property herself. She had spoken with her disapproving financial manager and local bank manager and knew that she could make it work through refinancing her house, cashing out some of her retirement savings, and then taking a massive personal loan. That plan wasn't financially ideal or even financially sound, but it was all she could think of as a last resort.

Will was already there when she entered, with a couple of people presumably from his company: an unfortunately very attractive woman who had the aggressive and confident look of a lawyer, and a fresh-faced young man who seemed to stand in Will's shadow. They were shaking hands with town council members and a few others in attendance. Will glanced at Casey and nodded his head in recognition before looking away. She could feel his eyes on her from time to time, and their eyes locked briefly more than once.

She felt a longing for him, despite her anger, and her eyes couldn't help but look at him. He radiated power, confidence, and certainty of purpose. Just as she had noted at the fundraiser, in his world he looked closed, serious, every bit the successful business owner. He smiled and interacted with people affably enough, but not with the natural ease and openness that she had witnessed during their magical moments together.

She wondered what she radiated: naiveté, desperation, sadness? The way the powers-that-be of the town were circling around Will, making conversation and shaking hands with him and one another, led her to believe that her case was already lost. Still, she had to try for the sake of the shelter, now overburdened with the hoarding rescues.

They all sat as the meeting was called to order. The council asked to hear from Mr. Ramsey and Will about their plans. To Casey's surprise, Will only introduced himself briefly then ceded the floor to his colleagues to speak on his behalf. The woman, who did indeed turn out to be general counsel for the firm, introduced herself as Mandy Tremaine and explained the agreement between Mr. Ramsey and Coach Lifestyle Solutions and how the process of licensing and building the campus would unfold. Next, the young man, who introduced himself as Brad Anderson, community liaison, explained how Coach intended to enhance the community. They would provide ethical care for the elderly of this and nearby communities, they would provide jobs, and they would build a beautiful campus in line with the architecture and mood of the historic downtown area. The few people in attendance clapped loudly as each of these was announced.

The council asked for comments, and Casey rose. Jakob, Bethany, and an elderly shelter volunteer named Leeann stood with her in support, and they moved as a group to the front of the room. They were hardly a formidable lot in comparison with the Ingalls group, especially since Jakob and Bethany were wearing scrubs and Leeann was wearing a floor-length denim sundress covered with appliqued cats and rainbows that she had made herself. But Casey stood up straight and forced herself to remember that she was a knowledgeable professional and that she cared much more about this community than the Coach group did, which had to count for something.

Casey went for her first argument, which was that the building project would have negative environmental impacts. They would destroy 60 acres of woodland bordering downtown that hosted upwards of 40 bird species, including two species that were declining in the area, and numerous mammals and other animals. She gave statistics about overdevelopment throughout the state of Tennessee, and how that development was harming species, water quality, and quality of life for towns like theirs. There were already-developed lots available elsewhere that could serve the purposes of Coach Lifestyle Solutions, so why should this beautiful downtown property by the river, which they all valued so greatly, be sacrificed?

Then she got a little mean. She reminded the group of some recent cases in the news: assisted living facilities that had closed suddenly or been involved in fraud cases. Unfortunately, vulnerable populations such as the elderly attracted those who would exploit them. She was not suggesting that Coach Lifestyle Solutions was anything but ethical in intent, but some of their facilities had in fact been managed by one of the companies caught up in a fraud case. Shouldn't the town council learn more about this before automatically saying yes?

Next, she reminded the group of the value of the animal shelter to the community of Pleasant Valley. She called to a couple of people in the audience who had adopted animals from the shelter and saw them nod as she talked about how wonderful it was to unite a needy animal with a loving family. Although there was a county-run shelter available, it was over half an hour's drive away and under-resourced. The Pleasant Valley Shelter was the one people could call about feral cats or abused dogs in their neighborhoods or to take in pets they could no longer care for.

Finally, she asked the town council to let her buy the land herself. She would only be able to offer Mr. Ramsey two-thirds of what Coach was offering. Looking Mr. Ramsey in the eye, she said, "It's still a reasonable offer and would allow you to continue providing a service to your community that I know you value: taking care of animals in need and providing local families with loving companions. I ask that the town council nullify the contract with Coach Lifestyle Solutions and that Mr. Ramsey make a new contract with me as owner of the property."

She sat down, accompanied by the others, and tried to stop shaking. Would she succeed? The general mood of the room suggested to her that she would not, and she felt a sinking feeling in her stomach.

Town council members asked for additional comments, and there were none. Mandy Tremaine raised her hand and asked if she could respond to some of Dr. Young's comments, and she was granted permission to do so.

She assured attendees that ethical concerns were taken very seriously by their company. In fact, after the scandal brought up by Dr. Young, William Ingalls himself had made the decision that they could not trust management of their properties to anyone else. They had bought the management company, kicked out the leadership, and now ensured ethical accounting procedures were installed and followed to a T. Since that time, the company had had a spotless record and even won an award for ethical industry leadership.

She restated what Brad had said about providing jobs and other benefits to the community. Finally, she informed the crowd that they were increasingly incorporating green elements in their building plans and that this campus would be their most state-of-the-art project yet. She smiled winningly at the town council members before spreading her beneficent look to those in attendance, including Casey and her little crew.

Then Will rose and looked out at the audience, his eyes lingering on Casey's. "I take very seriously the important concerns raised by Dr. Young, who I know cares passionately about this community and about the work of the shelter that she founded and runs." He nodded at her in a way that let her know he wasn't being patronizing or insincere. She appreciated that. But she knew that he was going to win, and it was easy enough to concede such things to one's defeated enemy.

"I don't usually come to these town hall meetings," he continued, "because I have excellent colleagues, as you see, who are experienced in working with local communities and ensuring that our properties benefit them. But because I've gotten to know many of you"—again he looked at Casey—"I wanted to come personally and tell you directly that I care about this community, too. I care about the people who will live in this facility and the people who will work there. I care that this facility benefits all of you rather than taking away from your community. I appreciate the ethical concerns raised, and I promise ethical and affordable care for every future resident of this property, for which I will hold myself personally responsible." Will looked at her again, and she could see anger in the set of his jaw. She had publicly doubted his ethics and therefore his character.

There were a couple of claps from town council members. Yes, he had won.

"Dr. Young has given me some other things to think about, in terms of how such building projects affect the landscape and environment, and we will try to reflect some of her concerns in our updated plans, although I can't right now give specifics about how we will do so. And finally, I personally regret that the shelter will no longer have this piece of land because I am a pet owner myself and value the work the shelter has done. But I feel truly that the benefits of this proposal outweigh those costs. So I hope that you will allow the project to continue as planned—and as our signed contract has laid out."

This last statement contained a slight threat, and Casey remembered his words from the previous week. He believed in the sacredness of the legal contract, the only surety in a world of unreliable people.

It was a foregone conclusion that the town council would announce their support for the project, which they did to general applause. Bobby Roberson, the head of the council, then stood and beamed at Casey. Unlike Will, his attitude *was* patronizing—and more than a little self-congratulatory.

"Casey, I'm going to forget this Dr. Young business because you're one of us. We do admire and thank you for the important work of this shelter. And in that spirit, through personal fundraising among the council members and the allocation of some town funds, we have a check here in the amount of $15,000 toward the work of the shelter and hopefully the purchase of another piece of land so that you can continue it." There was applause. "I wish it could be more, but given that the residents of this town pay taxes toward the county shelter, we didn't feel right taking any more of their tax

Chapter 4

money than we already have. I hope you will accept this as our good faith gesture and deep thanks for what you have done."

Everyone clapped again, and Casey felt forced to rise, smile, and come forward. She shook Bobby's hand, accepting the gift. Of course, $15,000 would get them nowhere. It was a humiliating gift, and she felt humiliated to accept it. But she tried to make herself feel grateful, too; these were nice people, and they were trying to do something to soften the blow. She couldn't help glancing at Will. She expected to find him gloating a bit, but he merely regarded her speculatively.

Afterwards he sought her out. "Are you okay?" he asked, and she could hear sincere concern as well as lingering coldness in his tone.

"I have to be, don't I? You won. Which, as we know, you love to do."

He made an attempt at lightness. "So you still see me as your greedy real estate developer enemy?"

"Yes."

His eyes narrowed as he looked at her. "You certainly fight dirty."

"Well, you have to admit your industry doesn't have a spotless record where ethics are concerned."

"But how could you think that I would intentionally have anything to do with fraud and the mistreatment of vulnerable elderly people?"

He was hurt. "Well," she said defensively, "we don't know each other very well, do we?"

He looked steadily at her for a few moments and then sighed unhappily. "I thought we did."

Those words hurt her in turn. He had opened up and revealed himself to her, he seemed to be saying: couldn't she see that he was a good person?

She thought she had seen a good person in Will. But her father could be a good person, too. He could be a loving father and husband when he had time to be; he could be kind and generous to people when he chose to be. He would never kill anyone or deliberately hurt anyone in any way. But the deal was the deal, the dollar was the dollar. He put work above all else. He evaluated people's character by how successful they were and how they handled their money. He ridiculed Casey because she had spurned his money and business. He missed important events in Casey's life because he was busy signing the next contract. That simply was not her definition of "good."

And now Will had come to her little town and turned her kind, generous neighbors into people who thought like he and her father did. How much money could Ramsey get? How many jobs could the town get? What did a few little dogs and cats matter? And they had even put a monetary value on Casey's relationship with the town, a lousy $15,000 that was probably spooned out of the ridiculously huge Fourth of July fireworks budget.

So yes, she knew Will could be sweet and funny and open. But now she also knew that he was as ruthless as her father when it came to pursuing money and contracts. And someone motivated mostly by money was capable of any ethical breach, in her opinion.

She didn't think she could explain all of that to Will, so she said nothing. Mandy came to Will's side and gave him her winning smile. She clearly was attracted to him, as Casey imagined most women in his company must be. Mandy smiled at Casey less winningly and put her hand on Will's arm a bit possessively. "Ready to go?" she asked him.

Then Brad came to stand on the other side of Will. He smiled at Casey and said, "Thank you for expressing your concerns. I hope we can address them to your satisfaction."

Casey smiled politely as Brad gave her his card and insisted that she follow up with any other concerns because he felt that his job was to remain in an ongoing conversation with the people who lived in communities served by Coach Lifestyle Solutions. She didn't feel like being "handled," so she merely nodded and walked away. She didn't look at Will again. What was the point? It was over.

She gathered up her allies, and they headed back to the office. As always, she would immerse herself in her work, first and foremost planning what to do about the shelter. Her primary hope was that she could find another place that would suit her purposes. There were now 16 dogs and 18 cats. There was Jackie the African Grey parrot, who was doing fine as the office mascot but deserved a home with people who could devote more time to her. There were some aquariums housing hamsters, seven in all. And there was an iguana she had already promised to take in that would be arriving next week.

The hard part was finding a place with ample space for cats and dogs. The current shelter was useful because it included an indoor play area, plus a large yard with fencing.

She retained her faith that things would work out, as they had for the current shelter. That opportunity had fallen suddenly and magically into her lap.

By her second year in Pleasant Valley, she had been starting to think seriously about opening a shelter but not taking any steps yet to make it happen. Then one day she was talking with her friend Suzanne, who had stopped by the clinic to pick up her dog after a dental procedure. Suzanne was complaining about all the stray animals in town and how hard it was to get the county shelter folks to come all the way over to Pleasant Valley.

"Wish we had something closer," Suzanne said. "There's no way you could take them in here, could you, Casey?"

"I'm thinking about it. I've always wanted to run a shelter as well as a clinic. But I'd have to find the right location."

The Ramseys were in the lobby, waiting for lab results for their poodle, Minnie. Mr. Ramsey overheard the conversation and suggested, "What about that old building out back?" Within half an hour, Casey and Mr. Ramsey had made a deal. He had no intention of using the property, and he let the clinic lease it for $1 a year plus payment of his property taxes. It had cost Casey quite a bit of money to convert the space into an appropriate one, but overall the place had been a godsend.

That was how things worked in a small town like Pleasant Valley: people generously solved one another's problems to their mutual benefit. They didn't need to talk contracts and money, and they didn't put business before relationships.

Now Casey reminded herself that she still lived in that same small town. Will was wrong; his way was not the way of the town. Something would turn up. Casey was convinced of it.

Shelter

She got to work on the task of finding a temporary space to move into. She called prominent townspeople, landowners, and real estate agents and asked for their help locating other possibilities. Most were sympathetic, but with only a handful of them did she sense a real commitment to help. That was expected: people had limited time and interest in any one issue. But a handful of interested people was a good enough start.

Jakob also started calling around to pet stores and churches in the area to ask if they would be willing to host an animal adoption event. Casey had been remiss about those recently. If they could push themselves to do three or four of them in the next month, that would go a long way toward emptying out the shelter in case she couldn't find another location.

The only thing left to do was call shelters and ask if they could take in her animals if the worst happened and she wasn't able to find a new space. She couldn't face that possibility yet. She didn't want to hear resigned, guarded voices as they told her how overrun and overextended they already were. She made a mental note to begin those calls one month from now, if every other road had led to a dead end.

Then she directed her attention toward the day's remaining patients. The Brody family brought in their black lab, who was starting to get old and slowing down a bit. She saw a rabbit with digestive problems and reminded the family of the importance of supplying fresh hay every day rather than relying solely on store-bought rabbit pellets. She helped Janie Thompson make posters announcing her missing cat and tried to hint as kindly as she could that it was safer for cats to be kept inside. She trained Jakob on some new equipment for taking and analyzing blood. And she covered a couple of annual checkups for cats, examining blood and teeth, weighing the animals, and searching for lumps or other problems.

Just as they were about to close for the day, little Katelyn King and her mom brought in a cat carrier with a tiny ginger kitten curled up inside. "She just had to show y'all her new baby," Josie King said to Casey and her crew. Katelyn had been begging her parents for a kitten for the last couple of years of her seven-year life. They were a dog family, unsure if they wanted to venture into cat care.

Chapter 4

Everyone oohed and aahed over the kitten and Katelyn's obvious happiness. "So you finally gave in?" Casey asked Josie.

"No, fate caught up with us. Someone dumped her in our yard."

Casey shook her head. "Why do people do these things?"

"Well, this person was better than most: he left an open can of food next to her."

Casey took out the little cat and examined her. No obvious fleas or mites, eyes clear. "Do you want me to fix her up now, or do you want to come back next week? She needs an exam, shots, and so forth."

"Oh, we don't want to trouble you now. Katelyn just insisted that we bring the kitten into town to show Grandma and then, of course, you."

Casey assured her it was no problem and stayed a few extra minutes giving the cat a check. "Take care of this little baby, Katelyn," Casey said when she had finished, patting the child on the back. "I can tell she already loves you."

"I'm her mommy!" Katelyn declared, kissing the kitten on the head. The little creature mewed in return.

Thanks to Katelyn, Casey ended the day with a smile on her face, despite all the turmoil in her head. An abandoned cat now had loving home, and a sweet little girl would begin a lifetime of loving and taking care of pets.

Casey's hopeful mood mostly held through the week. The new arrivals from the hoarding situation were mild-mannered animals with big trust issues, so she and the staff spent as much time as possible with them. She devoted lots of nighttime hours to providing them with medical care. She called a couple of high school kids who loved to come in and care for animals, and they joined her usual roll of volunteers. By early the following week, a couple of cats were allowing themselves to be petted, and some of the new dogs were now playing in the outdoor areas with the other dogs, although they were still a bit skittish about human touch.

Keeping busy was good for her state of mind, allowing her to forget about Will for minutes at a time. When she went home at night, though, her thoughts oscillated between anger and longing, and these strong emotions found their way into her dreams as well. She wondered in despair how long it would be before she could forget about Will completely.

Chapter 5

"Coach Lifestyle Solutions just announced plans to build a retirement home in my little town!" Casey informed the other members of the Save Wild Tennessee executive board at their monthly meeting the following Tuesday night. The faces of her colleagues reflected the horror she felt. "They're building it smack dab in the middle of downtown, right on the river, where there's a beautiful bunch of woods and a stunning natural view."

"Typical for them," Randy scoffed.

Shay let out a dramatic sigh.

Latasha added, "And let me guess: there was absolutely no local opposition."

"None," Casey said. "I gave it my best at the town council meeting: I called their ethics into question, I gave information about wildlife numbers in decline and how that was an environmentally sensitive area. I even tried to use sympathy for my animal shelter. Nothing worked."

"What do you mean, sympathy for your animal shelter?" Sallie asked.

"Oh, that's the real clincher for me. They've bought the land that was donated to me for the shelter. So now I have to find a way to move it or close it down."

She listened to their angry grunts and sympathetic words.

Shay asked, "What did you talk about in terms of ethics?"

Chapter 5

Casey explained the problem with the former management company, and Shay looked at her thoughtfully.

"Hey, this is a new angle," Randy said, picking up on what Shay was obviously thinking. "We've always focused our ad campaigns on environmental issues. Rightly so. But this is a big conversation right now: the fear people have that nursing homes are neglecting residents at best and actively abusing them at worst. Maybe we could use this to draw some new attention to our cause."

Casey had looked forward to telling the group about her problem with Will and getting their sympathy. The small part of her that wanted revenge was happy to envision some kind of effort to publicly shame Coach Lifestyle Solutions and Will through it. She had even entertained a small glimmer of hope that their actions could halt the project in Pleasant Valley and allow her to keep that land. But she wasn't sure Will deserved an ongoing public shaming about the past ethical breach of another company—a breach that he had worked to correct.

She explained her hesitation to the group.

"Yeah, sure, you're right," Shay conceded. "We don't want to slander anyone who doesn't deserve it. But it's worth looking into."

"I'll be happy to do some research," Randy offered.

"Well, at the commission hearing, the owner of the company made it clear that they have dealt with those ethical problems," Casey explained. "They ended up buying the management company and transforming it to keep within their ideals."

Latasha laughed. "Easy words, Casey. Of course, that's what he said. But as you know, these guys lie pretty easily. Look at how Ryan Builders produced that report about earning mitigation points by restoring two acres of sensitive environmental land for every acre they developed somewhere else in the state. Lies, lies, lies!"

Shay shook her head. "Yeah, we can't just take it at face value."

Sallie spoke up in a firm tone. "We need to move on to the next item on our agenda. Randy, do some research and report back at our next meeting, okay?"

"Will do," Randy said.

They continued their discussion of other companies listed on their petition and how to reach out to those who had signed and get them involved in whatever new campaign SWT would carry out in the next few weeks. They had gained 1,200 signatures total.

Casey left the meeting feeling excited about where they were going. She had a nagging concern deep inside, however, about how quickly the others had grabbed onto this idea of accusing Coach Lifestyle Solutions—and therefore Will—of ethical violations. She knew what they were like, especially Randy and Shay, when they were out for blood. She reassured herself with the thought that they were also careful about substantiating claims with good evidence. After all, Latasha had once practiced law and knew what she was about.

Anyway, Casey reminded herself, she didn't know Will all that well, nor did she know what he had been willing to do in order to build his wildly successful business. If he deserved a campaign against him and the company because of past ethical breaches, then so be it. Why should she try to protect him just because they had had a really fun first date?

***

When she arrived at the clinic the next morning, Jakob jumped right in front of her and said, "Guess what?" He looked at her, hand over mouth in a sorry attempt to hold in his giggles.

"I can't even begin to imagine," she answered, meaning it. She never knew what that mischievous look on Jakob's face might suggest.

"I just vetted a new volunteer. He starts tomorrow. He has grant writing and fundraising experience!"

She breathed a sigh of relief. More news to give her some optimism. She wasn't making any headway on finding another location she could afford, so the next plan would be to raise some money—and quickly.

Jakob peered at her expectantly.

"What?" she asked.

"Nothing. It's just that he's cute and I think you'll like him."

"Okay."

He kept looking at her, trying not to laugh.

"WHAT?" She was half amused, half annoyed.

"Nothing. It's just … well, it will be interesting to have him here."

"Sounds good," she said and moved away from him and the weirdness of the conversation. She didn't care what this new guy looked like or how interesting he was. If he could find her some money, asap, that's all that mattered to her.

That Saturday morning, Jakob was already there and hard at work when she entered the clinic. "Ready to meet our volunteer?" he asked her immediately. "He should be here in ten or fifteen minutes." That mischievous look was back on his face.

"What's up with you, Jakob? Who is this volunteer?"

"Just someone who is definitely your type."

She looked at him skeptically. "And what is my type?"

"Self-possessed enough to date a small-town vet who is also a crazy cat lady?" he suggested with a smile.

She threw some paper clips at him and turned away to get some coffee. "Want something to drink?" she asked.

"No, already caffeinated, thanks."

"How long have you been here?"

"An hour or so."

She walked back over to him and gave him a side hug. "Jakob, I cannot thank you enough for all the extra time you're putting in. I don't know what I'd do without you."

He gave her his angelic look, arms folded in prayer and batting his eyelashes toward heaven. "You're welcome. Katie is busy with work these days, too, so I don't have much else to do."

In that case, she hoped Katie would stay busy for a while longer. She really needed Jakob now.

"How is Katie?" she asked.

"Bitchy. She's working too much and she's tired. I'm going to surprise her tonight by taking her out for a nice dinner."

"Maybe you should surprise her instead by actually doing the dishes for a change," Casey offered with an angelic smile of her own. This was one of their favorite topics: how Jakob needed to do more to help Katie instead of just wanting to go out and have fun with her all the time. "Or maybe offering some childcare."

"What, with that little devil?" Emma was a truly angelic-looking, towheaded five-year-old girl who knew how to push all of Jakob's buttons.

"You're going to be her stepdad, you know. You're actually going to have to take care of her sometimes."

"That's for Bio-Dad to do. I'm just there for the fun stuff. And only when she's willing to behave."

Casey clucked her tongue and shook her head at him. "And you wonder why Katie keeps putting off the wedding date."

He shook his finger in her face. "That's where you're wrong, Doc. She's waiting for my boss to give me a freakin' raise!"

Casey flashed him her best mean-boss look. "Well, then, you're never getting married."

This time he threw paper clips at her.

"Pick those up!" she commanded in her best mean-boss voice.

She sat at the desk and settled into some paperwork. She wanted Jakob to work on some inventory needs early the following week and gather estimates for maintenance work the clinic needed. Jakob was a hard worker but only if he had clear guidelines, so she always had to put in some extra effort to get him started.

She heard a knock at the still-locked door, and Jakob rose to answer it. "Well, hello again, Will!" he exclaimed loudly, and Casey heard Will's voice answer, "Hello again, Jakob."

"And you know Doc—uh, Dr. Young. Casey."

Casey swiveled around in her chair, frowning. "What are you doing here?" she asked Will, not bothering with polite greetings. Jakob looked back and forth between her and Will with glee, wringing his hands in excitement.

Will stepped toward her, not at all cowed by her attitude. "Well, I saw a

Chapter 5

need, and I think I can help fill it. I have fundraising and grant writing skills, and it seems to me that you're in need of some funds. I'm here to help!" He smiled with confidence, sure this statement would please her.

"Hmmm. But you live in Nashville and have a very busy job taking over properties and wowing people with your impressive donations," she retorted. Why did she have to sound so shrewish? "Do you really have time for our little out-of-the-way shelter?"

He maintained his friendly demeanor. In fact, he looked pretty darn pleased with himself. "Yes, I have cleared out my schedule and will be here every Saturday for the foreseeable future. If you'll have me, that is," he added with a smile that suggested he couldn't think of a single reason why anyone wouldn't have him.

"Oh, we'll have you!" Jakob said, "We can sure use that kind of commitment."

"Well," Casey interjected, "I wouldn't say that we are in great need—we can certainly find our way ourselves. But we're always grateful for volunteers."

That seemed like the least she should say. She was flustered. She had thought she would never see him again, and now she would presumably be seeing him every Saturday from now on. She had also thought she never *wanted* to see him again, and here she was thrilled at the sight of him, her heart thumping inside her chest.

She had no idea how to interpret his motives. Was he trying to say he was sorry? Was he making fun of her? Was he trying to prove something to her? And why did she feel so antagonistic toward all of these possibilities?

She decided her best course of action for now was to distract him and get him away from her. "You can certainly be useful working on grants and some ideas for raising funds, but we also need help socializing the animals. We just took in some rescues from a hoarding situation, and they're in pretty rough shape. So you'll have to do some of that, too." She looked him up and down, taking in the expensive, dry-cleaned jeans, the tailored button-down shirt that fit him so snugly, the immaculately clean boots. "Uh, are those clothes you can get dirty?"

He stepped toward her, cutting into her personal space, and then leaned over her desk. Now his face was more level with hers, and he looked intently at her, his eyes twinkling with amusement. "Sure, I'll do whatever you need. Just make sure you play to my strengths and let me do what I can to help you with the future of the shelter rather than giving me busy work that anyone could do."

Casey was reminded of Will's scolding tone when he called her efforts unrealistic and unsustainable. He doesn't think I know what I'm doing here, she thought, irritated. She stood and retreated from him, then pulled her white lab coat from the back of the chair and pulled it over her slacks and t-shirt. Hopefully that made her look a little more professional.

She said in a matter-of-fact way to Jakob, "I'll handle the first appointments. Please take Will over to the shelter and get him started." Jakob smiled at her, not even trying to suppress his excitement at the drama in the room.

Jakob led Will out the back of the practice, and Casey breathed a sigh of relief. She glanced around the room, trying to see it as Will had. It was neat and clean enough—she insisted on this—but was otherwise a little drab and run down. It hardly looked like the kind of thriving, polished urban practice that he probably took Barney to. In fact, it looked like a place that did need some help, and she couldn't stand the possibility that he might see it—and her—this way. Fortunately, she was saved from dwelling on these thoughts by the arrival of Bethany, followed by the day's first patient, a cat who seemed to be drinking too much water. She hoped it wouldn't turn out to be diabetes, but there was only one way to find out. She dismissed thoughts of Will and moved into the rhythm of what she knew best: caring for animals and comforting their humans.

She didn't see Will again all morning since she remained in the clinic and he in the shelter. At noon she decided to make her way over there and directly address the absurdity of his presence in her work life. She entered the shelter to find him on the floor, looking at something on a tablet while petting a cat that was curled up in his lap.

"What are you doing?" she asked.

"I'm socializing a cat and looking up grant possibilities," he answered, proud of himself. "Multi-tasking!"

Chapter 5

She had to give him credit. "That poor cat has been slow to get used to human touch. I can't believe you've got her in your lap."

"I've always had a certain power over women." He looked at Casey and raised his eyebrows. "Well, some women." He patted the cat's head. "This one, at least. Right, girl?" He looked back at Casey. "The funny thing is I don't even like cats. I can't imagine why she likes me."

"Cats are contrary like that. They like to mess with your head."

He laughed.

She got serious. "What are you doing here, Will?"

"I meant what I said. I'm here to help."

"But you wouldn't help by even entertaining the idea of stopping that deal."

"I told you: I couldn't stop that deal. What I can do is help you find another situation. A *better* situation."

"I don't need you; I can figure that out for myself. I have the help of Jakob, Bethany, a host of volunteers, my contacts in the animal shelter world, access to potential donors." She wondered if she should cross her fingers behind her back since she was exaggerating almost to the point of lying.

"Yes, but I want to help you ensure the future of this shelter, not just move it to the next free space that it will be kicked out of down the road." His tone was light, but his words hit her like a punch to the guts.

"Well, why don't you stick to your world, where things are done in contracts rather than human relationships? Or, since you like to make donations, why don't you just give us a couple million bucks and then you can walk away without wasting any more of your time?"

"Now you're thinking," he proclaimed in triumph. "It's money in the bank that you need, not just nice volunteers and friends in the animal shelter world. I knew you would see it my way."

Oops, she had backed herself into a corner on that one. How exasperating!

He got up and placed the cat gently on the top of the nearest cat tree and then turned to face her. "Actually, I could and would love to make a donation. But I know you wouldn't accept it."

He was right, so she didn't say anything.

"So I'd like to help in other ways," he continued.

"Okay. Just realize that you have to serve in all the roles of a volunteer, and right now we need other things. Please talk to Jakob about your ideas about fundraising, and he can run them by me." She turned to go.

She felt his hand on her arm, pulling her back toward him. "Jakob is a very nice kid, but I'd rather be efficient and go straight to the horse's mouth. Not that you look anything like a horse's mouth." He let his eyes linger over her face and hair appreciatively, and she could feel her face redden. She had kept the lab coat on because it gave her more certainty of purpose, with "Casey Young, D.V.M." embroidered on the pocket. But she felt exposed and vulnerable under his gaze.

"What time is closing?" he continued. "You and I could arrange to meet just after closing each Saturday so I can update you on my ideas and the information I've found. Maybe over dinner?" The request was made with a smirk; he knew she would refuse.

Jakob burst through the door at that moment. "Doc, Francis Whisenhunt just brought his Golden in, and he's throwing up. You'd better come." All her attention immediately went to the dog and his needs. "Okay, whatever," she said distractedly to Will and then followed Jakob back into the clinic. Fortunately, the dog turned out to be fine.

At 5:00, Will came into an exam room to find Casey scrubbing an exam table with sanitizer and a sponge. "What are you doing?" he asked.

"Cleaning up. Protocol at the end of the day."

"You do it yourself?" He raised his eyebrows.

"Sometimes. Bethany had to leave early, so I told her I would finish up."

He shook his head almost imperceptibly.

"What?" she demanded.

"Nothing, I just think the vet should be the vet and the employees the employees. You could be talking to me about the future of the shelter—and your practice—right now, something that Bethany can't do."

She rolled her eyes and looked back down at the table. "So now you're going to volunteer to tell me how to run my clinic, too? Why don't you just come early next weekend and show me how to perform surgery while you're at it?" She finished wiping down the table in a frenzied way. Next

Chapter 5

she grabbed the mop and went after the floor, taking a childish pleasure in brushing the dirty mop against his nice boots.

He laughed and stepped back. "Like I said, I'm here to do what's needed." He grabbed the mop, against her protests, and began mopping the floor. She left to clean out the next exam room, and in a few minutes he had followed her there.

"So when can you be ready for dinner?" he asked.

"What dinner?"

"You said we could grab dinner and talk over my fundraising ideas."

She remembered that she was having dinner with Henry that night. She had said yes because she didn't want to be rude to such a nice person, but she had had difficulty mustering any enthusiasm for it. Now she was grateful to Henry; otherwise, she probably wouldn't be able to resist taking Will up on his offer. Will stimulated her, even amidst her anger. She was irresistibly drawn to him, Lord help her.

"I was distracted by the dog situation," she said, shaking her head. "I didn't mean to say yes. We can discuss anything we need to discuss here in the office, next Saturday."

"Well, can I go get you some dinner while you finish cleaning up?" He sounded disappointed.

"No, thanks." She kept her head down, busy with her task. "Actually, I have plans for dinner a little later. I just have a couple more things to do and then I'm leaving. You might as well head back to Nashville now."

"Okay," he conceded. "But Casey?" She felt compelled to look up. "Remember what I said: you should play to my strengths. I can really help you if you'll let me."

"Help the shelter, you mean," she corrected sharply. He couldn't seem to understand how his use of the word "help" irritated her.

"Okay, the shelter, then."

"Well, thanks for your work today," she said dismissively. "Good night." She couldn't help appreciating his dark chocolate eyes, the curls around his ears and neck, the window of dark hair where his shirt was unbuttoned.

"Good night," he said and exited the room. She heard the front door close behind him a few seconds later, and she leaned back against the exam table and sighed a long sigh of relief. The day-long effort to keep her feelings for him at bay had exhausted her. How was she going to survive the next few weeks?

***

Poor Henry. He had come all this way, and she was having a hard time concentrating on their dinner conversation. He really was a nice guy. Cute, too, with his neat black hair and glasses, his tanned skin and eyes that hinted of some Polynesian ancestry. Thank goodness he had dressed down, since she was only up for wearing jeans herself. They had gone to a diner instead of a nice restaurant. It felt more like a friendship-that-might-turn-into-something-someday kind of a date than an actual one, and she tried to relax and just enjoy his company.

He told her about his new job at the hospital and how hard it was to fit into the hierarchy. "Doctors really piss on their territory," he explained. "Even if they like you, it's hard for them to trust you and let you in. I feel like I'll have to work to prove myself for several months before it lets up."

"That's one of the reasons I wanted my own clinic," Casey replied.

"Yes, but it can feel good to be part of a team. Hopefully the others will have my back and teach me what they know. Maybe it's just because I'm at the beginning of my career, but that feels good right now."

"I understand that." She told him something of her troubles with the shelter, admitting that it was difficult to face the situation with all of the responsibility squarely on her shoulders. Henry seemed sympathetic and asked a lot of questions about her options. He was a good listener, too. If she hadn't just met Will, would she be more inclined to view Henry romantically?

She tried to get to know him a little better. He told her he had wanted to be a doctor since he was a child, patching up his younger brothers and sisters when they were hurt.

"Did you ever think about doing anything else?" she asked.

He shook his head. "And you?"

Chapter 5

She shook her head and laughed. "My father wanted me to take over the family company, a real estate development firm. But I never seriously considered that."

"Why doesn't he develop a little real estate for your shelter?"

Good question. And there was a very good answer. Suddenly, uncharacteristically, she wanted to share that answer with Henry. Perhaps it was her exhaustion and anxiety. Perhaps it was Henry's obvious empathy. Perhaps it was because she had bottled up too much that day, trying to downplay her feelings for Will. Whatever the reason, she began to tell Henry a long story that dated back to when she was 16 years old.

Obtaining an apprenticeship with a wildlife rehabilitator named Orville Tatum had been Casey's first step toward carving out her own life. As her junior year of high school was coming to an end, she was becoming more and more depressed at the thought of spending the summer interning at her father's company, CY Properties. He had been forcing the idea on her since the beginning of her junior year, after talking about it in vague terms for most of her life. She was going to start out in human resources and then perhaps move into sales and marketing. It was the beginning of her preparation to follow in his footsteps and join the firm. After all, he liked to joke, she already had the right initials.

But Casey had been developing another idea that year. Back in the fall, she had started walking at a nearby park on weekends. She always passed a house where there seemed to be an odd assortment of wild animals living in captivity and a white-haired, imposing-looking man caring for them. At some point in the late fall she had gotten up the nerve to strike up a conversation with him, even though he had seen her walk by numerous times and never even waved at her.

"Hello, sir," she called out from the sidewalk. The house was a large brick two-story, set off from the road. She could see a large metal building behind the house and several cages of different types and sizes scattered around the yard. She had picked out a raccoon in one and some kind of hawk in another.

The man, who seemed impossibly tall now that she was closer to him, looked at her with a stern expression and waited for her to say more.

"May I ask what you're doing?" she continued. "Do you work with wildlife?"

He reluctantly gave her a short explanation of what a wildlife rehabilitator does, and it was music to her ears. She had no idea there was an official title for this labor of love. He turned away without a goodbye, but she hardly noticed because her mind was overflowing with questions and dreaming of possibilities. How did one learn? Was there a school? Was this something she could do for a career? She had already decided on being a vet, but maybe she could be a wild animal vet, if there were such a thing. She spent the next week finding out everything she could, including the fact that state-certified wildlife rehabilitators had to apprentice themselves for a long period of time to an existing state-certified wildlife rehabilitator. And she discovered it was indeed a labor of love, performed as a volunteer rather than as a paid employee.

None of that information daunted her. The next week she was brimming with excitement as she returned to talk to the man. Once again he gave her his stern, unsmiling look. She decided not to ask him outright if she could be his apprentice but, instead, to ask him about the raccoon. He answered that it had been hit by a car and he was working to heal its leg before returning it to the wild. She asked a lot of questions about how he knew what to do with the leg and how he would train the animal once healed, and he answered them in short, measured sentences.

Then he said, "Well, you'd better be on your way," and she left. But she thought she detected a slight smile on his lips as he dismissed her.

She went back just about every Saturday for weeks with more questions. Gradually, Orville introduced her to the animals currently under his care, showed her his workshop in the metal building, and explained the different kinds of cages and equipment he used. During this period, the raccoon returned to the wild and Orville found the red-tailed hawk, clearly blind, a home in a raptor rescue and education center. Gradually, she came to feel that Orville appreciated her desire to learn more about wildlife rehabilitation. Somewhere along the way, his wife Lettie came out and introduced herself, and from then on the visits included a glass of lemonade and some cookies.

Casey kept these visits from her parents, who were fortunately too busy on weekends to notice how long she took to return from her walks. She couldn't bear to share this budding interest with them because she knew they wouldn't like it. It was like wanting to play basketball instead of take piano lessons, or wanting to dance tap instead of ballet, or wanting to play with the housekeeper's daughter rather than the girls who lived in their neighborhood. It just wasn't *done*, at least not by their daughter. And Casey didn't have enough of a sense of herself yet to stand up to them about such things.

But by early spring, she had to act. She presented Orville with a proposal that she become his apprentice, outlining the hours she could work and the tasks she could fulfill at first, until she learned more. He listened to her proposal with a smile—well, his version of a smile, which looked to the uninitiated more like a snarl.

"Nope," he said simply when she had finished. "I've enjoyed having you visit and take an interest, but all that sounds like too much to me. And you're a teenager: you'll probably get busy and lose interest, and then where will I be?"

She swallowed her disappointment and ran home. Imogen, the housekeeper, saw her tears and comforted her. Casey thought about the situation all week, came back the following Saturday, and asked again. This time Orville said, "I reckon we can make it work if you're that determined." He didn't seem particularly happy about it, but she was. She dashed back home, hugged Imogen, and began planning her life as a vet and wildlife rehabber.

In the midst of her triumph, she also made the decision to tell her parents. They took it pretty well, hardly even responded at all. Charles reminded her of the many benefits of the summer internship at his company and suggested that she do both: intern there at a reduced time of 30 hours per week and devote the rest of her time and weekends to her apprenticeship with Orville, whom he, of course, would have to meet before she began. She agreed.

Her happiness continued all summer. By the end of it, she was just beginning to learn the basics, and she looked forward to continuing through her senior year in high school and hopefully even while she was in college. She told this to Orville one day, and he chuckled and said, "So your father was wrong: you didn't get tired of it after all."

"What do you mean?" Casey asked, at full attention. What did her father have to do with anything?

Orville looked up in mild alarm and then sighed. "Well, I let that slip and shouldn't have. Your father and I had a talk last spring about me taking you on for the summer. He didn't think your interest would last through the summer, and he was wrong. That's all."

She could sense that Orville was holding something back. "Well, it's not just the summer, right? I want to keep going so I can get my license, and I need a lot more months of apprenticeship."

Orville stopped what he was doing and looked at her. "Don't look so riled up. Of course, you can keep going. But you ought to know that your father paid me to take you on this summer, and he may have an expectation that the service he paid for has now come to an end."

Casey was taken aback. "He paid you?"

"Sure did. I'm an old man, and I didn't much want a teenager around. But your dad gave me some money I wanted to buy more equipment, asked if I would see you through the summer. He thought you'd get tired of spending the time and come to your senses." He patted Casey's hand. "I'm glad you didn't."

Casey was furious. She had been congratulating herself on getting this apprenticeship all on her own, free for once of the overbearing influence of her family. She had felt excited to find something that was all hers, that would allow her to develop interests that her parents hadn't forced on her. But it had all been a lie.

That evening, she had made a plan for independence from her parents. Her grandparents had put together a trust for her, enough to pay for college in addition to the scholarships she would receive. When she left home and moved into the dorm, she swore to herself she would never again accept help or money from her parents. And she hadn't.

So, she explained to Henry, asking for her father's help now was out of the question.

Henry nodded. "Somehow I saw that ending coming."

They went on to talk about Henry's huge and chaotic family. His parents had been too busy raising their seven kids to tell Henry what he should do with his life. They were glad enough he had turned out to be a doctor but upset that he had moved so far away. "My mother keeps telling me I can stay here until I have her grandchildren, and then I'm honor bound to return to Hawaii."

Casey laughed, and then Henry looked at her seriously. "I don't mean to stick my nose in your business, but I wonder if you should give your father the chance to understand your situation and help you out. We grow up, and our parents can change, too. The whole dynamic of your relationship is probably different now, right? And family is basically all we've got, right?"

Casey hesitated, then replied, "I appreciate the advice, and you may be right. I'll think about it." She was being polite; she knew she would never consider this. She had had too many bad conversations about her life with her father, and they had finally found a mostly peaceful equilibrium she had no desire to disrupt. She feared there was no room for their relationship to grow.

She and Henry spent the rest of their evening talking about fun things to do around Nashville. "Well, thanks for the information," he said, "but I hope I'll get to experience more of the wild and crazy nightlife of Pleasant Valley, too." He said it with the touch of shyness that she remembered from the fundraiser and liked very much. Yes, he was an attractive, nice man.

"You're welcome any time," she answered, smiling at him and trying to mean it.

They parted ways with a hug, and she drove back home thoughtfully. If Will were permanently out of the picture, she could see herself being very glad to have met Henry and happily anticipating their next date. But with Will coming around every Saturday for who knew how long, would she be able to move on and forget about him? She knew the answer was no, and she determined to put a stop to his involvement in her life. She could hardly prevent him from volunteering. But maybe she could make him no longer want to.

She got home and headed to bed. Meow snuggled against her face. She breathed in his clean-smelling fur and listened to his contented purr as she drifted off, unfortunately already beginning to dream sweet dreams of Will.

Chapter 6

While Casey was driving to the clinic early the following Saturday, she was still wondering what, specifically, she could do to drive Will away. Showing her antipathy towards him didn't seem to be enough. The solution presented itself when she arrived.

Someone had left two kittens on their doorstep. She estimated them at four weeks old, much too young to be separated from their mother. Jakob had immediately gotten to work on bottle feeding them and warming up their little bodies. It seemed they had just been dropped off early that morning, so Casey thought they had a good chance of surviving.

She felt a burst of anger as she imagined the situation. These people had an outdoor cat they hardly took care of. They had found the kittens somewhere around the yard and taken them to the clinic without even thinking about the kittens' needs at that age. On the other hand, Casey tried to appreciate their choice to bring the kittens to the vet. Too often people just threw them out of their car windows as they raced down the highway near a wooded area, or threw them in the trash, or drowned them. At least these people had *some* heart. Still, she prayed her usual prayer that these and other people would embrace spaying and neutering. If only there were a better way to educate people about this necessity, or to get local government more involved. Too many cats suffered in this population glut. And, of course, all those feral or semi-feral cats were hard on wildlife, especially birds.

Casey's eyes filled with tears as she looked down at the poor little creatures, sleeping soundly in their little bed. A plan formed in her mind.

She was in the process of a long conversation with one of the recent rescues, a frightened beagle, when Will interrupted with a hearty "Good morning!" She wondered how long he had stood there and listened to her ramblings about the wonderful future the beagle could look forward to in his forever home.

"Good morning," she answered, rising from where she sat on the floor.

He held a plastic carrier against him with three cups of coffee from the café next door. He waved his hand over them. "Hazelnut with cream and sugar, regular with cream and sugar, or black?"

She decided to play nice. "Oh, thanks. Hazelnut with cream and sugar, please."

"I knew it!"

Why did he always have to be triumphing over her? Her gratitude for his kind gesture now melted away. She supposed that was a good thing; gratitude could interfere with her need to be tough.

She took a sip of the coffee. "By the way, we keep travel mugs in the kitchenette that you could use next time. Cuts down on paper and plastic."

"Yes, boss," he said. She looked up to find him smiling at her, despite the sharpness of her tone. He just didn't take her seriously at all. "Would you be available to meet at the end of the day today to talk about some things?" He winked mischievously and added, "I want to make sure to get in your calendar well in advance this time around." And why did he always seem to be baiting her?

"Well," she answered, trying to sound commanding, "I actually have a special assignment for you today and for the next few weeks. I'm not sure you'll have time to do much work on fundraising and grants."

"I anticipated that you might say something like that," he replied evenly. "So I did a lot of work on it during the past week. Now I just need fifteen minutes of your time to report on some of my conclusions and ideas." He sounded triumphant again: he had outsmarted her. "But what is this special assignment?"

"I need you to take care of two kittens who were dropped off this morning before we got here. They are much too young to be separated from their mother, so we need your *help*. Jakob will go over the basics with you, and then you can use today to figure it all out."

She emphasized the word "help" and tried to sound a little patronizing as he always did when he said it, wondering if it would irritate him as much as it did her. He noticed the emphasis and grinned, catching on to her once again. He was determined not to be offended by anything, it seemed, only amused.

"We'll give you the first couple of weeks' worth of supplies when you leave with them this evening," she added.

His eyes opened wide. Now she had gotten his attention. "You want me to take the kittens home with me?"

"Yes, they need round-the-clock care."

"From me?"

She stared at him, pretending surprise. "You said you wanted to help."

"Yes, but I don't know anything about how to care for motherless kittens."

"Well, that's what today is for," she answered soothingly. "It's simple enough. They're going to need bottle feedings every eight hours supplemented with a gruel that you make from wet food and formula. They're also going to need a lot of socialization, so you'll have to schedule in some play time. They should be able to figure out a litter box at this point, but you may need to supervise that over the next week or so." She smiled sweetly at him. "Don't worry: you'll be ready by the time 5:00 rolls around."

He let out a breath.

She dropped the next bomb. "If you're not willing to do whatever needs to be done, then we can't really use you as a volunteer. I'll understand if that isn't acceptable to you and you'd rather stop volunteering."

He looked at her speculatively. "So you're willing to leave two vulnerable kittens with an amateur who doesn't even like cats, in an attempt to drive him away?" It suddenly sounded petty coming from his lips.

"Not to drive you away," she fibbed. "But you should know the reality of volunteering here. Are you not sure that you can take good care of them?"

"Oh, I'll take *great* care of them, just to prove to you that I can." A flash of arrogance—real arrogance this time, not his usual mock version—crossed his face as he said these words, and she knew them to be true.

"See?" she said lightly. "I knew you were the right person for the job!" Finally she was the one who got to have the "I told you so" tone. To be honest, however, she had been hoping he would refuse. She should have known better. He was determined to volunteer, and she thought he had just expressed the reason why: he was determined to prove himself. She must have hurt his pride when she called his character into question, and now he wanted to make her eat her words. Maybe if she thanked him profusely for his "help" someday soon and went on and on about what a wonderful person he was, then he would go away and she could live her life in peace. But she didn't think she could muster those words quite yet.

He looked at her with resolve. "Do you have time now to show me what to do?"

She glanced at her watch. "Actually, I have appointments. I'll send Jakob. You know, the vet is the vet, and the employees are the employees." He rolled his eyes and shook his head, but he also had an amused glint in his eyes; he was getting a kick out of this banter with her. "In the meantime, will you go around and spend a little time with each of the dogs along this wall? I didn't make it all the way around."

"Sure." At least he would like that job. "And will you give me fifteen minutes at the end of the day?"

He was like a dog with a bone. She decided to concede, admitting to herself that she was curious about what he had to say. "Sure."

She left and asked Jakob to give Will a few minutes with the dogs and then head in to help him with the kittens.

***

The next Saturday, Will looked a bit more tired than usual, with some circles under his eyes.

"Wow, you look exhausted!" she and Jakob both said at the same time.

Chapter 6

He glared at her. "Yeah, it's been a rough week. They're still alive, though!"

Casey and Jakob peeked in the box. The kittens were clearly more advanced, moving around more, their eyes brighter. Poor lonely babies, she thought. There's no substitute for a mother's care.

"I didn't think you'd come in this week," Casey said. "You know, you could have stayed home with them."

"Yeah, I hated to put them in the car, but they didn't seem to mind it. They just slept. And anyway, I wanted to follow up on our conversation from last week. I had some more ideas." She was dismayed at his single-minded determination. Her plan to get rid of him was not working very well.

"Fine. How about 5:00 again?"

"Sounds good."

Jakob disappeared and came back with a cup of coffee for Will, who accepted it gratefully. They all worked at socializing the new animals for a while, soon joined by two teenaged girls from Casey's church who spent an occasional Saturday morning with the animals. Maddie and Sophia led the dogs out in small groups to the play yard to throw balls and make sure they got some exercise. Casey asked Will to continue his good work petting and playing with each of the cats in the shelter.

"I still hate cats, you know," he told her.

"I know, but that's what makes you so good with them. You're their favorite volunteer!" This was the truth. They couldn't wait for the chance to sniff him, rub their faces against his hand, and climb into his lap. The site of a cat curled up against his chest, kneading away, always made her laugh.

"We need to get some of them adopted out," he said. "Don't they start to get depressed after they've been in a place like this long enough?"

"Yes, they really do. You can see it in those three over there, who have now been here for five or six months. They're getting quieter and lazier, less interested in coming over to greet people who come in. We've got to get them out of here soon. Problem is they're older cats. People only want to adopt kittens."

Will walked over to the cage of a tortoiseshell female named Daisy, who started to sniff his hand and then appeared to lose interest. "This one seems to be losing hope the most. I'm going to find her a home by the end of the day."

Casey laughed. "Oh really? Well, good luck with that."

"Is it okay if I leave the shelter for a while?"

"Sure, do what you need to do." She grinned at him. "Just don't forget feeding time."

He grimaced. "Don't worry. I have feeding time permanently etched into my brain."

She had a break in appointments around 2:00 and decided to take a couple of the older dogs for a slow walk in the park, glad to get a little exercise and sunshine for herself as well. She took off her coat and entered the shelter to find Will on the floor brushing one of the other cats that had been there for a while, Mittens, while he talked on his cell phone. He looked up and gave her a thumbs up.

"Sounds good," he said. "I'll swing by later to pick up your application." He hung up and said, "I'm making progress with Daisy."

"Hmmm," was all she could answer. She let the dogs out and started putting on leashes.

"What are you up to?" Will asked.

"I have about 45 minutes between appointments and thought I would take these two old boys for a walk. Stretch my legs a bit, too."

"I'll go with you," he said, not asking but telling. "Should I take some dogs, too?"

She sighed and motioned toward another two who liked to walk rather than to run. "Yes, take Nosey and Pickles." She went about the business of putting leashes on Ramses and Buddy, a middle-aged pit-lab mix and a senior mutt who had come to them when an older man had moved away to live with his son. Ramses was doing okay with them, but Buddy was having a harder time than most adapting to the noisy chaos of an animal shelter, and she loved to get him out in the world where he could smell the smells of nature and have a little peace and quiet.

Once they got on their way, Will asked, "Have you given any thought to what I suggested last week?"

Chapter 6

He had laid out a list of grant possibilities. The problem is, those would take several weeks to several months to obtain. He had also given her a list of area donors to other animal-related causes. She had no idea how he had gotten these names, and she hadn't asked. No doubt he had charmed the equivalent of her mother in the fundraising world surrounding animal causes. His suggestion was that they make some cold calls from the list. She was considering this, although she didn't like begging for money; she would rather the support come from the community organically, since this was supposed to be their shelter. In that case, he told her, he had come up with some fundraising event ideas. Those seemed like a good idea to her but limited in scope. There was no way they would raise enough money to buy land and build their own building—and it would take ages to raise much of anything at all. The only rental property they had managed to find was a bit too small, not located in the right kind of place, and way too costly.

So Will's main proposal for the short term was to empty the shelter, close it down, and wait to find the right situation, rather than try to move the existing animals to a new place now and spending lots of much-needed money to do so. She simply couldn't bear the thought of rushing to get the animals into homes. What if they were tempted to give the animals to a less-than-perfect home because they were in a hurry? And how could they possibly find enough homes in only five weeks? Will had some ideas for that as well: a series of adoption events and cold calls to institutions, such as schools, that might like a pet for the classroom. They would have to work hard over the next few weeks, but if they had success for two or three animals at each event, they could do it. The trick, he explained, was to get outside the immediate community, which was very limited. What about events in the suburbs of Nashville?

She had thought of almost nothing else over the last week but still not come to any firm conclusions. She felt paralyzed by the lack of easy possibilities to meet their needs in the short term and by her sense of responsibility for these animals. She just kept hoping that someone would hear of their plight and present her with the perfect setup, as Mr. Ramsey once had. She couldn't tell this to Will, however, because she knew what he would say and the patronizing tone with which he would say it.

As they stopped to let the dogs have their first good sniffing session alongside the riverbank, she began to tell him what she had decided for now. "Let's definitely apply for the grants. I've put together some of the information we'll need for them: background and history of the shelter, my credentials, our plans for staffing and volunteers, and our intake and success rates in the past. That was easy enough. The harder part is stating what it is, exactly, that we want. So I'd like to call a meeting in the next week to discuss it with Jakob, Bethany, and a couple of our most significant volunteers, to discuss that."

"Sounds good. That might be the beginning of your Board."

"My Board?"

"Yes, you should have a Board of Directors who help you plan for the organization that you'll need to found in order to run the shelter."

She grimaced. "Okay, slow down. That's too far down the road."

"Not really," he answered. "You'll make a stronger case in the grant application if you have a Board in place or at least in the plans. Nobody will want to give a substantial amount of money to an individual who's running a shelter as a side gig."

She didn't like his tone; it again seemed preachy and insulting, dismissing her shelter as an after-hours hobby. But the afternoon breeze was so nice, and the dogs were so happy; she didn't feel like arguing. "We'll talk about that later," she said firmly. "Moving on!"

He laughed, but she felt it was a slightly derisive laugh.

"I made some cold calls this week just to try it out, and they mostly didn't work except for one," she informed him.

"What do you mean they didn't work?"

"I felt like a beggar, the people seemed disdainful, we ended the call within too short of a time. I don't think I should have to sell myself. If people care about animals, they care about animals; if they don't, they don't."

"You didn't say that, did you?" he asked.

"Not in so many words."

"Casey, I just—."

Chapter 6

"I don't want to talk about that right now either. Moving on!"

He laughed again, this time with even less amusement. But perhaps he was distracted by Pickles, who was trying to run in the direction of a schnauzer being walked on the other side of the river.

"Does he think he can run across the river and get to that dog?" Will asked incredulously.

Casey laughed. They watched him for a few moments in silence. Then Casey said, "The adoption events you suggested I can really sink my teeth into. I went ahead and scheduled some of those for the next three weeks, two events a week. Most are around here, but two are closer to Nashville. Jakob or I will be at each of them with various volunteers I've contacted and asked to sign up."

"You actually liked one of my ideas!" She looked over at him. His smile seemed sincere although his tone was sarcastic.

"Well, we've been doing adoption events for a while now."

"Okay, so you liked one of your own ideas. Either way, I'm glad you're willing to move forward with adoption. All of this fundraising and grant writing and planning will take a lot of time, time that you currently devote to the shelter. You have to think about what's best for the long term, even if it means shutting down the shelter in the short term."

"You can't just accept that I'm running with one of your ideas and then quit while you're ahead, can you?" she asked, both annoyed and amazed by his need to scold her.

He turned toward her and held her arm so that she would stand still. The dogs sat down, panting.

"Casey, please stop seeing me as the enemy."

"I don't!" she protested, looking away.

"I don't think you realize how much I believe in you, believe in your heart and your love for these animals." His hand gripped her arm more tightly, nudging her to look back in his eyes. She hoped he couldn't see how it affected her to be so close to him, to feel his touch.

"Thank you," she said in a voice that came out more as a whisper.

"I'm only being so insistent because I can see that you're too close to the situation emotionally. That emotion is part of what makes you so wonderful, but emotion is not going to save this shelter or these animals."

Okay, now he had gone too far. He was back to the usual refrain: she needed his help because she was impractical and emotional rather than a licensed professional with her own business who had done just fine in life, work, and running a shelter until *he* had wandered onto the scene. No, he wasn't her enemy. But he had created her problem, and now he was blaming her for it and rushing to her aid so that he could play the knight in shining armor. Why? Because his ego had been bruised by her earlier questioning of his ethics.

He realized his mistake at once, as she jerked her arm away from his hand and said, "It's time to get back." She busied herself with dogs and leashes and turned to go. "We'll do the events, and I'll start working on the grant applications. That's it for now."

"Fine. Well, sign me up for any of the adoption events on a Saturday or Sunday." He sounded perturbed. Had he thought he was pouring out his heart and she had shut him down? Well, good. Now he had a more realistic sense of how she felt about his overbearing offers of help.

When they had returned to the shelter, watered the dogs, and led them back into their cages, he spoke again for the first time. His tone was measured, a bit on the cold side. "I should warn you that some of my team will be here this week to walk the property and do some surveying. I didn't want you to see them and wonder who they are."

"I appreciate the heads-up," she replied in an equally measured tone. She imagined herself turning all of the dogs on them, which gave her a moment of pleasure.

Will didn't say goodbye before leaving that day, which was just as well. She would have Jakob e-mail him the dates of some upcoming events after instructing him not to pair Will with herself at any of them.

***

The following Saturday, she hardly saw Will because he was with Jakob all morning at an adoption event and then she was inundated with appointments that afternoon. She did have time to talk to him briefly early in the afternoon, however. He and Jakob had returned triumphant, with adoption applications for three of the cats and two of the dogs. They had spent a lot of time talking to these would-be adopters and were certain they would provide genuinely good homes. Casey said a little prayer that this would be true.

"You should have seen Will, Doc! What a salesman! He would target the people who looked most like hippie animal lovers, and just talk to them and talk to them until they said yes." Jakob looked at Will with wholehearted admiration.

Will grinned at her, waiting for her approval.

"Hmmm," she replied. "You know, we don't want to give people the hard sell. That leads to a phone call three months down the road when the cat throws up or the dog leaves a little present on the rug one too many times and they realize that they didn't actually want to adopt a pet after all."

Jakob defended his new friend. "No, but that was the genius of it. He could tell who really wanted to adopt and who didn't, and then he knew how to get them to agree to what they didn't even know was already in their mind. It was amazing!"

Will added, "And all of them already have pets. They know that it's hard sometimes. They had been thinking about adding another pet but were just in that state of inertia about it, you know? I just bumped them out of it."

"I hope you're right," Casey said, and then decided to use her ammunition. "You weren't so right on this one." She lifted a filled-out adoption application from the desk and handed it to Will. "Did you really think a preschool would be the right place for a skittish old cat who is traumatized from living in a shelter for several months?"

"I talked this over with one of the teachers. She said Daisy would have a nice home in the quiet room and would be there for kids who were upset and needed to calm down. You know, like a therapy animal."

Casey continued, "Did you not think you ought to run it by the director?"

Will looked at her warily, unsure of what was wrong. "This teacher seemed to have the authority. And she was very enthusiastic about it."

"Who was it?" Jakob asked.

Will pursed his lips in thought for a moment. "Um, Rachel something at that preschool down at the corner of Main? In the white brick building?"

Jakob laughed out loud. "Oh, she just wanted *you*, not the cat. She would have said yes to anything you suggested, if you know what I mean."

Will laughed in return but then looked at Casey sheepishly, like an only slightly remorseful child awaiting his punishment.

"Anyway," Casey said, not laughing with Jakob as she normally would have, "When I called the *director* to follow up, she did not feel it was such a great idea. See, that's why we can't just rush these things and try to shuttle all of the animals out the door to suit your timetable!" She couldn't keep the pique out of her voice.

Will wasn't going down without a fight. "Well, at least I got close," he said. "I still have some things to learn. But the point is I'm out there hustling, thinking of new possibilities, making the ask!"

"And we're not?" Casey asked. "You think we didn't know how to 'make the ask' until you showed up?"

Jakob stepped in again. "Come on, Doc. You have to admit it's good to have some new faces and some new ideas around here. We might have gotten five adoptions today!"

Casey smiled. She would concede to Jakob, if not to Will. "You're right, Jakob. Good point. And thank you both for that."

She turned without looking at Will and headed back to the clinic for her next appointment.

At 5:00 he was waiting for her so that they could have their weekly discussion, which she both dreaded and looked forward to.

"Your people were here during the week, as promised," she remarked to start the conversation off. "They spent a lot of time here."

"Yes, they have to look very closely at the property, survey it, start building a vision for how and where the facility will be sited."

"They seemed to spend a lot of time looking at the woods along the back."

"Of course. That will be the first thing to go."

Casey looked at him in surprise. "Go?"

"Yes, we'll have to pull down the woods. It will become lawn, with walking areas and gardens. Also, we need a view of the river from the facility."

She couldn't believe what she was hearing, even though she had known that this was the *modus operandi* of Coach Lifestyle Solutions and one of the reasons Save Wild Tennessee was working against them. The wildlife in that woodlot had become an important part of her life. She had spent hours out there, watching birds and other creatures that made their home there. She had watched fox kittens grow up, seen the waves of migrating birds come for the nesting season and depart as the summer waned, enjoyed the loud hum of the cicadas that inhabited the tall trees each summer. Now the property would become yet another lawn space, where nature was mowed down and neatened up, replaced with a monotony of yard trees and flowers maintained with herbicides and pesticides. The river would lose yet more of its protective layer of nature; the bank would erode further. She wanted to burst into tears.

"What's wrong?"

She tried to explain, but she could see from his face that he didn't get it. To him, as for many people, it was just a little woodlot like so many others, easily shaved off the landscape in the name of "development."

"But," he responded, "people are going to be living there. Elderly people. They need a nice place to walk and sit and relax, and they need to feel that it's aesthetically pleasing. You know, some people find woods messy or ugly or even scary. And aren't there plenty of other woods around here for those animals to go to?"

Casey shook her head. "No, it's not that easy to just move somewhere else. Animals live in very specific niches and territories. Some birds fly to Central America in the fall and then migrate in spring back to the very same tree where they made their nest the previous year. Or if you take a turtle and move it a mile down the road, it will die; it's not able to figure out a new space, where to hide, where to find food and water. So every woodlot is its own little ecosystem and cannot be replaced."

"That's really interesting," he said sincerely. "But it must all turn out okay in the end. I mean, there's no shortage of birds and wildlife around here."

"It may seem so, but just about everything is in rapid decline, in large part because of development and habitat destruction." She sighed. "Why do people like you have to develop new land instead of using already developed land? There's an old motel out on the bypass that you could raze and replace with this facility. That property is just about as big as this one."

"But being centrally located to the town is important. It makes residents feel more part of the world. That makes a difference. That's what makes our model unique."

She didn't know what to say to that. They would never be able to come to terms about this topic. She had had this discussion with her father her entire life, always to no avail. She saw her father as anti-nature, and he saw her as anti-progress or even as anti-people.

They remained silent for a moment, and then Will conceded, "I appreciate your point of view. This is all new to me, and I would like to learn more, actually." In his words and tone, Casey sensed an opportunity to change his mind, an opportunity she could not pass up.

"Any chance you could get here early next Saturday? Like 5:00 in the morning early?"

He looked puzzled. "Of course. What do you have in mind?"

"I want to take you out birding and wildlife watching. Maybe I can convince you that nature deserves some consideration in all of your plans." This meant that she would have to spend time alone with him, and she felt anxious about that for a plethora of reasons. But overriding those anxieties was the possibility that she could make him see reason. Then maybe he would move the facility to the old motel property and she could keep her shelter.

"Okay. Will you give me some time afterwards to show you a couple of things, too?"

"Why?"

"Well, I can see the wheels turning in your mind. You're hoping I'll fall in love with woodlots and nature and call the whole thing off." She couldn't help laughing. Was she really that obvious? "So it only seems fair that I get a chance to make you fall in love with real estate development so that you'll enthusiastically embrace Coach Lifestyle Solutions and demand that we pull down woodlots all over the state so we can build retirement homes."

She laughed again. "Fair enough. But you're not going to change my mind."

"So I have to be open minded but you don't?"

"Exactly."

"Well, I get a couple of hours alone with you, so I still win," he announced proudly. She blushed, realizing with dismay that she was looking forward to a couple of hours alone with him, too.

He noticed her blush and smiled. Why did she always have to give herself away so easily?

"All right, 5:00 then, in the parking lot here," she said quickly, trying to cover her embarrassment.

"I'll be here."

***

The week was a busy one. Casey was finally able to call together her "Board," although it wasn't a terribly productive meeting. She asked them what they wanted, ultimately, in a shelter. They all described what they already had, and then they expressed their sadness for the loss of this special little place. Casey had to guide them with very basic questions, such as, "How many dogs and cats would you like to be able to house in our new shelter?" The general answer to every question was: "Oh, whatever you think, Casey."

They were also busy holding two adoption events during the week. They had some success, getting applications for two of the cats and one dog that had been in the shelter for some time. The animals rescued from the hoarding situation were still too skittish to take out to adoption events, but they were pretty rapidly finding homes for some of the other animals. She also convinced one of her cat-loving friends, Monica, to adopt the two kittens Will was fostering. Monica's resident cat was still young and playful enough to put up with kittens, so Casey felt sure it would be a good match.

More good news: Casey had had one successful conversation with a potential donor, who offered a $5,000 match for their first annual "Race for a Claws" 10K scheduled for the following spring.

On some days she felt hopeful. They were making progress towards emptying the shelter, even if it seemed small and slow. On other days she felt overwhelmed with hopelessness. She worried she would never get together the money to open a new shelter, even with the loans she had discussed with her bank manager. She was newly realizing how expensive property was in the area, and how difficult it was to build anything, even a metal building, without breaking the bank.

Her biggest hope lay in the possibility that she could bring Will around to her point of view. If she could lead him to appreciate nature as she did, maybe he would change his plan for the property. He might agree to save the woods, or, in her wildest dreams, give up on the project altogether. She also let herself indulge in the fantasy that he would renounce the part of himself that was problematic for her and become the man she had thought him to be on their first date. Then all would be right with the world.

She arrived the next Saturday morning at 4:55, and he was already there, leaning against his car, as she pulled into the lot. His car was a sleek black Mercedes: elegant, luxurious, masculine. He was wearing shorts and a t-shirt and had a Cardinals cap on his head. "No time for a shower," he said as he caught her looking at the cap. "But I thought a cap with a bird on it was a good start."

She laughed, his good humor surprisingly contagious given that it was so early in the morning. How could he still look so well put together, even in casual clothes and a cap?

She had made time for a shower, but otherwise was also wearing shorts and a t-shirt and no makeup. Her hair was still wet from the shower and pulled back in a loose ponytail.

She offered him a carry cup of coffee. "Black, right?"

He took it gratefully. "Right. Thank you."

"Least I could do for someone willing to get up at 4:00 in the morning," she said, trying to start the day on a light and friendly note.

"More like 3:30," he said with a grimace. "So where are we going?"

Chapter 6

"Just here for now." She pulled two pairs of binoculars out of a canvas tote in the back of the car and handed him one. "Ready?"

She headed into the woods with him following closely behind her, chose a spot once they were surrounded by trees, and plopped down. The dawn chorus of the birds was playing like a symphony all around them. "Listen," she said. "Just listen."

They sat in silence for ten or fifteen minutes, and she appreciated that he was able to wait so patiently and remain silent. Finally, she asked, "What do you hear?"

"Birds. Lots of them."

"Note the number and the variety," she instructed.

The sun was coming up quickly and the sky losing its bright hues of gold and pink. "Now sit as still as you can and watch."

"What am I watching for?"

"Any movement. We might see birds, we might see foxes—."

"We might see snakes or ticks or rabid raccoons."

She laughed. "They're part of nature, too, you know. Now shhhhh."

They made themselves as still as possible, and then magical things began to happen. Birds flew down to perch on branches near them, then hopped onto the ground, having made the decision to risk going about their usual routines of finding food despite the presence of humans. They heard a rustling sound a few feet away from them and saw an opossum moving through the woods in its ambling way, probably heading toward shelter after a night of feeding. They heard the distant hoot of the great horned owl, one of Casey's favorites.

After a while she whispered, "Look up there," pointing toward a branch above them and then lifting her own binoculars to the spot. "It's a small black and white bird."

It took him a minute, but then he said, "Yes, I see it."

"That's a black-and-white warbler. Their numbers have gone down by one third in the last 50 years because of habitat loss and forest fragmentation. Oh, and crashing into all the tall buildings that we're putting on the landscape."

The great horned owl hooted again. "Do you hear that? It's a great horned owl. It lives and hunts in the woods. Each owl needs a vast amount of space in order to have sufficient hunting grounds. If this woodlot goes, that one will have to crowd into another woodlot with another one. They'll fight over territory, maybe one will be killed, or they will try to live together and share the space but there might not be sufficient food for both of them and their mates and offspring."

"Hmm. You know, I hear birds all the time but don't really think about what kind they are or where they came from. It's fascinating."

She felt a surge of hope.

"Ready to go?" she asked. There was another place she wanted to take him.

"Not really. I like it here," he answered, taking a sip of coffee. "But if you insist."

He shot up to a standing position and offered his hand to pull her up, which she accepted. A jolt of electricity shot through her arm and buzzed through her belly. They walked back to the car in silence, and she gave herself a stern warning not to touch him again.

"Hop in," she said when they reached the car, moving around to the driver's side door.

She drove a few miles to a small meadow next to a housing development. The meadow was overgrown with grass and wildflowers. She parked the car and got out, sitting on the hood and motioning to him to do the same. "Now, what you can't see right now, because it's morning and they're still too wet from the dew to fly, is the hundreds of butterflies that normally hover over this meadow. One of the most important of them is the monarch butterfly, the orange and black one that is famous for flying all the way to Mexico and Southern California each year for the winter."

"I've heard of them."

"This field is full of milkweed, which is the only plant where they will lay their eggs. Because of development and agriculture, all the old milkweed stands are disappearing, and the monarch is going to go extinct."

"Oh!"

"This field is also home to grassland birds, like the Eastern meadowlark, the grasshopper sparrow, and others. Do you hear that buzzy sound?"

Chapter 6

"Yes."

"That's the grasshopper sparrow."

"And how are people like me destroying them?" he asked, and she could hear the smile in his voice. Of course, she laughed. What was this power he had to make her laugh, even when she was discussing something of such seriousness and importance to her?

"Oh, believe me, I intend to tell you," she said pedantically, and he laughed in turn. "These birds nest in the grass. So, two things happen to destroy their ability to nest. One is—you guessed it—greedy real estate developers come along and build over the few remaining meadows in Tennessee." She indicated the housing development just adjacent to the meadow. "There used to be acres and acres of meadowland through here until Ryan Builders came along."

"What's the other problem?" he asked.

"Hayfields. The birds nest in the grass and then the hay is cut. If farmers would delay that first cut by a few weeks, it would give the birds time to raise their first brood. But, of course, most farmers don't know or aren't willing. So, within a hundred years those bird species will have disappeared, too."

"I'm impressed by how much you know about all of this," Will said.

She smiled at the compliment and the sincerity of its delivery. "So are you going to become a birder and avid wildlife lover now?"

"Anything is possible, I guess. I would definitely love to do this again. It reminds me of the couple of times I went hunting with my dad—my biological father—when I was young. Of course, we were there to kill, not to look. But what was most fun was getting up early, sitting out in the woods with my dad and his friend, and quietly waiting to see a deer. We saw lots of other things, too: birds, raccoons, foxes. I remember the peacefulness of it all in the midst of a pretty chaotic life." He nudged her with his elbow, and she turned to look at him. "Thanks for reminding me of those rare moments of peace."

"And do you see my point of view at all? Do you see why nature can't just be shut down or moved over or replicated somewhere else?"

"Yes, I see where you're coming from." That didn't seem like much of a concession, but at least it was a start.

"Okay, that's the end of this morning's nature tour. Now what do you want to show me?"

"It's a little ways off, if that's all right. Do you want me to drive?"

"Sure." She handed him the keys.

They drove for about 20 minutes out of town toward Nashville. Since she didn't have to concentrate on driving, she surreptitiously looked him over. His legs were muscular, with lots of dark hair, and his right knee had some pretty serious scarring on it. He drove in a relaxed way, one hand placed casually on the wheel, but he sat tall and upright. He took his eyes off the road a lot to look around at the scenery as they passed. He sped a little but otherwise wasn't aggressive. Everything about him this morning seemed just right to her.

Once he caught her looking at him and smiled. She couldn't help smiling back, glad he couldn't see the reddening of her face.

At last he pulled into the parking lot of a shop. It was on a slight hill, with a nice view of pastures and the road they had just traveled on. He stopped the car. "Now, watch the road," he said.

"What am I watching for?"

"Shhhh," he said, exaggeratedly mimicking her shush from earlier. "Just watch." He looked over and winked at her. She liked it when he did that, both acknowledging and softening his arrogance. But she forced herself to stop thinking about all the things she liked about him and instead focus on the road.

As she watched, she realized there were a lot of cars on the road, too many for a two-lane country highway. Some drivers obviously wanted to go faster than others but couldn't until they got to the one passing area in their view, and then they zoomed around. At one point the passing car barely got back into the lane before another car came from the opposite direction. There was quite a bit of honking, and Casey could imagine the four-letter words implied by it. There were also a lot of 18-wheelers on the road, which seemed dangerous given how small and crowded it was.

"Now, what do you see?" Again he was mocking her, but in a funny, not unkind, way.

She explained what she had observed.

"Yes, exactly," he said. "And the reason the road is like this is because of limits on zoning for development. I happen to know the name of the company that planned for a large housing development of 2,500 homes out this way: CY Properties."

Casey slowly blew out her breath as she shook her head.

"Keep in mind this is a growing area, a bedroom community for Nashville. These are people who work hard, who have families, who want to move away from the city so that they can improve their quality of life: bigger house, more land, maybe a nicer school system, small-town values. Nothing wrong with that, right? But because of restrictions put in place at the last minute by development opponents lobbying the Tennessee Development Commission, the development was moved to the edge of this county. Instead of being served by a much wider highway as originally planned."

Casey knew who the development opponents he referred to were: her organization, Save Wild Tennessee. Had he chosen this example on purpose, knowing of her association with them?

"The people in those 2,500 homes now have to use this highway. So this is a Saturday morning, and you see how crowded it is. Imagine it on a weekday morning, when this is the only route to get to Nashville? It's a nightmare. Traffic fatalities have gone way up, deer and other roadkill incidents have gone up, and people are spending more time in their cars spewing exhaust fumes, edging closer and closer to a heart attack because of all the stress of spending three hours a day on their commute, feeling—."

"Okay, okay," Casey interrupted, laughing. "I get the point."

"Getting a little carried away, was I?" he asked.

"A little."

"Well, I'm up against a cute little black-and-white—what was it?"

"Warbler."

"Black-and-white warbler. I have to fight with everything I've got."

She laughed again. "Okay, I get it. Development will save lives and allow people to live the American dream and keep their lungs clear. And it's better for the deer, too, apparently."

"Exactly." He turned the car ignition on. "And now for our final stop."

She looked at her watch. "We should get back to the clinic pretty soon."

"Well, we're in luck, then, because that's the final stop."

He turned onto the highway, and now they were in the midst of the traffic. "Oh, no, look at all this traffic! If only the crazy anti-development fanatics hadn't had their way!"

She punched him lightly on the arm.

"Mind if I turn on the radio?" he asked.

"Sure," she said. It was an old car, so all it had was a simple radio and a CD player. It must seem so antiquated to him, she thought, once again viewing her rather shabby life through his eyes.

"I'm going to snoop and see what stations you have in memory."

"Go right ahead."

He went through all of them and, except for ads, heard classic rock, except for one country/bluegrass station.

"Classic rock?" he asked. "That is not what I was expecting."

"Oh really, what were you expecting?"

"Girlie pop." He looked over and winked at her.

"Seriously? Is that what you listen to?"

"Of course."

She asked, "No, really, what do you listen to?"

"News and talk radio. News and talk podcasts." He looked at her and grimaced. "I know: terrible, right?"

"Yes, terrible. You really need to get a life."

"Believe me: I'm trying to," he said, looking over at her with an expression that was hard to decipher.

She looked out the window and thought about the day. Had he taken her seriously? She thought he had, although she didn't get the sense his mind had changed. Hearing his point of view certainly hadn't changed her mind, although it had made her consider that there might be some noble reasons behind the his choice of careers. She determined to learn more about his corporation and its work, which she probably should have done originally, before writing it off as another evil real estate development corporation like her father's.

In what seemed like no time, they were back at the clinic parking lot. They got out, and he led her over to the eastern side of the property that sprawled behind the clinic. He stopped and pointed beyond the clinic into the downtown area.

"Now, imagine you are a retiree sitting here, which will roughly be the front porch of the facility. What do you see?"

"A thriving vet clinic run by a caring vet whose shelter was plucked from her by an unscrupulous real estate developer."

"Have I just been demoted from greedy to unscrupulous?"

"Actually, you were demoted weeks ago."

He chuckled. "Well, at least I have nowhere to go but up. Now look to the West, beyond the clinic. What do you see?"

"Downtown."

"Yes, now imagine your children have forced you to leave your home because they feel you can't take care of yourself, or imagine that your spouse now needs assisted living and you have had to move into this facility. Or you're recently widowed and lonely. Are you sadly cut off from society, stuck away in an isolated place? No! You're here, downtown. You can watch people walk by, see families with small children. You can go to the coffee shop. You can go to the old movie theater that you used to go to when you were a kid. You can shop in the bookstore or boutiques, or you can walk all the way down to the library. You can go for a walk in the city park. This is still your town. Can't you see the value in that?"

She nodded. "But if all that is here, then why do you need grounds and gardens and a view to the river?"

"Valid question. I guess we just want to provide as many options as possible."

"What about the option of woods to go birding in? Or a nature trail through the woods in place of a mowed lawn that is expensive to maintain?"

"You know, it's not a bad idea."

She looked at him in surprise.

"What? I told you, I came here with an open mind."

She nodded, impressed.

"And what about you?" he asked. "Has anything I said made you rethink your position, even a little bit?"

She thought about it. "Yes, I understand better that human needs drive development." He nodded. "But," she continued, "there are better ways to address those needs than to rip nature apart and turn everything into housing developments."

"Yes, but sometimes we have to make a choice. Sometimes we have to be pragmatic."

"Well, the destruction of our planet is not pragmatic," she shot back. Her temper was rising, and she didn't want to end what had turned out to be a nice morning on a sour note. "But I'd better get in and get to work. So … agree to disagree? For today anyway?" She held out her hand for a handshake.

That was her mistake. Covering her hand with his own, Will stroked it lightly with his thumb while he looked intently at her. She felt transfixed by his gaze; she wanted to run away or even look away but was unable to do either. He moved toward her, and all she could think about was how good his warm, strong hand felt on hers, and how good his lips would feel on her lips. "Casey, I—."

She caught a movement in her peripheral vision and saw Jakob standing in the window, looking at them in disbelief, mouth wide open. Then he gave her a thumbs up and grinned and moved away, no doubt to tell Brittany what he had just seen and then to text Katie and tell her. Oh dear, Casey would never hear the end of this.

But she was grateful to Jakob for breaking the spell. She pulled her hand out of Will's, turned, and entered the practice, ignoring his protest. A few minutes later, she was in more professional clothes and ready to work. She was determined to leave her feelings for Will, now even more confused and confusing, behind for the day.

Jakob never said anything directly about what he had seen. But every time he was alone with Casey, he sang a little song under his breath: "I knew it I

Chapter 6

knew it I knew it I knew it." When Casey would inevitably glare at him, he would raise his eyebrows innocently and ask, "What?" Once he did it when he was in the room with both Casey *and* Will. Casey glanced up at Jakob and then over at Will to find his eyes on her and a mischievous smile on his face. She blushed. What was happening to her?

She had to walk over to the shelter that afternoon and saw Will there with Daisy curled up in his lap while he made phone calls. "Just one more call and I think I'll have everything I need to complete the Herscheimer Foundation grant!" he whispered merrily.

She smiled gratefully.

He pointed to Daisy. "She refuses to leave."

Casey smiled again and couldn't help wondering who was the better judge of character: her or the cat?

Chapter 7

The next Saturday Casey entered the clinic with a sense of dread. Her parents had called at the crack of dawn to inform her that they would be near Pleasant Valley sometime in the early- to mid-afternoon and would love to stop in and say hello. Spontaneity was unlike them, which already made Casey a bit suspicious that something was up. But her mother assured her there was nothing in particular behind their visit. They were simply coming back from a conference and had realized they could change their route a bit and stop in to see her. It had been too long since they had been to Pleasant Valley, Katherine said sunnily.

The day was off from the beginning. The coffee pot was broken, so Casey, Jakob, and Bethany had to deal with one another's heightened grumpiness until Jakob called Will and asked him to pick a new one up on his way in. Will charged in like a hero come to save the day, holding the new coffee pot up victoriously while everyone cheered. Casey laughed and tried to snuff out the silly, resentful thought that he always got to play the hero.

The wifi was down, which meant some portions of the patients' records could not be accessed and they would be unable to process debit or credit cards.

"What am I going to do?" Bethany whined helplessly when Casey informed her of the problem. Bethany could be bright when she focused, and she could be hardworking when properly motivated. But generally she wasn't the most proactive employee imaginable, particularly if things weren't running exactly according to what she was used to. And, of course, she needed sufficient caffeine in the morning to be civil, so her mood was already challenged.

"Whatever you can," Casey replied, trying hard to infuse her voice with a patient tone. "I'll worry about the patient records; you simply put together the form and folder as always and let me take care of it from there. Encourage everyone to pay cash or check, if possible. But if they have to use a card, just write down their name and all the card info and tell them we'll charge them when the system is back up."

Bethany looked at her sullenly, eyes narrowed. "What credit card info exactly?"

Casey sighed. "Full name, number, type, expiration date, security code on the back of the card. And make sure we have their correct phone number on record in case there is a problem."

Bethany sighed in response. "I'll try."

"Why don't you write all of this down?" Casey suggested and then watched as Bethany slammed down a notepad and began to write.

"It shouldn't be a big deal, Bethany. Jakob can help if you need him."

Casey glanced over at Jakob, who smiled and gave her a thumbs up.

"The biggest problem for you, Bethany, is you'll have to pay games all day on your phone instead of on the computer," Jakob called, leaning back in his chair. "Hope you brought your charger!"

She flipped him off and did not join in when he laughed.

"Okay, I just hope everyone's not in a bad mood about it when I'm trying to work with them," Bethany said.

"Well, Bethany, part of your job is to be in such a good mood yourself that it's contagious!" Jakob called in a sunny voice.

"Excuse me, Doc, are you my boss or is he?" Bethany asked hotly, making a face at Jakob.

This time Jakob flipped her off.

"Okay, you two, enough!" Casey said, laughing. She saw a slight smile form on Bethany's face and felt a sense of relief. "Anyway, Bethany, it's going to be fine. Just don't worry about it. Hopefully the wifi will be back up again soon anyway."

The morning's appointments went smoothly enough for the most part. Most of their community were kind, understanding people who had a long-term relationship with the clinic. And most of the appointments that morning were pretty straightforward, so Casey could make do with the records she had.

Will came and joined them in the clinic for lunch, as had become his habit when he was in the shelter all day rather than out meeting potential donors or manning adoption events. The four of them would eat their lunches, then go over to the shelter to play with some of the animals until the 1:00 appointments started showing up.

"Will, I've been taking your advice," Jakob announced as they all settled in, spreading out containers and drinks around the table in the tiny lunchroom.

"What advice is that?" Will asked. Casey noted that he was exceptionally good looking that day. His hair had grown a bit longer, and he had not shaved that morning, which was unusual. Unkemptness definitely looked good on him. He had also dressed down for a change. His old, faded jeans fit well, and his t-shirt was tight enough to show the muscles in his arms, chest, and abs underneath. He looked casual and at ease, which matched the smile on his face as he looked at Jakob.

"Yes, Jakob," Casey repeated skeptically. "What advice is that?"

"I've been trying to do a little more around the house to help Katie. You know, wash the dishes, clean up after myself. I even helped the monster with her homework and read her some bedtime stories a couple of nights when Katie was super tired." He smiled and preened a little bit, proud of himself.

"Wait a minute!" Casey couldn't help protesting. "What do you mean *Will's* advice? I've been telling you to do that for years!"

Jakob looked at her with genuine surprise. "You have?"

Casey laughed. "Yes, all the time. Right, Bethany?"

Bethany shrugged and pointed at her earbuds. "I don't really pay that much attention to what y'all say."

Casey continued, "Yes, Jakob, I've always told you that you had to help Katie more instead of always expecting her to go out and play with you."

Chapter 7

"Oh, yeah, that's right," he replied unconvincingly. "I remember."

Casey glanced at Will, who was looking at them with amusement.

"But I don't know, I just—well, Will was giving me a lot of advice about how to make my relationship better with her."

"Oh, was he now?" Casey asked.

"Yeah, well, you know, Will's got it going on. You know, he's pretty good with the ladies."

Casey almost choked on her food. She looked up to find Will's eyes on her, still amused, and Jakob's characteristic evil grin.

"Haven't you noticed, Doc?" Jakob asked her pointedly.

Casey swallowed in what she hoped was a dignified recovery and took a sip of water. "No, I haven't, actually," she lied. But the blush that began coursing up her neck told her—and everyone else—otherwise. Even Bethany seemed tuned in to what was happening. Casey studied her food closely, refusing to look up at any of them.

Jakob continued. "Yeah, Will's been making me see that I've got to grow up a bit, you know, be more of a man. After all, this is serious. I want to marry her, she's got a kid. That's a whole new set of responsibilities. So we've been talking about that. And it's working. Katie really appreciated it."

Casey sighed, feeling a strange sensation: jealousy. Jakob was *her* employee, *her* friend to advise. Why hadn't he listened all the times she had given him the exact same advice?

"I'm so glad that *Will* was here to help you see the light," she muttered.

Will laughed. "Well, we've been spending a lot of time together lately, haven't we, Jakob?"

Jakob nodded gravely.

"Something else we've been talking about is his work performance, how he could be more responsible with his hours, with following through on longer-term tasks that you have set him but that can be easy to forget in the day-to-day work. You know, time management, list making, that sort of thing. Hopefully you'll see the benefit of those changes soon, in the clinic." He smiled a proud smile at her, waiting for her reaction.

"Wow, you're really making all our lives better, aren't you, Will?" She took another bite of her sandwich.

"Hey, I'm here to *help*!" he teased.

Bethany scooted back her chair noisily and began collecting her things before heading off to the bathroom. Casey followed suit. "I'm done, too. See you in the shelter."

"Right behind you," Will said, stuffing the last of his sandwich in his mouth.

"Me, too," Jakob added.

A few minutes later, they were all back in the shelter petting and talking to the animals. Casey brought three of the cats who got along well into the play area and waved toys at them so they could get a bit of exercise. She could feel Will watching her as he and Jakob talked to and petted some dogs.

She had been in a state of uncertainty about him since their time together the previous Saturday. She felt herself thinking about him again in positive ways, remembering his kindness, his open-mindedness, his ability to embrace the things she was showing him and explaining to him. She had also simply enjoyed his company as he teased her, made her laugh, and shared light conversation. For the first time since their date, she had felt no pressure from him to do things his way or think about things from his perspective. She hadn't felt that he was mocking her or scolding her or doing anything else but accepting her and having fun with her. It had felt so simple—and so good.

Unfortunately, she had also remembered how easy it would be to fall in love with him, and now she felt off balance. Was he a fundamentally wonderful guy who had one problematic side and occasionally said things that made her angry? Or was he a fundamentally problematic guy who had just been having one good day? Was his charm sincere or a weapon he was using against her?

And then there had been that moment at the end, when he had appeared to want to say something to her. Where might that have led them without the sudden appearance of Jakob inside the window? She had gone over this moment again and again during the week, imagining different outcomes. She had also remembered what it felt like to have his hand on hers, its warmth as it caressed her. And those memories had led her back to kissing him in

Chapter 7

the parking lot on their first date, the desire that had coursed through her body.

It had been a confusing week.

Now she could feel his eyes on her, and she wondered what he was thinking. Was he as confused as she was? Surely he could see as well as she could that they were incompatible. But he still seemed to have something to prove to her. She wondered when he would feel that it was proven and walk away from her at last. Part of her longed for that day because it would make her world so much easier to live in, but part of her couldn't bear to imagine never seeing him again.

She continued to play with the cats, willing herself not to look at him. She easily replaced these thoughts of him with worries about the future of the shelter. They were making good progress in finding homes for the animals and in their long-term plans for raising funds for the shelter. But so far, no short-term savior had come along to lead her to a new location for the shelter so that she could keep it in operation. She was quickly having to get used to the certainty that she would have to close the shelter and that it might be months or years before she could open one up again. It was such a depressing reality to face.

Suddenly the door to the shelter opened, and Bethany barged in, yelling, "Something's wrong with the commode! There's water everywhere!"

They followed her back to the clinic to find water all over the floor, spreading from the bathroom into the lobby, and down the hall to the exam rooms.

"Must be a leak," Will said, approaching the toilet and turning the water valve off. "It happens!" He smiled reassuringly at Bethany.

"Oh, so it's not a big deal?"

"Well, I'm glad you told us when you did, or things could have gotten a lot worse," Casey said. "But no, it's not a big deal."

"I'll go get the mop," Jakob said. "Bethany, why don't you print out an 'Out of Order' sign for the door?"

"I'll call a plumber," Casey said and followed Bethany to the front desk.

Casey got on the phone, and just as she was finishing up, Thomas Kline came in with his two big chocolate labs, followed by Barbie Cassady and her tiny frisky little poodle. Some barking ensued, and Casey laughingly tried to say hello to the humans over the sounds of the dogs. Bethany began the process of checking the humans in and explaining the payment situation to them, and Thomas immediately began complaining that he didn't have cash or a checkbook. He was one to make a big deal out of a small issue. While Casey was trying to help, Will came into the room with a mop, trying to push the edge of water coming out into the lobby back toward the bathroom.

At just that moment, Casey looked up to see her parents standing in the doorway of the clinic. In all the chaos, Casey had completely forgotten that they were to visit that day—and they were a bit earlier than she had expected. She felt instant dismay at the looks on their faces as they took in the noise, the chaos, and the site of Will Ingalls, real estate mogul, mopping.

"Mom! Dad!" Casey called, trying to sound welcoming rather than panicked.

"Have we come at a bad time?" Katherine asked, a fake smile plastered across her face. Charles didn't even pretend to smile. He surveyed the scene with a stern look of disapproval, shaking his head in disgust.

"Yes, but that's okay," Casey said, trying to sound cheery. "Just one of those days."

Will seemed to pick up on the panic she was trying to hide, and he nodded at her in understanding. "Katherine, Charles, it's a pleasure to see you again!" he said, leaning the mop against the wall and coming forward to shake their hands. "Let's sit in the lunchroom while Casey finishes up some tasks." He subtly pushed them out of the lobby and toward the lunchroom, sending a reassuring glance over his shoulder at Casey as he did so. She looked at him gratefully and then watched as he guided her parents across the driest part of the hallway, careful to keep her mother's expensive shoes out of the flood. "Can I get you some water or a Coke?" she heard him ask as they entered the lunchroom.

It took a few minutes to get Thomas Kline to calm down, mostly by promising him a discount on the day's services to make up for any inconvenience. Since Barbie Cassidy was in earshot, that meant a discount for her, too. Jakob was making good progress with the mopping. Casey asked Bethany to lead the dogs and their humans to their respective exam rooms and sent Jakob in to begin the process of going over their records, weighing the animals, and checking other basics. She had five minutes or so to say hello to her parents and face their disapproval before getting back to her patients.

The sight that greeted her as she entered the lunchroom was a surprising one. Katherine and Charles were seated at the table, sipping Cokes and laughing as Will said, "So you see, I learned my lesson on that one!" He looked up at Casey and smiled.

"Hi, Mom and Dad," she said, and she could hear the trepidation in her voice. "How was your drive this morning?"

"Fine," Charles said, "until we got here." The lingering smile fell from his face. "What chaos! Is this how you run the clinic every day?"

She decided to attempt humor. "Yes, Dad, it is. Every morning, I come in and break the toilet so that we'll have water everywhere. If there aren't any dogs in the office, I play a loud recording of dogs barking just to keep the place noisy. And I turn the wifi off so we'll have lots of problems processing our clients. Sure keeps things interesting!" Her attempt to be funny just sounded like petty sarcasm when she heard it come out of her mouth.

Katherine threw in some sarcasm of her own. "And do you always have Will here to do the janitorial work?"

Casey beamed at her. "Only on Saturdays."

Her father started to say something else, and Casey interrupted him. "I have a couple of appointments that should be quick, and then I'll have a few minutes to spend with you. Why don't you stay here and wait? And Will, please feel free to head back to the shelter when you're ready." She didn't like the thought of him staying there and learning the full extent of her parents' disapproval of her.

She left, relieved to get away. She took care of the dogs as efficiently as she could and said goodbye to them and their humans. As she turned to head back into the lunchroom, the front entrance door opened and Peggy Beane entered with her two chihuahuas. The little black and white dogs immediately began yapping at Casey, as chihuahuas will do. Napoleon complex, Casey thought.

Will exited the lunchroom and came toward them, and the dogs began barking vociferously at him, too, skittering toward him and then away from him and wagging their tails.

"Oh, stop it, you two!" Miss Peggy said halfheartedly, to no avail. To Casey she said, "Hello, dear. I came in without an appointment. I hope you don't mind, but Bonnie's been drooling again and I just felt so worried. Do you have time to see us?"

Miss Peggy was in fine form, wearing pastel shades from head to toe, her dyed red hair immaculate, her blue eyeshadow unafraid to assert itself, and her body doused in strong perfume. She was one of Casey's favorite patients, a sweet, absentminded, aging Southern belle. All that was missing was the big floppy hat that she sometimes wore.

Casey was grateful for a further delay in facing her parents. "Better take a look at those teeth, huh, girl?" Casey directed this question to Bonnie, the female half of the infamous chihuahua duo Bonnie and Clyde. Bonnie barked again but a little less loudly this time. "Well, come on back then." She took the leash from Miss Peggy, who preferred to wait in the waiting room with Clyde. Will watched with a smile on his face.

When she came back out ten minutes later, Will and Miss Peggy were having a conversation about Miss Peggy's search for a new beauty salon where they might have a better lifting technique. She felt her hair was too tight to her scalp; she wanted it fluffier. She beamed with pleasure and patted the back of her head as Will gave the obligatory compliment about how beautiful her hair looked just as it was.

Casey broke up the charm session. "Once again, she just needed to have those teeth cleaned up a little bit. And as always, she disliked having me do it, didn't you, you scary little monster?" Casey loved these hyper little dogs. She handed the leash over to Miss Peggy.

"What do I owe you, dear?"

"Oh, this one's on the house. Seeing these two is payment enough."

She heard a not-so-subtle clearing of the throat behind her and looked

Chapter 7

up to see that her parents had entered the lobby and were listening to the conversation.

Miss Peggy grabbed Casey's hand and patted it. "Thank you, dear. You're an angel." She looked at Will. "I'm glad you've finally found such a nice young man." To Will she said, "I hope you treat her well; otherwise you'll have to answer to me and a whole lot of other people in this town."

Casey looked at Will, horrified. She could feel her cheeks begin to burn.

He smiled and winked at Casey, seemingly at ease with the misunderstanding. "Why don't I walk you out to your car, Miss Peggy?" he replied easily, guiding her toward the front door.

The office was now quiet—too quiet. Casey could feel her father glaring at her. She turned to her parents, smiled, and said, "Let's go sit down."

Once back in the lunchroom, her father laid into her. "Casey, this is no way to run a business. It's utter chaos in here. And you provide services without charging people for them? How are you even staying in business?"

Casey tried to keep her voice calm. "Dad, you walked in on an unusually chaotic day. Don't judge me based on that. Normally everything runs quite smoothly here. And Miss Peggy has spent a fortune here over the years, which entitles her to the occasional perk. The clinic is doing just fine." She smiled what she hoped was a confident, reassuring smile.

Her father rolled his eyes. "A well-run business shouldn't have unusually chaotic days. Casey, you're better than this. I've *taught* you better than this."

Katherine leaned in. "And why would you ask one of the most eligible bachelors in Nashville to mop your floors for you?" she whispered. "I couldn't believe my eyes!"

"He's volunteering for the shelter."

"Yes, he told us all about that," Charles said. "Why didn't you come to us? We could *give* you money for a new shelter."

"You know why, Dad."

Charles glared at her. "This ridiculous grudge that you hold against me is incomprehensible."

"It's not a grudge. I just prefer to live my life independently from you. That's proven to be the best thing for our relationship."

Katherine sighed and shook her head. "That's not independence, dear. That's stubborn pride."

"Call it what you will, Mom, I still prefer not to accept your financial help." She placed her hands on their respective arms. "Anyway, let's not argue. What conference were you attending, and was it a good one?"

Charles refused to change the subject. "Casey, I don't understand why you would continue in this dumpy little office and waste your time worrying about that shelter out back. You know, if you came to work with me, you could have enough money to sponsor a beautiful, state-of-the-art vet clinic and run hundreds of shelters. Why do you limit yourself to this when you could do great things?"

Casey's mind flashed back to the numerous times they had had some version of this conversation. They had all been painful, with her forced to face her parents' disappointment about the many ways she had not met their expectations. But even more painful was that these conversations had forced her to admit that she was fundamentally opposed to the way her father ran his business. He was one of the biggest environmental violators in the state, building recklessly in sensitive environments, fighting any environmental legislation that would put limits on developers, and ridiculing any arguments she offered about her point of view. She simply couldn't bear to go through another such conversation, especially not here, where she had built a life to get away from them and their expectations.

"Dad, we've talked about this before. There's no point in rehashing it."

He grunted, but at least he didn't continue.

There was a knock at the door.

"Come in," Casey called. Jakob popped his head in, a wary look on his face. Casey had no doubt he had been listening to their conversation from the other side of the door.

"Doc, sorry to interrupt, but can I see you for a sec?"

She nodded, grateful for the interruption. "I'll be right back," she said to her parents.

"Yes, Jakob?" she asked once they were in the lobby.

"Uh, I know this is a really bad time to ask, but can I leave early today?"

Chapter 7

Jakob often asked to leave early, which she normally didn't mind because he devoted so many extra hours to the shelter. Still, she had requested that he give her advance notice rather than asking, as he was now, in the middle of the afternoon.

"Jakob!" she cried out in frustration.

"I know, I know. It's just that, with everything going on today, I forgot to ask. Katie has to drive to Knoxville to pick up her niece for the weekend, and I don't want her to go alone because then she'd have to drive all the way back alone, after dark. And we really want to beat the late afternoon traffic."

"But Jakob, Bethany is already scheduled to leave early today!"

He smiled his most winning smile at her. How could she say no to that? She liked how Jakob tried to look after Katie, even though his efforts were seemingly unnecessary. Katie was over six feet tall and covered in tattoos and piercings. She was about 100 pounds overweight, and she stuffed her body into skintight biker outfits, almost always black. She had a loud, commanding voice, and was not afraid to tell anyone, even Casey, exactly what they ought to do in any given situation. Beneath that tough exterior, she was a kind and caring person. But looking after was definitely not something Katie needed.

"Okay, you can leave early," she answered with a sigh.

There was a horn honk outside. "Oh, that's her!" Jakob exclaimed.

"So you asked me when she was already here to pick you up?" Casey asked, astonished.

He looked sheepish. "Well, she wasn't actually here yet. She was just around the corner." He kissed her on the cheek. "Thanks! Love ya, Doc!"

"You're leaving?" Will asked, sounding equally astonished, suddenly standing behind Casey.

"Yes, thanks to my very generous boss."

"Suck up," Casey muttered under her breath. Jakob only smiled and then scooted out the door.

"I think we'll be on our way as well," her father said, startling her. She had not seen Will or her parents coming into the room, and now she realized with dismay that they had all witnessed what they would interpret as Jakob taking advantage of her. She was weak, they would conclude, and unable to control her employee, another sign of a poorly-run business by an inept veterinarian who was also unable to take care of the shelter animals in her care. Casey sighed.

"Okay, Dad, Mom," she said wearily. "Thanks for coming by."

A man she had never seen before, carrying a ferret, entered at that moment and glanced at them questioningly. "Bethany can help you at the front desk," Casey directed him, then kissed her mother's cheek and watched her parents leave.

She turned to Will. "Thanks for looking after them," she said then headed back to an exam room.

"You're welcome," he called after her. She was grateful he didn't ask for any conversation beyond that.

Bethany left around 4:00, and Casey handled the last couple of patients and then began cleaning the exam rooms. She would work on paperwork for an hour or so and then head home and try to decompress after such a terrible day. She really did feel like a failure. She was out of control of her clinic, her employees, the future of the animals in her shelter. And her parents and Will had seen her at her worst. Was it possible that she was as incompetent as they all clearly believed her to be?

"So everybody has left you early once again?" Will asked archly as he entered the lobby to find her sweeping the floor. "You sure do run a tight ship."

Anger flared, but her emotions were already in such turmoil that she decided to let this one go. She simply didn't have the energy to defend herself. "Well, we schedule Saturday after 3:00 pretty lightly in case this happens," she replied neutrally, continuing her work. "It's all good."

Just then the door opened and Linda Myers came rushing in. "Oh my God, Casey, I saw a dog hit on the side of the road. He's hurt bad. I've got him in the truck. Can you come see?"

Casey burst out of the practice with Will close behind her. In the back of the truck was a dog she recognized, a rough-looking Rottweiler, a victim of abuse that Casey had never been able to convince the authorities to take

Chapter 7

away from her owner. He kept the dog chained up to a tree when he wasn't letting her roam all over the countryside, attacking people's chickens and causing other trouble. His kids picked at the dog mercilessly, according to neighbors' accounts. She was neglected, left out in the cold, and not given food sometimes for a couple of days at a time. She had never known a happy day in her life, and here she was, with a laceration down the length of one side of her body that had almost split her in two and what looked to be a broken leg.

Casey couldn't believe she was alive. The dog whimpered, her eyes closed, and Casey knew there was precious little time to save her.

"Stay here," she told them both. "I'll be right back." She entered the practice, filled a syringe with a sedative, and grabbed a stretcher. At the truck, she administered the shot, not willing to take a chance that a Rottweiler in pain wouldn't lash out them, no matter how close she was to losing consciousness. She wondered how Linda had managed to get the dog in her truck bed. The sedative took hold in seconds, and Casey motioned to Will to help her move the dog onto the stretcher.

"Thank you, Linda," she said dismissively. "We'll see what we can do."

They carried the dog back to the room used for surgery, and she started getting fluids ready to inject into her. She cursed Jakob's decision to leave early; she really needed him. But at least Will was here.

"Will, I hate to tell you this, but you're going to have to play assistant for a while. Is that okay?"

"Yes, fine, whatever you need." His voice was confident and calm, which gave her a sense of relief. She knew she could depend on him.

Casey did a physical exam as quickly as possible. She noted paradoxical breathing, unfortunately indicating internal injuries, and administered oxygen. She checked the dog's mucus membranes for other signs of respiratory distress. She assessed the length and depth of the laceration and realized that, in addition to a break in the leg, there was a tendon cut almost completely through. She took a deep breath, delivered anesthetic, and began one of the most difficult surgeries of her career.

Her attempts to clean and sew up the laceration made a bloody mess. She was grateful for Will's steady hand and quiet demeanor as he followed her orders. She had to set the broken leg and repair the tendon. All through the procedure, she continued to recheck the signs of respiratory distress, particularly worried about the effects of the anesthesia on a dog that was already compromised to such an extent. Things seemed to be going well as the operation continued, and she began to relax slightly as she finished her treatment of the leg and laceration.

Suddenly the dog stopped breathing. Casey checked her heartbeat and realized it was slowing. There was no way to perform CPR given the dog's injuries, so she attempt to intervene with medications instead. She worked increasingly desperately as the dog came nearer to death, but to no avail. The poor creature died at 5:35.

Ripping off her gloves so she could lower her hands and smooth the now peaceful face, Casey felt her body grow heavy with grief. She bent to place her cheek against the poor dog's face. The sobs followed, and they quickly grew so intense that she struggled to catch her breath. All the emotions from the entire day, all the emotions from the last few weeks of worry, rolled through her and out in her tears. She could feel the release. But, instead of bringing relief, it was accompanied by a deep sense of grief and helplessness. In all ways, she seemed to be failing the animals who needed her most.

Will moved to her side. He pulled his equally filthy gloves off and offered his arms to her. She gratefully dove into him and clung to his strong body, welcoming the gesture and needing the comfort. "I'm sorry, I'm sorry," he said, holding her tightly and stroking her hair.

A few minutes later her sobs began to subside, but she continued to let him hold her. His embrace felt so protective, and she drew some modicum of comfort from it.

"I'm sorry," he said again.

She didn't know what to say besides "thank you." Then she pulled back and found herself pouring out the story of the dog, and the tears began to flow again.

"Will, she's never known a single happy day in her life! And then she had to die like this. It's so unfair. What did she ever do to deserve this life and this death?"

He held her again as the sobs wracked her body. He didn't try to answer her unanswerable questions, and she was grateful for this.

Finally, he pushed her back so he could look at her face. Gently he wiped away one of her tears and then looked at her tenderly. "You were magnificent," he told her quietly, almost reverently. "I've never seen anything like it. You knew exactly what to do. You were calm and collected. You fought with everything you had." He held and looked at her hands. "And your hands are so skilled and precise." He repeated, with more intensity this time, "I've never seen anything like it!"

The rush of words surprised her, and she didn't know how to respond. Her surprise deepened as she felt his lips on her face, pressing gently against the remaining tears on her cheek. Suddenly she found herself pressing her lips against his, tentatively. He responded immediately, deepening the kiss as his hand shifted to the back of her head and pulled her even closer to him. He explored her mouth with his, and she felt the reassurance in his kisses that she had just heard in his words.

She pushed her body against his, trying to get as close to him as possible, seeking comfort in his strength and warmth, the insistence of his mouth. He put his arms around her again and pulled her tightly against the length of his body, stroking her back, half soothingly and half reflecting a sensuality that was growing as they continued to kiss. He clearly wanted her. She ran her hands up his neck and into his thick curls, reveling in the feel of them, the masculine smell that emanated from him. She knew she wanted him, too, and not just for comfort.

But then a new round of tears came as she realized what he had just said. She broke the embrace. "But I couldn't save her!" she cried out. "So all that effort was worth nothing in the end."

He chose to answer this time. "Maybe she wanted it to be the end. You can't save someone who doesn't want to be saved." She could see on his face that he was referring to something much deeper and more painful in his life than the loss of this poor dog. "All you could do was try, and you tried as hard as you could."

She nodded, and they stood there for a few moments without speaking.

She tried to regain her composure. "Will you help me take her body off the table and bag her for the freezer?"

"Yes, of course." He helped her with that and watched as she made a quick call to the crematory and left a message about scheduling a pickup for Monday. Then she just stood there, uncertain what to do or say in light of the intensity of the moment they had just shared.

"Is there anything I can do for you?" he asked gently. He didn't try to touch her again, and she felt grateful to him for that, too.

She sighed and looked around the room. "To be honest, I'd like to be alone. I'll clean this up, grieve a little, and then head home. I just want to be home. It's been a rough day."

"I understand that," he answered. "And you'll be okay alone? Do you need help getting home?"

She pulled her shoulders back and wiped her eyes. "No, but thank you." She looked him straight in the eye and tried to convey her sincerity. "I really appreciate it. But this comes with the territory. Usually I can deal with it a bit more professionally, but there was something about this dog."

"Don't apologize for being—well, such a wonderful human being," he said. She replied with a slight smile, touched.

"Good night," he said, reaching out an arm to squeeze her hand briefly. "Call me if you need to talk or need anything else." He said it kindly and with concern, not in the patronizing tone he so often used. She liked this kinder and more respectful way of offering help.

"Good night," she said. After he left, she gave herself a few more minutes to stand in a stunned silence. And then she got to work, letting the familiar rhythm of cleaning soothe her as she allowed the grief to flow again. When she finished about 30 minutes later, she did indeed head right home to comfort herself further with her own dear pets and a nice, warm bed.

Chapter 8

Casey's phone buzzed the next morning. "How are you?" Will's text read. She rubbed her eyes and looked at the time. Eight o'clock! She never slept this late. The surgery and loss of the dog must have worn her out physically as well as emotionally.

"Fine, thank you. I overslept!" she texted back.

"Happens to the best of us. Sorry to wake you."

"No problem. Thank you again for your help yesterday. Really."

She was hit with the memory of his lips on hers. She could feel their warmth and softness, hear his breath, imagine his hands pulling her into him as the kisses gained intensity. She had repeated that moment again and again in her dreams. She also remembered his kindness, his helpfulness, his words about how magnificent—had he really said that?—she was.

"You're welcome."

She didn't know what else to write. What was going to happen now? Would they talk about that kiss or pretend it never happened? Did this change anything between them?

"See you later," he texted.

"Have a good day," she replied, disappointed. Was that it?

She didn't like to rush in the mornings, but she realized she could make it to church if she hurried to feed the animals and get dressed. She could use an hour or so thinking about positive things like hope and love. Then she would have time to eat a quick sandwich before working an adoption event with Ellen, an energetic former volunteer who liked to help out at the shelter when she was home visiting from college.

Casey pushed herself out of bed and let Meow lead her to the bathroom and then the kitchen. She couldn't believe the cat had allowed her to sleep so late. He yowled and brushed against Casey's leg as she prepared his food. She then fed all of the outdoor animals and said a quick hello to them. She felt guilty that she was always so busy with the shelter and not spending much time with her own animals. Reluctantly, she admitted to herself that Will was right: something had to give, especially if she needed to find even more time to secure the long-term interests of the shelter.

She arrived at church only a couple of minutes late. She spoke briefly with the greeter and then pushed open the sanctuary doors to hear one of her favorite hymns. She took the first seat available, at the edge of the back pew on the right.

As she sang, she made a cursory glance around the congregation, seeing so many familiar people who had embraced her since her move to Pleasant Valley. She saw the back of one head several rows ahead that looked like Will's. She could only catch glimpses of him through the movements of people in between them as they swayed to the music or jiggled their babies. Could it be? His height and longish dark hair were unmistakable, but she couldn't imagine why he would be here today. He headed back home on Saturday evenings, and anyway he had never mentioned attending church. Could he have come because he knew she would be there? That seemed unlikely.

It was hard to concentrate on that hymn or the next. During the prayer she tried her best to concentrate so she could infuse her own worries into the petitions of the pastor. The sermon was a good one, as they always were: the right combination of Bible study, conviction, and food for thought. Usually Casey was caught up in the message, taking notes of points to think over during the rest of the week. But this time she was preoccupied with memories of Will's lips on her own, his eyes searching her face, his words of admiration and comfort, his sensitivity.

Chapter 8

Perhaps they had reached a turning point. She might be able to look past her anger and reconsider who he really was. Yes, he was arrogant and bossy, and she didn't like his wholly no-nonsense approach to life as a series of practical business decisions. But clearly there was more to him, the sides she had seen the previous evening and on their first date, and in his humor during their morning of wildlife and traffic watching.

Of course, she didn't like how he forced his help on her at the shelter and indicated that her way of doing things was inferior. Yet she had to admit that he *had* been helpful so far. She really was too close to the situation and had benefited from his more objective perspective. Plus he had sacrificed time for her and the shelter every Saturday for weeks, even though he was undoubtedly a very busy man. So he wasn't exactly like her father after all, driven to neglect his loved ones in favor of work and making money.

After the sermon and prayer, there were announcements and then a final hymn. What should she do? She could try to slip out without him seeing her, or she could face him. She didn't wholly want to do either. She longed to see him face to face, look into his bold eyes, feel them look at her so appreciatively. Yet she knew she would face him with uncertainty and vulnerability.

She hesitated too long. He turned in his pew and immediately locked eyes with her, as if sensing she was there. She smiled at him and half waved, then had her attention pulled toward a young couple who were trying to greet her and whose toddler daughter was reaching out to pull her hair. Casey admired the girl and chatted with the parents for a couple of minutes, and then Will was at her side. She turned to look at him and caught her breath. He looked so handsome in a red button-down shirt that contrasted with his dark looks. He looked at her with a lopsided smile.

"Fancy meeting you here!" he said, and she couldn't tell from his tone if it really was a surprise or if he had indeed expected to find her there.

"Yes, fancy that. Imagine me showing up at the church I attend regularly!" This lashing out to cover her uncertainty thing was unfortunately becoming a habit.

He didn't seem to mind. "Do you think I'm stalking you?"

She remembered their first date. "No, I'm supposed to be the dangerous one, remember?" She thought more about the situation. "But really, why are you in town on a Sunday? Did you spend the night?"

"Yes, I had dinner plans with someone from the town council and then stayed here for the adoption event today."

"I think you've got your dates confused. Ellen and I are working today."

He flashed her a huge smile, showing beautiful white teeth. "What would you say if I told you I traded days with Ellen so that I could work today with you? Would that make you think I'm stalking you?"

She sighed. "It would make me think you're up to your usual project of showing me that I need your help to do anything and everything related to this shelter. Or you want to show off your sales skills, the ones Jakob was raving about the other day."

He refused to bite. Instead, he looked at her sincerely. "It's really much simpler than that. I just wanted to spend time with you."

She looked at him, surprised at the admission. "So you really are stalking me?" she joked weakly.

He didn't laugh. "No, I'm really not. Okay, maybe a little. But not this morning. I honestly had no idea you went to church here. I have a situation going on right now that's on my mind, and I needed a little church this morning. I came to this one because it's near the hotel."

She looked at him skeptically, and he laughed. "You don't believe me?"

"You don't seem like a church kind of a guy."

He shrugged his shoulders. "One of Coach Ingalls' many reforms."

"And, when the service was over, you turned around and immediately found me in the crowd, as if you knew I was here."

"I did know you were here. The preacher told a joke during the sermon, and you laughed. I would recognize your laugh anywhere."

"Really?"

"Um, you kind of have a loud laugh."

"I do?" She laughed and then listened to herself. Yikes. She *did* have a loud laugh.

"It's a great laugh," he assured her and then continued. "I did switch with

Chapter 8

Ellen so I could be with you this afternoon, so I guess that was a little bit stalker like. But it's just because I like spending time with you. I want us to be friends." He gazed at her for a moment and added, "No, to be honest, I want us to be more than friends."

She felt the blush move up her neck and into her cheeks. Suddenly she felt so embarrassed to be here, in this church sanctuary full of people, because she was imagining his arms around her, his lips against hers, his tongue in her mouth, his hands all over her body. She tried to save herself by making eye contact with someone else, in hopes that they would come over and extricate her from this situation.

Luck was with her. The pastor himself caught her eye and headed over. She was glad he couldn't read her private thoughts.

"Hi, Casey, we haven't seen you in a few weeks." Oops, busted. The church she had just said she regularly attended. "Glad to see you here!"

"Thanks, Bill. I've been so busy with the shelter and everything else."

"I've wanted to ask you how it's going. I'm glad the kids are able to help."

Casey smiled her thanks. "They have been a great help. I appreciate it so much."

"Who's your friend?" Pastor Bill asked, looking toward Will and extending his hand.

Casey smiled awkwardly at Will. "This is Will Ingalls, who is helping with some of the business at the shelter."

"Will Ingalls? Bill Folsom. It's nice to have you here." Bill paused, thinking. "But where have I heard your name before? You're not local, are you?"

Will dropped their handshake and explained, "You might have heard my name associated with the company heading up the project to build the retirement home and assisted living facility downtown." Will looked at Casey and raised his eyebrows.

"Yes, that's it. It was in the paper." Bill paused, thinking again. "But isn't that the company that is using the land where Casey's shelter—?"

He faltered a bit and Casey chimed in, "Yes, that's right." She tried to be light. "That's why Will is volunteering at the shelter. He's trying to make amends for his very great sin!"

Bill chuckled in response. "Well, Will, the Good Lord forgives sin. But whether Casey will, that's another matter."

Will laughed out loud and Casey couldn't help joining in.

After chatting with a couple more people who were obviously curious about the good-looking newcomer, Will accompanied Casey to the parking lot and her car. "Can I take you to lunch?" he asked.

She considered the offer and realized it would seem churlish to say no given his kindness to her the previous day. "Sure." She checked the time on her cell phone. "We have a little over an hour and a half before we head out this afternoon. But I do need to make time to pick up a couple of things from my house before we load up the animals."

They decided to walk to the nearby Downtown Diner, which was packed with the after-church family crowd. They squeezed into a tiny booth for two in a corner and ordered their food. Casey always had to eat breakfast at this diner, no matter the time of day; their pancakes were to die for. Will ordered a salad.

"You're having a salad?" Casey blinked in surprise. "Are you on a diet?"

He laughed. "Nah, I just had a big breakfast in the hotel a couple of hours ago. I'm not that hungry."

"Did you ever see that episode of *Seinfeld*? You must be very comfortable in your masculinity."

"Well, once I realized I had a wimpy dog, I gave up on appearing masculine to the rest of the world. And I don't want to go to an adoption event with my pockets full of meat, so best not to order it," he added, referring again to the *Seinfeld* episode. So he was just as cultured in yesterday's sitcoms as she was, she thought.

That was something neutral they could talk about: 90s sitcoms. So that is what they did. It was a nice, light conversation. It wasn't full of banter like their first one, it wasn't full of irritation like their more recent ones. It was just a normal, relaxed conversation between two people who volunteered together at an animal shelter.

Their food came, and his was a huge Greek salad with enormous chicken tenders. "Ha ha, not so unmanly after all, you see," he thundered in an extra

Chapter 8

deep voice. Then he looked at her food. "So you like your breakfast, huh?"

"Oh, yes, especially here. Wanna try a bite? They're the best pancakes on earth."

He tasted them and agreed. The sight of his lips closing over her fork steered her mind back towards thoughts she was trying to forget. Fortunately, he said no when she asked if he wanted more. "I had pancakes for breakfast, actually. Blueberry."

"Wow, that's also the least masculine kind of pancake. I'm seeing a new side to you."

"I had sausage on the side," he said defensively. "Anyway, you're going to give me a complex about it if you keep this up. Maybe I am starting to doubt my manhood."

"Don't worry, you are *all man*," she replied in an uncharacteristically lust-filled tone. She had been thinking it but hadn't intended to say it out loud, and she could feel the cursed blush rising in her cheeks as he looked at her in amused surprise. She looked down at her food and willed him to change the subject. Instead he pressed his foot over one of her own. It was an intimate, overwhelmingly physical gesture—a secret touch under the table, just between them. Her entire body was flooded with the memory of being held against him the day before, the way it felt to be in his arms. She couldn't help but raise her eyes to his, drawn to the look she knew he would be giving her as he shared that memory. He kept his foot against hers, and her body buzzed with desire. No one had ever looked at her the way Will did.

Finally, he moved his foot away, looked at his watch, and sighed. "Not to rush you, but we'd better get on our way soon. How much time will it take to run by your house?"

She forced her thoughts to clear, grateful for something else to concentrate on. She pulled the phone out of her purse and checked the time. "Um, we should leave here in 15 minutes."

"I'll go ahead and ask for the check, but take your time finishing up." She smiled at him. He had already wolfed down much of his salad in his mannerly—but manly—way.

They kept the conversation neutral for the remaining time, and she avoided his eyes. Finally, they left the restaurant and headed back to their cars. "I'll be back in a few minutes," she said as she moved to get into her car.

"Can I come along and help you?" he asked. She could think of no good reason to say no other than her cowardly desire to avoid him, which again seemed churlish after such a nice lunch together. But she fervently hoped there would be no more intimate moments. Her thoughts were confused enough as it was.

"Sure."

As they drove to her house, he asked, "Did you always want to live in the country?"

"Yes," she said, then corrected herself. "Well, actually, when I was in high school and college I thought the city was way more fun. But I always knew that I would settle down in the country eventually. I love the quiet, I love nature, I love having space to roam around. Of course, Pleasant Valley is facing a lot of development, so even the country is getting a lot noisier and more crowded."

That was venturing into dangerous territory for them, so she decided to stop there. "What about you?" she asked. "Would you ever want to live in the country?"

He chuckled. "Hmmm, that is an interesting question. I have bad associations with life in the country because my mother always seemed to move us into junky, filthy little places. And I would do odd jobs for the neighbors that were disgusting, like raking out chicken houses and spreading manure in their gardens. Our house always had mice and bugs everywhere, and I could smell skunks in the yard at night. So I couldn't wait to get to the city, where nature is neat and landscaped and not allowed to smell bad."

She glanced over and saw him looking out of the window. They were moving through an area of low hills and agricultural fields. The landscape was dotted with neat farms, although they did pass the occasional junk-filled front yard that was straight out of a reality show about the South.

"But you're right that it is beautiful," he finally continued. "And calming. I'll never get used to the sounds of cars flying down the street and honking at all hours. And it is nice to smell some fresh air for a change."

Chapter 8

"Even if it smells like manure and skunks sometimes?"

"Even then," he admitted. "Turns out that's better than exhaust fumes."

As they pulled into her driveway, she wondered what he would think of her place. It was a one-story house that sprawled out horizontally. It was bigger than she needed, with three bedrooms and three baths, a huge living room and kitchen, and a partially screened-in back porch that stretched the full length of the rear of the house. The original part of the house was stone, and one of the later add-ons was brick, and then the third section was covered in siding. This eclectic look was one of the things that had attracted her to it.

She had pulled down all the landscaping around the house and covered much of the front yard with what she hoped looked like an English country garden, overflowing now with purple and red coneflowers, cosmos, and lavender. She could see butterflies and bees hovering over much of it, which always filled her with pleasure. The garden was huge and more than a little wild looking, but at least it was contained neatly in the jagged stone borders she had placed around it. It had taken all five years to get it to look just right, and she was proud of her efforts.

As they got out, he looked around but didn't say anything. She walked around and opened up the back of the SUV.

"Would you mind following me around back?" she asked and then pointed to a 50-pound bag of chicken feed. "And would you mind carrying that bag?"

He lifted it as if it weighed no more than a feather.

In the back, her vegetable garden looked fresh and neat thanks to the work of a couple of teenagers from down the road she had just paid to weed and water it. The flowers in the backyard were in outrageous color, too. She again felt proud. Beyond the garden was a bit of lawn, which then ceded to a woodlot of about twenty acres. She had it all: a garden, farm animals, and plenty of nature. She loved this place.

She led him toward the barn, where she had stored some of the carriers in order to free up space at the shelter. She kept the barn neat. The chickens had plenty of straw and shavings and a huge outdoor area to roam around in, and the rabbits were in a neat, roomy space with a fan blowing to keep them cool. She used the rabbit and chicken waste to fertilize the garden, allowing her pig to come in every now and then and scratch and root through the straw to mix it all up. It was raked out regularly to keep it from smelling, especially given the Tennessee heat.

He transported the carriers back and forth to the car with her quietly, but she could see him looking around. Finally he said, "This is a beautiful place. So different from our homes when I was growing up in Kentucky."

"Oh, thanks! Yeah, the one problem for me with being such an animal person is that I'm also a clean freak."

"Well, you make it work."

"Thanks. I have to. I couldn't live without all this. I really couldn't."

He looked at her with a question in his eyes that she couldn't quite understand. "Yes, I can see that. This place suits you."

"Well, ready?" she asked, closing the barn door behind them after they had grabbed the last load of what they needed.

He followed her back to the car, and they rode in silence most of the way back. She wondered what he was thinking about as he stared out the window, his chin resting in the palm of his hand, elbow against the car door. He looked like a young boy, his hair blowing in the wind of the slightly opened windows.

At one point he reached over and squeezed her hand. "I like your life," he said, looking at her. "It's peaceful and happy." Without waiting for a reply, he pulled his hand away and returned to looking out the window. She couldn't think of a reply for such a statement, so she settled back into her thoughts.

It felt good to be with him, going through the motions of her life with him. It felt natural. She remembered their first date and her intuition that he was freer and easier with her than he probably was in his usual world. She had the same feeling now: he could live this life, drive down country roads with his hair blowing in the wind, and be happy. There was so much more to him than the serious businessman who liked to win.

What if they had continued from that first night and let their relationship develop organically, without the anger and bad feelings and accusations? This was where they would be, she realized, and she would be content. But

Chapter 8

that baggage was still there, she reminded herself, forcing her thoughts away from him. Instead, she thought about each of the animals she was planning to bring today and said a quick prayer for them in her mind: that they would be matched with the perfect home and live the life they deserved.

They reached the shelter and loaded the animals: four dogs and six cats. The poor things looked miserable packed in the car together, especially the dogs, two of which were in small kennels and two of which were left out and lying on the floorboards. Will kept reaching around to pat their heads reassuringly. The cats yowled the entire way, but there was nothing to be done about that.

They drove toward Nashville to a mall parking lot where they were joining the weekly farmers' market. This was always a good bet for adoptions: well-heeled people whose worldviews included the idea that animals were meant to be cared-for companions, not objects that could be abandoned or worked or tied up in the backyard. And these people would have the money to care for them properly. Casey felt hopeful as they pulled in and saw all the farmers and bakers and craft makers setting up their booths. The market would go from 3:00-7:00 that evening, which would give them a lot of time to reach a lot of people.

The afternoon seemed to be a success. Casey could see Jakob's point about Will's ability to sell the pets, especially to women, an observation that was accompanied by more than a little bit of jealousy. He had a certain kind of charm that he used with them, still sincere but definitely superficial and intentional. She was happy to contrast that with the natural, easy charm he used with her. He was good with men, too, and children. He was just so darn affable; everybody liked him. She couldn't help but be impressed by his people skills.

After a conversation had reached the "We'll think seriously about it—can I take an application?" point, Will would turn and wink at her. Then he would say, "It will only take five minutes to fill out the application now and save you the trouble of doing it later. But first, let's take one more look at him." He would pull the cat back out or call the dog over to him and make sure everyone in the family got one more chance to pet and cuddle and ooh and ah. While that was going on, he would pull out a clipboard, application, and pen, and then exchange that with the cat or the leash as he took the animal back from the person. It was almost unconscious on their part, then, to take the clipboard and pen and start filling out the application.

As they turned in their application and then walked away, he would turn to Casey victoriously, back in arrogant mode, and she would shake her head or roll her eyes. Yes, he seemed to have made the sale, she thought. But had he found the right home, someone who was truly committed to the animal rather than just manipulated by a friendly and good-looking salesman? That remained to be seen.

Casey's own style was to let the animals do the work. She stood quietly by as people admired a particular animal, sometimes making a comment or two about how sweet the animal was or how much the volunteers at the shelter loved him. "Let me know if I can answer any questions," she would say and then let the relationship form organically—or not. The "contract," using Will's language, had to be between the animal and the people, in her opinion, not her and the people. She felt sure that her method might not yield as many applications but would yield many more adoptions.

Still, she enjoyed watching him, listening to him, admiring him. She laughed a lot at his antics. There was no one like him, and she felt proud to know that he was performing to an audience of one: her.

At about 5:00, Casey's phone rang. It was her mother. She indicated to Will that she was taking it and walked a few paces away from the noise.

"Hi, Mom," she said.

"Casey, dear, I have something worrisome to tell you." Casey could hear the anxiety in her mother's voice and immediately felt alarmed.

"What's wrong, Mom?"

"Well, your father has had a heart attack!" Her voice faltered. Casey had never heard her mother sound anything less than fully composed, and this told her even more than the next words how serious the situation was. "He's heading into surgery at Vanderbilt Health. When can you get here?"

"I'll leave right now." She asked her Mom for more details and got them quickly: they had been playing tennis after lunch at the club, and

Chapter 8

he had collapsed on the court, clutching his left arm. Katherine had known immediately it was a heart attack, even though he had never had one before and didn't seem to have any heart problems that they knew of. Fortunately, the ambulance had come right away and the huge Vanderbilt facility wasn't too distant. But Katherine was scared; Casey could hear it in her voice.

She hung up the phone and called Jakob.

"Jakob, are you free to come and wrap up the adoption event with Will this evening?"

"Yeah, sure, what's up?" He must have sensed something in her voice because he didn't take the opportunity to tease her about working an adoption event with Will.

"My father has had a heart attack, and I need to get to Nashville. Can I just leave?"

"Yes, go," he assured her. "I'll be free by 6:00 and can head over with my van. Will and I can take care of everything."

She returned to Will, who was smiling and talking with a vivacious redhead in short shorts who couldn't have been more than twenty. When he saw the look on Casey's face, he turned his full attention to her. "What's wrong?" he asked.

"My father is in the hospital. I need to go."

"Where, Nashville? Let me drive you; I can get you there right away. Can someone come and take care of the animals?"

He seemed to share her sense of urgency but also seemed calm and ready to take command, to relieve some of her burden. She was surprised to realize that she actually wished he were free to take her to Nashville. She explained the situation to him: she needed him to stay with the animals until Jakob was free at 6:00 to come and help him pack up.

He seemed regretful that he couldn't go with her but said, "Sounds like a plan. We'll take care of everything. Go do what you need to do and don't worry about a thing here." He smiled and gave her a quick hug. "Call me if you need me, if you need anything at all." She hugged him back gratefully and then ran to her car.

"Drive carefully! Don't rush!" he called out to her as she got into the car.

Yes, she thought: slow down, slow down, slow down. But she was very worried as she pulled out of the parking lot and drove as quickly as possible into the city.

She joined her mother in the waiting room about 40 minutes later. Katherine stood and hugged her, then pushed the hair back from Casey's face in a tender, motherly gesture.

"Oh, Casey!" Katherine had been crying; even what had obviously been a recent reapplication of powder around her eyes couldn't hide the signs of tears.

"Mom, what's the latest news? Is he out of surgery?"

"I'm still waiting to hear from the doctor."

"Can I get you anything? Water or coffee, Kleenex?"

Katherine waved her off and sat down again, crossing her legs tightly as she did so. "No, no, I don't need anything except an update. Where is that doctor?"

Casey sat next to her. "It's going to be okay, Mom. Dad is the healthiest person I know."

"Well, you never know what's going on inside a person, do you? And he is under so much stress. I've been telling him lately that he has got to slow down, but he's involved in a new project and burning the midnight oil. This is the first day, even on a weekend, that he has allowed himself to rest and have some fun, and look what happened!"

"Now he'll say it was resting that hurt him and he needs to go back to work," Casey joked, trying to lighten her mother's mood. She looked at Katherine and noticed, with a start, that she was looking older. Her parents had always seemed the same to her: ageless and formidable. But in fluorescent lights she could see the wrinkles through her mother's thick makeup and Botox injections, the very slim line of gray in the roots of her dark brown hair. Of course, the worry of the situation would add ten years to anyone's face. But, apart from that, Katherine was clearly moving into a new phase in life: an older lady rather than a middle-aged woman. This would crush her mother's vanity, she knew.

And now her father, her slim, strong, marathon-running father, had had a heart attack. How would that change his life? Some men in the same situation had to limit activity, eat special diets, watch their salt intake. It could mean more frequent doctor visits, daily pills, and other new regimens. He might grow frail, worried, fretting.

Casey was the only child of aging parents. She needed to think more about how she could care for them, be there for them. She needed to talk to them about wills and advanced care directives, although she was certain they had already worked such things out for themselves. She realized with a start that her life was about to change, too.

Katherine looked at her. "Are you all right, dear?"

"Yes, fine, Mom. Just in shock. I mean, how could Dad, of all people, have a heart attack?"

"It was terrible to see him fall down. He just—crumpled, I suppose is the word. And there was nothing I could do for him. Fortunately, there were people on hand who knew how to make him comfortable. I don't even know who called 911, but I'm thankful someone did so quickly. All I could do was stand there and beg God to let him live." She sobbed a bit as she said the last word. "Oh, Casey, he is going to live, isn't he?"

Casey held her mother's hand. Katherine had never in Casey's life seemed so vulnerable, so in need of comfort. She was always strong as a rock.

"Yes, Mom, he's going to live. Of course he's going to live. These days, having a heart attack is nothing. They'll fix him up, he'll recover, and he'll go on about his business."

Katherine looked up and glared at Casey. "Well, that's where you're wrong. I simply will not allow him to go on about his business as before."

Casey again attempted a joke. "Well, *that* will be much harder than performing heart surgery!"

The waiting room door opened, and a doctor entered. She was tall and imposing, with sharp black eyes and thick gray hair tied back in a bun. "Mrs. Young?" she asked.

They stood. "Yes, and this is my daughter, Casey."

"Nice to meet you both. I'm Dr. Lotfalian. Mr. Young has come through surgery just fine. We performed a double bypass, no complications. A full recovery is expected. More good news: we were able to perform minimally invasive surgery, meaning a shorter hospital stay and recovery period. I'll have a nurse come out and tell you more about how long he'll need to stay in the hospital and other details, but I wanted to personally let you know that the surgery is over and he is doing well."

"Can we see him?"

"No, not yet. He's still unconscious, in any case. I recommend that you go to the café, get something to eat, walk around a little bit, and try to relax. Come back in a couple of hours and then you can see him."

The door opened again, and a younger woman came in, dressed in scrubs with a Snoopy pattern. Casey could only imagine what her mother was thinking about the fact that her husband's care was in the hands of a grown woman wearing Snoopy scrubs, with her hair pulled up sloppily into a ponytail. Casey caught sight of a tattoo on the back of her neck as well. Oh dear. This conversation might not go too well.

The doctor left, and the nurse sat and explained several details of what Charles had been through and what would happen next. She spoke calmly and intelligently, and Katherine seemed able to overlook the woman's physical appearance. Charles would be in the hospital for four to six days, first in the ICU and eventually a regular unit. Katherine insisted on a private room, and the nurse said they would work that out later. She described the machines and tubes that he would need, the schedule for transitioning him from liquids to solid food, how much he would be able to walk over the next few weeks.

After the nurse left, Casey smiled at her mother. "See, Mom, everything will be fine. Let's go walk around outside, get some fresh air. I'll buy you a coffee."

Katherine gave her a tired smile. Uncharacteristically, she followed Casey's lead. They grabbed coffees in the café and then walked around a flower garden beside the hospital. It was a hot and humid night, and Casey's clothes clung to her skin. But she liked being outside.

She also liked being with her mother. She was seeing a new side to Katherine, and frightening as that side was, it made Casey feel that she was with a real live person rather than her imposing, dominating, hyper-confident mother. Casey wanted to comfort her and enjoyed the feeling of doing so.

They chatted for a few minutes and then walked in silence. Casey's mind was flooded with memories of her father. Her first memory was of him lifting her high above his head before throwing her into the lake where they spent many Sunday afternoons when she was young. Well, she and her mother spent many Sunday afternoons there, or Casey went with her aunt and uncle and cousins. Her father was rarely able to join them, which was one reason that this one early memory remained so clear after all these years. She was scared of the water but also determined to show him that she wasn't, and she screamed all the way in and then giggled all the way out, relieved that she had made it back out of the water alive.

She remembered her father's posture, tall and straight, as they sat in church. He sang hymns in a deep bass voice and then nodded off during the sermon. But if she fidgeted or sighed too long, he was alert and looked over at her with such a look of disapproval that she hardly dared to move or breathe for the rest of the service.

She remembered her biggest fight with him, when she was nearing college graduation and informing them of her acceptance into veterinary school. He was so obviously disappointed, which made her furious. What had she done that was so wrong? Why did he seem so disappointed in her all of the time?

As Casey thought through these memories, a tear ran down her cheek. There were happy memories, too, when he had held and comforted her, called her beautiful, announced her 4.0 GPA at Vanderbilt to everyone with pride. Why was her mind now determined to dwell on memories of his harshness, when she had come closer to losing her father than ever before in her life? She felt ashamed of herself. She loved her father, and she would do what she could to help him recover and to support her mother during this transition. There really was nothing more to think about.

After a while longer, Katherine said, "I would like to try to see him now. Are you ready to go back up?"

"Yes," Casey replied and followed her mother back into the hospital and to the elevators. They retraced their steps to the nursing station outside Charles' room and got permission to enter. He was still knocked out, so they pulled up chairs on either side of his bed, held his hands, and waited.

Chapter 9

The following few days were a whirlwind. Charles briefly regained consciousness on Sunday night but was hardly able to talk or interact with them. Casey insisted that her mother return home while she stayed and spent the night on the couch in her father's room. He woke a couple of times during the night and cried out for help. She comforted him until he fell back to sleep.

She received a text that night from Will. "Don't want to disturb you, but hope everything is okay. I'm just down the road if you need anything." She had returned the text with a thanks and then texted Jakob and Bethany to ask them to clear her calendar for the next few days. She tossed and turned on the uncomfortable fold-out chair in the too-cold room. What if he died, when there were so many issues unresolved between them? Or what if he lived, and they had time and opportunity to resolve some of those issues? Each possibility was its own source of anxiety.

Charles didn't make life easy on her, Katherine, or the hospital staff during the next few days. He was a fretful patient, refusing to believe that he should stay in bed or not make phone calls related to work. "I'm fine," he would thunder. "My heart was fine, too, didn't need that surgery. I'm going to have my lawyer look into this."

Sometimes Katherine smiled indulgently, sometimes she got frustrated. At one point, when her frustration peaked and became anger, she said, "Charles

Young, you will lean back in that bed and stop getting yourself all riled up, or I will jab you with that syringe full of sedatives myself. Things are going to have to change, and that change starts now!"

While Charles rested, Katherine and Casey took cat naps in their chairs or went down to the café to eat a quick meal and read the paper. Twice-daily visits from doctors on rounds and almost hourly check-ins by nurses to get vital signs or dispense pills broke up the monotony. A few people from Charles's office and the country club visited, as well as the pastor of her parents' church. Charles was impatient with their visits, though, and waved them away as soon as he had gruffly informed them he was fine. Casey suspected he didn't like for people to see him in a weakened state.

"Casey, go take a break," Katherine said cheerily on Tuesday afternoon, after returning from a quick trip home to grab a few things.

Casey looked at her gratefully. "You know, Mom, I will. It would be nice to stretch my legs a little and get some fresh air, grab a coffee."

"What you should do is brush your hair and put on some makeup," Katherine said pointedly. Katherine herself looked immaculate, in a designer suit and with her hair and makeup perfect, as always. Although still worried, she had clearly regained her sense of control over the situation. Casey could still see the bags under the makeup beneath her eyes but only because she knew to look for them.

Casey rolled her eyes but said nothing. The tender moments were likely now behind them, and she regretted their loss.

She spent about half an hour walking around the garden, trying to get her blood moving after so many hours of sitting. She had gone for a quick run on Monday evening to pound some of the stress out of her body, and she was already stiff and cramped and in need of another one today, just a few hours later. But walking would have to do for now. Katherine had insisted on spending the night tonight, so Casey knew she only had to wait a few hours until she could get back to her parents' house and run again before hitting the sack.

She cycled once again through the same thoughts that had been on a repeat loop since her father's heart attack. She might have lost her father.

Chapter 9

He was such a huge, dominating presence in her life and always had been. It was impossible to imagine that he might not be there anymore, and yet his heart attack was forcing her to imagine it. But rather than feeling tender toward him, she was dealing with anger and resentment. Her father had not played a loving, nurturing role in her life. Instead, he had played a berating, admonishing role, always diminishing her and reminding her that she had been a disappointment to him. She hadn't even enjoyed being around him since leaving home and becoming an adult because they seemed to have nothing to discuss other than all the ways that she fell short of his expectations.

She was also resentful that she had almost lost someone whom she had never really had. Charles had always put his work first, missing key events in her life so that he could sign a contract or visit a site or attend a meeting. Even after becoming one of the wealthiest and most successful men in Tennessee, with more money than he could lose in a thousand lifetimes, he continued to put his work first. It seemed unfair that he would hold himself back from her for all of these years and then die, cutting off her hopes for some calmer, quieter retirement years. She had big expectations for those years and the possibility of more quality time for them to spend together.

She didn't know what to do with all of this anger and resentment. Did his surviving the heart attack mean a second chance for her to overcome the past and forge a new relationship with him? And would that process require forcing him to acknowledge how he had hurt her over the years, or would it be best to ignore the past and start all over again? Would this experience change him at all, or would it be Casey who would have to change? She wasn't sure if she had the courage to face all of these questions and their possible answers. It would be so much easier simply to see him through his hospital stay, go back to Pleasant Valley, and continue on as before. But wouldn't she—wouldn't they all—be happier if they could instead use this opportunity to improve their relationship?

She headed to the café for a hot cup of coffee. She bought the coffee and sat at a small table, picking up a home design magazine to leaf through in hopes that it would distract her from her thoughts.

"Casey?" she heard Will's voice say and looked up to find him next to her, smiling down at her. Her heart melted. She had been thinking of him over the last few days, going over and over the romantic moments they had shared the previous weekend. She had longed for the kind of comfort he had provided. And now he was here! On impulse, she jumped up and threw herself into his arms.

He encircled her in his arms and held her tight, and she felt the tears begin to pour down her face. There was something about his strength that once again dissolved her need for control over her emotions. She hadn't fully realized how worried she was about her father, how hard the last days had been, until she felt the warmth and comfort of his body pressing against her.

He remained silent, simply holding her until she was all cried out. As she pulled back, she could see wet streaks all over his tan blazer. "Oh, sorry!" she said, pointing at his lapel and laughing self-consciously. "Good thing I'm not wearing any makeup."

"No harm done," he smiled, pulling back her chair and gesturing for her to sit. He sat in the chair next to her and reached into her lap to cover her hand with his own. "I would ask 'how are you?', but I think your tears just told me."

She chuckled. "Yeah, it seems so. Actually, I'm okay now, but I guess I had some pent-up emotions that still needed to be released."

"I bet."

She tried to lighten the atmosphere. "I seem to be forming a habit of throwing myself into your arms and sobbing like there's no tomorrow!"

He smiled at her warmly. "I don't mind."

"What are you doing here?"

"Well, I came by to check on you and to give my best to your father. It felt a little awkward because I don't know him that well, and he was kind of gruff and scary."

Casey snorted. "Yes, he's been that way with everyone. He's not thrilled to be in the hospital."

"It shows. Finally, he said, 'Well, Ingalls, you'd better get back to your office now. Time is money!'" Will's impression of her father was spot on,

Chapter 9

and she burst into laughter.

"Did he really call you Ingalls?" she said after gasping for air between laughs.

"He really did. And then your mom told me how happy you would be to see me and that I could find you either in the garden or the café. She made me promise not to leave without finding you and saying hello."

The peals of laughter continued. "Oh, too much," Casey finally said when her laughter was spent. "Too much. Well, thank you for braving all of that to come by and see us."

"I've been thinking of you and hoping you're okay. But I hope I'm not intruding."

"No, it's nice to have you here, making me laugh." She smiled and held his gaze, marveling at how the sunlight brought out so many different shades of brown in his irises.

"Have you been staying here in the hospital?" he asked.

"Yes, Mom and I are both here all day, and then we alternate nights. Tonight's my night off. He should be able to go home by the end of the week."

She glanced over Will's expensive suit, tamed hair, and clean shave, and realized he had come from the office. "How are you? How's work?"

"Oh, fine. You know, just another day killing birds and destroying Mother Earth." He smiled ironically at her, and for once she refused to let her mind think about his profession and the problems associated with it. For better or worse, she simply wanted to enjoy having him there.

"You were really crying hard just now," he continued. "Are you sure you're okay?"

She sighed. "Yes, but having this happen so unexpectedly made me think about how many problems there are between Dad and me. It's a relief that he's survived, but it feels like a warning: he's not going to last forever. So what am I supposed to do about all of this baggage? I just keep worrying about it all."

He nodded. "Hey, why don't you come over for dinner tonight? I'm a good listener, you know."

She looked at him skeptically. "You can cook dinner?"

"No, I didn't say I would cook dinner. I will *order* dinner."

She laughed.

"But something delicious, I promise. Will you come?"

She imagined herself going for a long run then returning to her parents' house to warm up something tasteless from the freezer and cry herself to sleep. And then she imagined herself sitting across a table from Will, eating good food and staring into his dark brown eyes as they talked for hours and hours. She knew what she wanted to do, and in the moment she felt like indulging her desires.

"Can I bring anything?" she asked.

"Nope. What time works for you?"

"Seven?"

"You got it. I'll text you the address."

"Thanks, Will, for coming by and for the invitation. I'll see you then."

"See you then." He looked down at the magazine and pointed at the "after" photo of a living room. "By the way, those curtains are hideous."

"I know, right?" she said, laughing again. She had the pleasure of watching him walk down the long hallway to exit the café. He was tall and straight and strong. Polite, too, she noted as he held the exit door for a pregnant woman. It occurred to Casey that she was back to being in danger of falling in love with him. Her guard was definitely down these days; she would have to be careful.

***

Casey felt nervous as she announced herself to the doorman and waited for him to call up to Will's apartment. The man smiled knowingly at her, and she couldn't help wondering how many women had come over for dinner and, well, other activities in Will's apartment. The doorman walked her to the elevator, and Will greeted her as the elevator doors opened on the tenth floor. The big smile of greeting that had become so familiar was on his face once again, and she began to feel more comfortable.

Chapter 9

He looked her up and down in that appreciative way of his. She had dressed casually but with care in jeans and a bright blue peasant blouse. She had fixed her hair and put on a touch of makeup. She hadn't been sure: what do you wear to have dinner with someone you know but don't know, who seems to like you but also thinks you're incompetent and a spoiled rich kid, who wants to listen as you tell him the details of your fraught relationship with your father but may hope for other things as well?

He looked at ease in jeans and a white polo shirt, and he was barefoot. He could look so handsome all dressed up in a suit, but Casey felt the casual look suited his personality better.

When they entered the apartment, she laughed.

"What?" he asked.

"It's exactly what I imagined: it's like a spread in *GQ* magazine."

The living room was all masculine neutrals—gray, black, and brown—with indifferent artwork and photography on the walls. Clearly it had been decorated by a professional. Even at immediate glance, she could tell there was almost nothing personal here, that this was a place where he slept rather than lived. It was very clean, though, and she was interested to note that he might be as much of a neat freak as she was.

He shrugged sheepishly. "It's a place to live. But *this* is what makes it all worth it." He walked toward the windows, and she followed him to see an incredible view of the Cumberland River and downtown Nashville. The evening sky was a slightly faded blue, and the colors of the city were highlighted by the rays of the sun as it dropped toward the horizon.

"Wow, it's beautiful!" She marveled as she always had that cityscapes could be beautiful in their own way, even though they were so different from the natural landscapes she preferred.

"Very different from your own view, of course," he said, seemingly picking up on her thoughts.

"Yes, I guess my place is more like a spread in *Country Living* or maybe even *Flea Market Style*."

"Can I get you something to drink? Water, beer, wine, Coke, seltzer, whiskey—actually, it's probably easier if you just tell me what you'd like and

I'll see if I have it."

"Red wine?"

"You got it. Be right back."

She stood and continued to stare at the view before her. She had gotten so used to seeing Will in her territory, and now she was in his. It made her realize once again how little she knew about him and his life. What was she doing here? What would happen tonight? Why was she putting her heart at risk for someone who was undoubtedly incompatible with her? And she was particularly vulnerable now, with everything that had happened with her father, the deep emotions the situation had stirred up. Tears came to her eyes, unbidden, as her mind sifted through these worries.

"Here you go," Will said, and she turned to take the glass of wine he offered.

He saw the tears. "Do you need another hug?" he asked, half joking, half serious.

She laughed and pointed to his white shirt. "Better not. I'm wearing makeup this time."

"It's just a shirt," he said, and she shook her head, smiling. The tear-inducing thoughts were subsiding now that he was in the room; all she wanted to think about was him and the pleasant fluttery feeling in her belly.

"Make yourself at home. Have a seat." He seemed uncharacteristically awkward. Could it be that he was just as unsure of what they were doing here tonight as she was?

She sat on the sofa. He sat next to her and placed his bottle of beer on the coffee table.

They looked at each other for a few seconds and then both burst into laughter.

"Why does this feel so weird?" he said.

At the same time, she said, "I have no idea what to say to you!"

She shook her head. "We need some animals here to make things seem more normal."

"Oh!" He stood up and left the room, then returned with Barney in tow. Barney came over to Casey for a few head pats and then sat, resting his face on her leg.

Chapter 9

"He was asleep in the back," Will said. "Excellent guard dog."

She laughed, remembering their first encounter and Barney's submissiveness.

"Oh, I almost forgot," he said and stood up again. He came back with a nibble tray covered in olives, cheese, crackers, and grapes.

Now Barney was intent on getting some food, and Will gave him a stern "No" as his head moved toward the goodies. Barney looked back at Casey regretfully and then laboriously headed out of the room, no doubt to return to his nap.

"Looks good," she said. "Did you put this together?"

He smiled sheepishly. "No, I ordered it, too. I'm just not much use in the kitchen."

"I get it. I'm sure you're busy with work and volunteering at the animal shelter."

"Definitely. Someday I hope to slow down a bit, but right now I'm still trying to build the company. I can't quite rest yet."

"Well, don't wait too long," she warned. "My father has never slowed down, and look where it got him."

He nodded sympathetically. "Is he recovering well?"

"Yes, I think so. But he's not out of the woods yet. He has to stay mostly in bed for several more days and then can only have limited activity for the next few weeks."

"So no work, I take it?"

"No, my mother won't allow it. She's already called in his immediate team and told them that they absolutely cannot bother him until she says so." She laughed and shook her head, imagining how this situation was going to play out. "He's going to be like a chained bear, roaring and fighting the whole time!"

Will smiled and spread some Brie on a cracker. "Tell me more about him."

She took a sip of her wine, which was excellent: a smoky Chianti. He had remembered that was what she liked.

"Hmmm, where to begin? Well, as you know, he works too much. Always has. He's kind of a self-made man, like you."

"What do you mean 'kind of'?"

"He grew up with money. But he had a falling out with his parents and they cut him off, so he had to start all over again as a young man. He was always determined to show them up, and he did. He ended up buying his father's company before he died, purely as an act of revenge." She made a face at one of the many unattractive aspects of her father's greed.

"Yikes. What was the falling out about, if you don't mind my asking?"

"Nothing, really. He wanted to go his own way, and they wanted to control him."

"And they cut him off because of that? That just sounds like normal parent-child stuff."

"Yep. See what it's like to grow up with a lot of money at stake? It's not all it's cracked up to be."

She stopped and looked at him, again wondering about his story, how he had gone from poverty to riches in such a few short years.

Will ate an olive, and she reached to get one, too.

"I'm just gonna dive right in here," Will said, "and hope I don't say anything wrong. But I get the sense that you think your dad wants to control you, too."

Casey nodded, considering what to say and how to say it. Well, she would just dive right in, too. "He has never approved of anything about me. He wants me to run his company and be just like him, and he reminds me continually of what a disappointment I've turned out to be."

Will tried at some lightness. "The look on his face in the clinic the other day!" he said, laughing.

Casey laughed, too. "I know. What timing! But that's what he thinks my whole life is like all the time: chaos, incompetence, you name it. He also has this idea that I'm destitute, that the clinic is sucking me dry and I'm forced to live on whatever nuts and leaves I can forage from the woods."

"So when you go hiking and birding, he thinks you're out hunting for your next meal?"

"Exactly," she replied, giggling.

"You said you moved to Pleasant Valley to escape them a little bit. Did it

Chapter 9

work?"

Tears pricked her eyes again, so suddenly that they took her by surprise. "I don't think you can ever escape from your parents' disappointment."

He gave her a few seconds without saying anything and then asked, "What is it you'd like to change now that you have a second chance?"

She guided Will through a long list of things that had been on her mind recently. She wanted to be able to spend quality time with her parents without them telling her that she needed to run CY Properties or get married or do anything else that they wanted her to do. She wanted to be able to share her opinions about development and the environment with her father without the discussion breaking down into a fight. She wanted him to take her seriously as she was rather than demanding that she change to be more like him. She wanted him to respect her independence rather than trying to "help" her all the time. And she wanted him to realize that there was more to life than work, that he had proven himself and had nothing left to prove, that he had enough money and status and didn't need to keep killing himself to gain more.

Will listened and nodded and looked thoughtful. "This explains a lot," he finally said, peering at her intently.

"What do you mean?"

He kept looking at her for a few moments, as if trying to decide what to say. Then he shrugged his shoulders and joked, "You really do have daddy issues!"

She laughed halfheartedly. "What did you really mean?" she asked.

"Nothing really. Let's eat! I'll go lay out the spread."

She remained on the sofa and sipped the rest of her wine. What had he been about to say? What did all of this explain? Suddenly she felt self-conscious about telling Will so much about her parents and her. Yes, he was a good listener, and it was easy to talk to him. But what was he thinking about her now? That was hard to fathom.

She walked over to the window and looked out again. The sky was darker now, with the fading colors of sunset, and the city's lights were beginning to appear bright and sparkly. She tried to empty her mind of its worries—including new worries about what Will must be thinking of her—and simply enjoy the view.

They view had a hypnotic effect, so she didn't even notice Will was near until she felt his arm come around her from behind to wrap around her waist and pull her body into his. He rested his chin gently on top of her head. They stood there for several minutes, silently sharing the view together. Hyper aware of every bit of his body that touched hers—his muscular strength, his warmth, his leanness—she let herself melt against him. She sought his comfort and warmth as before, but she also began to want more. She wanted to turn around and kiss him for hours. She wanted him to make love to her. Would he have the same combination of masculine power and tenderness in bed that he had in his other interactions with her? She almost lost control at the thought of it.

Instead she simply stood there, until finally he kissed her hair and said, "Dinner's ready." He pulled away from her and headed toward the dining room.

Dinner was delicious: steak and pasta, grilled asparagus spears, salad, cheesecake. They made light conversation about nothing serious: his wacky neighbors, her animals, Jakob and Katie's relationship, their favorite novels, and a series of other neutral topics. She could not take her eyes off of him as he talked, and the wine as well as the company lulled her into a warm, contented state. She felt happier than she had in weeks, since their first date, really, and she wished that they could simply erase all the negative things that had happened since.

"Let me help you clear the table," she finally said, after the meal was over and the conversation had reached a lull.

"Thanks," he said, hopping up and grabbing plates from the table. She did the same and followed him into the kitchen. Finally, on the kitchen counter, she saw something personal: a photo of Will with an older man and two men around Will's age. They were smiling for the camera, although the older man looked a little pained behind the smile. She could only guess this was Coach Ingalls, the man who had raised him. His wan look and bald head suggested that this photo had been taken after he had already become sick

Chapter 9

with cancer. Will looked young but just the same really: the curly hair, the dark looks, the smile that brought sunshine into what could otherwise be a hard and dangerous face.

He saw her looking at the photo and said, "That's Coach and his two other sons, Danny and Peter."

She turned and looked at him. "Would you mind telling me about them? I feel I don't know anything about you and your past."

He looked deep into her eyes. "I don't talk about them much, but yes, of course. Come here." He grabbed her hand and pulled her into the living room and back onto the sofa.

"Don't you want to finish putting away the dishes?" she asked.

"Nah, I'll take care of it later."

They sat on the couch, and she looked at him expectantly. He took a sip of beer.

"Coach was my eighth-grade history teacher and the football coach. It's a long story, but I was in foster care at the time and pretty troubled. He just saw something in me, he told me later. I reminded him of himself when he was a kid. And I really liked the class. I liked *him*. So I worked hard, and I did well, and he thought I had some promise. He also encouraged me to play football, said I had the right build and the right brain. Turns out he was wrong about that—I was a terrible football player!"

Casey laughed. "But you were a history genius, right?"

"No, I wasn't exactly a superstar in the classroom either," he admitted. "But I was trying really hard to be a good kid, go to school, do my work. And then my foster family started talking about how I was too much trouble, how they didn't want me to be a bad influence on their son. I didn't understand it; I was trying so hard to be good, and I couldn't imagine what I had done wrong. I came to school really angry one day about the unfairness of it all, and Coach asked me what was wrong. I told him the whole story, just poured it right out. I'll never forget: he went over to his desk and came back with a Bible and threw it on the desk in front of me. He said, 'Thousands of years of wisdom in that book. Now open it up and show me where it says that life is supposed to be fair. Or that you're supposed to sit around feeling sorry for yourself every time it's not.' That changed something in me. I can't even explain it, but at that moment I wanted something different for my life."

"Wow," Casey said, impressed by Coach's words and the effect they had had. "And how did he come to be your father?"

"A couple of days later, he told me he had called social services and made arrangements to start the process to foster me, if that would be okay. It was pretty amazing how it all worked out." Will shook his head and smiled, remembering. "He was just the man for the job. He actually had already adopted a couple of foster kids who were grown up by then, back when his wife was alive, so he knew the ins and outs. That was Danny and Peter. Social services were able to place me with him while they expedited his training and completion of all the paperwork. And suddenly I was living there with him, and he was calling me son."

He smiled at her, and for a moment she was caught up in the excitement of the idea: this lonely boy finding a loving home.

"I can't even tell you what an amazing man he was. He was tough on me but in a good way. We both had to sign what he called a Father-Son Contract that outlined what he expected of me and what I could expect of him. Then there was a list of potential consequences if either of us broke the contract. We both signed and dated it. From that point on, I shaped up: did better in school, quit messing around. When I got a little older, I worked jobs on the weekends and invested the money. Then I went to college. I just wanted him to be proud of me."

"I bet he was."

"Yeah, he was," Will said, his eyes alight. "When I was 14, I went from being William Ray to William Ingalls, and I'll always consider him my father. But as you know, soon enough he got lung cancer, and within a couple of years after that he was dead."

"I can't imagine how tough that was."

"Yeah, he was it for me. I didn't have anyone else."

Will was telling his story in a matter-of-fact way. As on their first date, Casey sensed that he didn't want any words of pity or sympathy, so she didn't offer any.

Chapter 9

They sat in silence for a few moments, Will looking thoughtful as he took another swig of beer.

"Why didn't you have anyone else?" Casey finally asked. "What about your biological parents or your brother?" She didn't mean to be pushy, but she felt there were mysteries about this otherwise straightforward man. She wanted to know what had made him who he was, what he had defied in order to become the person he was today, why his face often registered sadness when he talked about his past.

"Well, my biological family was a disaster. My father was a coal miner and drug dealer, and my mother was an addict. She'd go a little crazy every time she got mad at my father and just disappear for days. Then he'd take his temper out on Tommy and me. Tommy's my brother. We lived in Kentucky then, in the southwest, in this horrible little coal town. Like I told you, it was dirty and awful."

He shook his head at the memory and then continued. "Then it got even worse. My dad was killed in a car accident when I was eight years old, and my mom got even crazier. It was just one man after another, whoever could supply her with drugs. She would disappear for a few days and then come back with no explanation. Tommy and I had to get used to taking care of ourselves."

"How did you even live?" Casey asked, horrified.

"Government checks and selling drugs, I guess."

"Was there no other family to take you in?"

"Every once in a while, we'd go live with some aunt or cousin or somebody. But then Mother would steal from them and get us kicked out. Someone in the family offered to take Tommy and me in, but Mother was too proud. I don't know how, but we got by. You know, some church would bring us food, or we'd get toys at Christmas from some neighbor. A little here, a little there. We made it. At least she wasn't abusive or anything like that; she just wasn't *there*. That's what drugs do to a person."

Casey sighed. Suddenly her problems with her own parents seemed so minor. They had tried to give her *more* than she wanted, not *less*. She couldn't even imagine growing up as Will had.

"Then one day she disappeared for good," he continued. "We never saw her again."

"What?" Casey gasped. "What happened? Where did she go?"

"No idea. A few years ago, I hired a P.I. to look into it. He was able to trace her to West Virginia within a couple of years of leaving us, but there was no sign of her after that. I have no idea if she's even alive, although it doesn't seem likely."

"How old were you when she left?"

"Eleven."

Casey shook her head. She wanted to hold his hand or comfort him in some other way but still sensed that neither was the right thing to do. So she just waited, ready to listen.

"Life with her was hard enough. Then, after she was gone, we went into foster care. Some of those relatives made inquiries about adopting us but ultimately decided two near-teenagers with a troubled past were too much trouble for them. We were bad kids. We'd steal from our foster homes, cut school, buy pot. Tommy sold a little bit, too."

"At age eleven?" Casey couldn't believe it. It was so far beyond anything she had experienced in her own life. How could this man before her, who cried out stability and success, have come from such beginnings?

"Oh, you have no idea. We were *bad*. But then Tommy started going too far. He was breaking into houses, getting into fights where he really hurt people. He kept getting suspended from school. Finally, the powers-that-be decided we should be separated in the system because he was a bad influence on me, so we went our separate ways, went into different school systems in Lexington. And I met Coach Ingalls."

"What happened to Tommy?" she asked.

"Nothing good, as you can imagine: crime, drugs, juvenile detention after he set a house on fire after robbing it. He didn't last in any foster homes; he was moved to a group home, but they still couldn't control him. We stayed in touch for a while, but he hated me, really, because I had found a good situation. He came over once, and Coach sat me down afterward and said, 'Your brother's trouble, and he's always going to be trouble. You have to

Chapter 9

make a choice, and I hope you'll choose yourself.' So I broke ties with him. Later I heard Tommy went into juvie, and I tried to get back in touch with him, but he wouldn't write or call me back."

Casey couldn't imagine such a situation. How could anyone bear such pain?

He looked at her as if a spell had been broken. "Would you like some more wine or anything else?"

She laughed. He was thinking of her even at a time like this, after telling such a story.

"You look a little shocked," he said. "I forget what a dramatic story it is; it just seems like life to me. Are you okay?"

She smiled. "Yes, of course. I'm just trying to figure out how you turned out to be such a good man. I don't know how you did it, honestly!"

He shrugged. "I don't know how good I am. But it's all due to Coach."

Casey didn't buy it. It sounded to her as if Coach had seen something that was already in Will, a goodness that he could draw on to pull himself out of that bad history. But she didn't offer this insight; she knew Will would reject it.

"What an incredible man. Are you in touch with Danny and Peter?"

"A little bit. They weren't around much when I was growing up, so they don't really feel like brothers to me. Our only connection is through our memory of Coach. I hear from them every now and then on Facebook, or I get a Christmas card. That kind of thing."

"So you really are all alone," she said without meaning to. "I'm sorry," she added, "that was a terrible thing to say."

He laughed. "No, it's okay. It's true. Anyway, I've got Barney." The dog had wandered in again and rested his head on Will's lap.

"Thanks for confiding all of that in me," Casey said. "I didn't mean to pry into your private life."

"No, it's okay. I'm not ashamed of the story; it's what made me who I am. And I'm grateful for how it turned out in many ways. I just don't talk about it much because it's a lot to lay on people. Especially when I'm supposed to be comforting them while their father is in the hospital!"

"I'm glad to know you a little bit better. Things make more sense now."

"What do you mean?"

She reached over and punched his shoulder lightly. "Hey, you wouldn't tell me what you meant when you said it about me while ago, so I'm sure as heck not going to tell you what I mean!"

He laughed and continued to pet Barney's head. "This guy probably needs to go out. Wanna go for a walk?"

"Sure," she said, eager to get some fresh air and respite from the intense subject matter of the night's conversation.

They walked in silence until they were in a small park adjacent to the building. Will let Barney off the leash, and he ran off to do his business.

"What I meant," Will finally said, "was that you seem to need to prove something to yourself and your father: that you're independent and competent and don't need any help from anyone. In fact, have you ever noticed that you absolutely hate the word 'help'?"

He had that mischievous look on his face again, and Casey laughed. "Yes, that's because 'help' in my house always came with strings attached."

"But the question is: when are you going to stop needing to prove yourself? When are you going to give your father a chance to appreciate who you've become? When are you going to let someone else in?"

He was staring after Barney, and she was relieved that he wasn't looking at her because then he would have seen the look of dismay that she knew was on her face. Was this an accurate character sketch of her? Had she shut her father out? Had she shut Will out? Was she really as closed and stubborn as Will implied?

She remained silent for some time, thinking about herself and about him, and about her father and his father. Then she said, "I meant much the same thing about you. You need to prove you're a good man, not the bad kid you used to be. You need to prove it to me and to the world. So when are you going to stop needing to prove yourself? When are you going to let yourself just relax and enjoy what you've got?"

This, she had just figured out, was the true parallel between her father and Will. It wasn't just the real estate, the desire for "progress" at the expense of

Chapter 9

nature. It was that push to prove oneself. It had never let go of her father, and it might not ever let go of Will. That was why she, fundamentally, could not trust him with her love. She was now more certain of this than ever and knew it was time to leave.

"I'd better go," she said. "Thank you for a lovely dinner and for listening and for sharing your past with me. Really."

He turned toward her, and she stood on tiptoe to kiss him on the cheek. He was a good man, and she wanted him to know it, even if he could not be the man for her.

He must have felt the dismissal in her light kiss, and he was having none of it. "Oh, you're not leaving yet," he said mockingly, as he grabbed her shoulders and pushed his mouth against hers. His lips devoured her lips, his tongue her tongue. She couldn't help responding to him, despite the warnings her mind was screaming at her. When he sensed her response, he began to kiss her neck, his hands clutching at her hair and then the small of her back. She wrapped her hands around him and pulled herself tight against his body. Her hands found their way to his beautiful curls, and she pulled his lips back to hers and kissed him hungrily. His hands moved down her back and finally to her bottom, pulling her even closer to him. She felt her insides turn to liquid as her desire for him heated up.

They heard a discreet cough and looked up to see a small woman opening the gate into the park, guiding a Cocker Spaniel. Casey could feel Will's amusement and suppressed a giggle of her own.

"Hello, Mrs. Whittaker," Will called. "Neighbor" he whispered to Casey.

"Hello, Will, dear," she said as she veered her dog over to the opposite side of the park, trying not to look at them. Casey watched as Barney bounded over to greet his friend.

Will looked intently at her, and she could see little slivers of white in his eyes, a reflection from the lamplight. "Mmmm," he said, tracing her lips with his thumb. He bent down and kissed her again, but it was a much more chaste kiss this time.

"I really do think I should go," she said reluctantly. Her mind was at war with her heart, but her mind had a way of winning these things, ultimately.

"I should get a good night's sleep because tomorrow will no doubt be a taxing day."

He gazed at her without speaking and then kissed her again, softly and slowly. Her whole body was on edge, wanting more. She knew she only had to say the word, that he was giving her the chance to lead them in the direction she wanted to go. But she couldn't let herself give in to what her body wanted.

He sensed her decision and pulled back. "There's so much more I want to say to you," he said, stroking her hair. "But I suppose it can wait for another time."

He walked over to Barney and bent over to pick up his mess. "What a crappy end to the evening!" he joked as he pitched the bag into the trashcan.

Chapter 10

Their remaining days in the hospital continued much the same way, and then on Thursday afternoon it was time for Katherine and Casey to see Charles home. Katherine had set up a downstairs guest suite for his comfort and 24-hour nursing care to see to his needs. He was installed comfortably in the bed, with books, magazines, and a sketch pad at the ready.

"What's this?" Charles snarled. "Where's the newspaper, the remote, my telephone?"

"None of that for a while, dear. For years you've been saying you wanted time to read and think and would love to get back to drawing like you used to do in college. So here you go: you're on vacation in your own home!"

"No," he answered. "At least let me make some calls and get some things settled at the office. Then I'll do whatever you say."

"*I* have settled everything at the office," Katherine declared. "There is nothing left for *you* to do. If you behave, follow your protocol, and graduate your first check-up next week with flying colors, then you can check in with the office. Until then, they are not to call you and you are not to call them. Gary and Marie know exactly what to do; that's why you hired them."

"But—."

"Charles," she interrupted, her voice containing a threat.

He muttered something under his breath and settled back into his pillows, flashing a hostile glance at the nurse, Amanda, as she came forward to pull the blanket up and over his chest. Charles picked up a book off the end table, looked up at Katherine and glared, and then opened up to page one with a dramatic sigh. Casey stifled a laugh.

By the next morning, Charles already looked a little better, and he seemed somewhat more resigned to his situation. He was even being friendly to his nurse. This time it was a heavyset, muscled man named Grady, who seemed like the type who whipped recalcitrant patients into shape on a regular basis. Casey chatted with Grady a bit and was informed that all signs still indicated her father would make a full and uneventful recovery.

"Sounds good, Dad," she said to Charles.

"Well, I could have told you that."

"Of course. Are you getting used to your situation, the new normal, as Mom calls it?"

He rolled his eyes. "Do I have any choice? Actually, I agree with her that I could use some rest. I have been working too hard lately. But the timing is bad; we're adding some condo portfolios, and I don't like to move in a new direction and not oversee it personally."

"I know, Dad. It's your company, and you feel that everything reflects on you. But you really do have good people working for you."

"Not the people—the person—I want most," he stated meaningfully.

"Good people nonetheless," she insisted, then changed the subject. They chatted a little longer, and she left him to join her mother in the kitchen. Katherine was seated at the kitchen table with a cup of coffee and the crumbs remaining from a slice of toast, the same breakfast she had had every morning for Casey's entire life.

Katherine smiled tenderly as she entered the room, signaling that she was still feeling a bit more vulnerable and worried than usual. Casey decided to take advantage of the moment and open up to her mother a bit about some of her recent thoughts regarding her father.

"Mom, can I talk to you about something?"

"Of course, dear."

"Since Dad's heart attack, I've been having very particular thoughts about him, and I don't quite know why or what to do about them."

"Worries about his death?" her mom questioned, wide-eyed.

"No, they're not so much about him as they are about me. Let me ask you: have you ever resented him for working so much?"

Her mother stared at Casey in surprise. "Resented him? No, not exactly. It did take me some time to get used to it. We had fights about it early on." She smiled, remembering. "Once we were in the kitchen, and I wanted to throw something at him, as I'd seen couples do in the movies. But I was just standing there doing nothing, and our housekeeper Georgia was standing between us, putting the dishes away. So I ordered Georgia to throw a plate at him, and she did!"

She shook her head and chuckled. "But to me he was just like my father. It had never occurred to me to be angry at my father for devoting himself to his work, so I decided not to be angry at Charles about it."

Casey was silent, and Katherine asked, "Do you resent him for it?"

"Yes. I thought I had put it behind me, but it's been resurfacing the last couple of days. He wasn't there for so much of my childhood, and now he might have died. He could have taken himself completely out of our lives because he put work over everything else for all of these years."

Again Katherine seemed surprised. "What of your childhood did he miss?"

Casey wondered if this meant that her mother hadn't noticed. That would surprise her; her hawk-eyed mother noticed everything. "Well, time, really. Track and field meets, church events, the father-daughter dance. He didn't take me to school or pick me up."

Katherine studied Casey's face. "No, those are small things. You never cared that he didn't pick you up at school. What's really on your mind?"

"Well, I think it's more that he never took the time to get to know me and understand me."

"How so?"

"He's never understood what I want out of life, why I don't want to simply take over his life and live it the way he lived it."

Katherine shook her head and sighed. "This is what's wrong with your generation, dear. You think your parents should be your best friends. Your father and I were raised to have a different point of view. His role was to provide for you and take care of you and protect you, not to have deep, emotional talks with you about who you are and what you want out of life. It's not that he chose to work instead of loving you; he worked in order to love you."

Grady called for Katherine from the stairs. "He needs you," Grady said. Katherine rolled her eyes at Casey and rose from the table. "Stay here and eat. I'll be right back."

By the time Katherine came back, the mood for sharing intimate thoughts was broken. Anyway, she had already given Casey some food for thought, so Casey decided not to push her mom for more that morning. Instead, she went for a run, hoping to pound some of the anxious thoughts out of her head.

When she returned, her parents were on the front porch, Charles tucked into a wicker chair.

"Look at me!" Charles called out to Casey, mimicking a child. "I walked all the way out here on the porch by myself!"

"Yes, you're a good boy," Katherine replied sarcastically.

"You're looking even better than you were earlier this morning, Dad," Casey replied.

He flashed a genuine smile this time. "I feel well."

Casey stayed standing so she could finish cooling down a bit, absentmindedly deadheading the geraniums lining the porch.

"How was work this week?" Charles asked. "Were you busy making up time?"

"Oh, I haven't been back to work. Mostly I missed annual checkups and that kind of thing, which can easily be rescheduled. Plus pet owners are an understanding lot. I'm starting back tomorrow."

Charles grunted, and Katherine changed the subject. "What about that Will Ingalls, dear? It was nice of him to come by the hospital. Am I to infer anything from that?"

"No, Mom, he's just a friend from the shelter," she fibbed. She had been thinking about Will nonstop, and now it seemed strange to be talking about

Chapter 10

him.

He had texted her a couple of times and asked her to call him when she was back home and things had calmed down. She wasn't sure what to say when she called. Would "I seem to be madly in love with you, but we're incompatible so I'd really rather never see you again" work? It was hard to imagine herself being able to say anything like that—or to imagine Will accepting it and walking away. She had sensed something in his kisses, something more than sexual interest, and she guessed he wouldn't go quietly. But he must go; she was sure of that, no matter how her heart might feel.

Katherine made a tsk-ing sound with her tongue. "Well then, what about that Dr. Carruthers? You haven't mentioned him again. Are you still seeing each other?"

"We never really were, Mom. I've seen him a couple of times, but I think we're just meant to be friends. Anyway, he's so busy." They had talked on the phone a couple of times, with a promise to get together in a few weeks when things would hopefully calm down for both of them. She enjoyed their conversations, but it was clear to her that they had no real romantic potential. In fact, she had begun trying to think of friends she could fix him up with.

"Well, he was a nice catch, so I'm sorry to hear that. What are we going to do with you, Casey?"

Casey smiled, even though she couldn't stand it when her mother used that wording, and brought her attention back to Charles. "So you're recovering well, Dad? I'm so glad to hear it."

"Yes, just fine. Looks as if I'm going to spend the rest of my life sleeping and being bored. I'll be treated like a prize orchid and not allowed to do anything for myself because that's how Katherine wants it."

"Yes, I'll feed and water you and set you up on a nice table in the foyer for people to admire," Katherine replied sweetly.

"She might actually let me go on a walk every day because I've been so good."

"Yes, a *little* walking is good. But he won't be on the treadmill again for quite a while. Now, speaking of sleeping, Charles, it's time to get back into bed."

Charles muttered a curse under his breath as Katherine motioned to Grady.

Casey went up to her room to shower and dress. Then she returned downstairs to grab a couple of bites of lunch before heading to her father's room.

She knocked very lightly on the door and, after a couple of moments, heard her father call out, "Come in!"

"Where's Mom?" she asked as she entered the room.

"She had to run a quick errand." Charles motioned for her to sit in the chair next to the bed, and she did so. She heard the sound of paper rustling as he shifted his position in bed and looked to discover that he had tucked a newspaper out of sight.

"Uh oh, I caught you! Were you reading the paper?"

She couldn't help laughing at the trapped animal look in his eyes.

"Casey, don't you dare try to take this paper away from me," he said, half pleading and half threatening.

She shook her head. "I won't. Surely reading a little news can't do much harm. But how did you get hold of such contraband?"

"Grady got it for me, so don't tell your mother or he'll get in trouble, too. Grady says it's fine, but Katherine has become Chief Medical Officer of the household and overrides the nurses' decisions."

"Your secret is safe with me," she assured him. "Do you want me to come back later, after Mom is home?"

"No, I need to talk to you."

He sounded serious, and Casey straightened up in her chair, ready to listen. "Okay, Dad. What's going on?"

"I realize how frightening all of this was. I feel fine, and I expect to make a full recovery. But for the rest of my life, your mother is going to be watching over me and curtailing my activities. I hate it, but I'm having to face the reality."

"I'm sorry, Dad. I really am. I know all of that will be hard for you to get used to."

"I'm a pragmatist."

Chapter 10

"Are you worried about Mom? She was really scared while she was waiting to hear about your surgery."

"Yes, I'm worried about her. She'll be okay, but now she'll have it in her mind that this could happen again, that I could die. She'll never live free of those fears again."

Casey nodded.

"Thus, I've decided to indulge her. I'm ready to step back from some of my responsibilities at the office. Maybe I'll work part time and oversee the easier work that doesn't require so much time on the phone and in meetings."

Casey felt a rush of joy and relief. "Dad, that's fantastic! There are so many other wonderful things you can do with your time, and you deserve that time." She put her hand over his. "I'm so happy you've made this decision, both for her and for you."

She thought of herself, too, and their relationship. Maybe they would finally carve out some time to be together.

He put his other hand over hers and looked her in the eye. "But this all depends on you, Sugar."

"What do you mean?" she asked, but she didn't really need to ask. She knew what was coming.

"I can only do it if I know you're there to run things. We can be a team: I'll be behind the scenes, you'll be on the front lines, and I'll know that everything is in good hands because you're there. It's the only way I can let go."

She shook her head. "Dad, there's no point in talking about this. That's not what I want for my life."

"But what is your life, Casey? You run a vet clinic that barely makes enough money, you live on a ramshackle farm in a small town far away from the people you need to meet and surround yourself with. I thought you would have outgrown all of this by now."

His words stung, as they always did. "If I'm so bad at managing my practice, then why would you ever let me run your billion-dollar empire?" she asked bitterly. She had never understood how her dad could simultaneously belittle her actual accomplishments and hold her in such high abstract esteem.

"You're not bad at managing it. I can tell you have a brilliant head for business on your shoulders. I've worked with thousands of people of all ages, backgrounds, sexes, classes over the years, and I know whom I can trust to work the same way I do. You've got it, Casey. It's in your blood! But at that vet clinic, you're able to indulge other characteristics that aren't so helpful. You won't charge this person because she's living on a fixed income, you sell products at a discount because you want to make sure medicine gets out there to all the animals. You spend all your free time wearing yourself out at a shelter that doesn't even represent a drop in the bucket of all the work that needs to be done. What kind of life is that for you?"

She sighed and looked up at the ceiling. "Actually, it's the life I've always wanted, Dad. I wish you could understand that."

He disregarded her response. "You could meet your goals so much better with the kinds of resources your mother and I have. You could open hundreds of shelters and staff them well, you could distribute all kinds of medications and supplies at a discount or for free, you could donate to programs that help people keep their pets in times of financial hardship. Think of what you could do with that money, Casey, and with the status and power that being head of one of the top real estate firms in this country could give you."

"Dad, I've explained this before. That's not the way I operate. I want to do those things through relationships, through education, through my own hands—not by writing a check while I sit miserably in my corner office looking over downtown Nashville!"

She tried to look as determined as he did so that he wouldn't keep going. Instead, he tried a different ploy. "Why have you always wanted to get away from us and what we do, Casey? What's so wrong with the corner office? It's all turned out pretty well for us, wouldn't you agree?" He motioned, and she knew he was inviting her to consider their beautiful home, all the material things with which they were blessed.

He had asked, so she decided to tell him. "What's wrong with that life, Dad? It took you away from me and Mother. You simply weren't there. I think back on so many moments in my life when you weren't there because

Chapter 10

you were at the office. I wanted you to be with me, but you were consumed with putting money in the bank. I made a decision somewhere along the way that relationships were more important to me than money." She felt tears come into her eyes and wished them back. Her father's best chance of understanding would come through logic, not through emotion.

"But you don't have relationships. You have pride and stubbornness and distance. Where is your husband? Where are your children? Where is your social network? You're on the run from something, Casey. Is it from me? From me and your mother?"

She had never thought of her life that way before. Yes, she was on the run *from* them. But what had she run *to*? Basically he was saying she was alone, and he was right. From that, he was inferring that she was lonely. Was that true? No, she loved her life. And yet meeting Will and having the brief thought that she might have found The One had forced her to recognize that she did want something more. She remembered Will's comment about her workaholic tendencies. Had she followed in her father's footsteps and put everything into work instead of relationships?

As always, uncertainty made her defensive. "I am on the run. You're right. I don't want the life you and Mom have: money, clubs, fundraisers, people who may be your friends but may also just want some of the status and benefits friendship with you can give them. Remember George, Dad?" She watched as his face registered confusion and then clarity. Had he never made the connection before that George had wanted her father rather than her?

"Most of all," she continued, trying to keep her tone calm rather than pleading, "I want independence. I want to be who I want to be, without the pressure of what I was supposedly born to be. I love you and Mom, I want to be part of your lives, but I don't want to be dependent on you in any way."

He still had a trick up his sleeve, and he drove it home forcefully, his voice raised for the first time. "You *love* us? Well, if you love us, if you love *me*, you will see that we need you now. I can't step back from work without you there. If you want to take care of this family, give back to this family, you will join me! You will grow up and take your responsibility to this family seriously.

And yes, that is a responsibility you were born into, just as I was, just as your grandfather was, just as his father was before him. That is adulthood, Casey!"

This was the final straw. Now he was using her love for him to guilt her into the family business? Preaching to her about responsibility to her family when he had abdicated most of his parenting responsibilities to her mother—or, more accurately—to a series of servants? Asking her to give up her life for him when he had everything he could ever want, including enough money to live like a king even if he never worked another day in his life?

Casey wanted to reply that he did not *need* her, he simply wanted to *control* her. But she knew he wouldn't understand.

Finally, he looked at her sadly. "I want to help you, Casey. Your life is not where it should be. Come work with me. I'll help you get your life on track and find more efficient ways to meet your goals. We'll work on it together. Please."

He was pleading with her, something he had never done before. Her thoughts returned to the brief conversation she had had with her mother. She realized that, in his own mind, he was trying to show his love for her. But their ways of loving were mutually exclusive and always had been. She had tried to compromise; he never had.

"I don't need your help, Dad. I have made it just fine on my own, and it's important to me to make it on my own." She repeated firmly, "I don't need your help."

He chuckled and shook his head. "You're not as independent as you think, you know. Who do you think has given those big donations to the shelter each year?"

She didn't understand at first. And then she thought about it. Each year a foundation sent her a large check in thanks for her outstanding service to the community. There were other sources of money as well, but this check provided the lion's share of the funds used to keep the shelter running, covering the basic costs of food, supplies, and medication. A big piece of the independence on which she prided herself was actually paid for with the

Chapter 10

earnings from her father's business. And he had never been honest enough to tell her or ask if that was okay.

"And, if Will Ingalls has his way, there will be more where that came from," Charles continued.

Now she was really angry, and she had to struggle to keep her voice calm. "I don't want your money, Dad. Why would I want money from an industry that is destroying the state I love? Ripping out the forests, covering up the wetlands, bulldozing grasslands so that people who already have enough can have bigger houses, bigger yards, more, more, more? Why do you, who were born with enough, have to make more money and consume more, more, more yourself? I consider it ill-gotten gains, and I don't want any part of it, either as the President and CEO or as a shelter dependent on your charity."

Her ears heard the line about Will, and she briefly wondered what he meant. But it seemed a minor point in the conversation as a whole, so she decided to figure that part out later.

Casey took a good look at her father and realized how riled up he was and how bad that was for him right now. She felt ashamed of herself and determined to end the conversation.

"Dad, I'm sorry," she said. "I didn't mean to be disrespectful, and I don't want to upset you. I just want you to try to understand me. I am begging you to let me live my life and not place these expectations on me. Please don't ever talk of this again."

He smiled at her and leaned forward to pat her hair as he would a little child. Her father did nothing without thought: she was trying to explain and justify her life to him, and he was showing her that she was nothing more to him than a willful child. He hadn't heard a word she had said.

Then he attempted a joke. "Well, I tell you what. Marry a man who can run the company for me, and I'll quit bothering you about it." Immediately Will's face came to mind. Wouldn't her father be thrilled with that choice? But the image of Will merged with the view of her father in front of her. That's why Will cannot work out, she thought. He is my father all over again. She imagined herself with her mother's empty life, the bored sidekick to a man who worked nonstop and gave her trinkets from time to time to let her know he loved her. Casey would choose loneliness over that every time.

"I'd better go, Dad," Casey said, rising and leaning down to kiss his forehead. She felt bad about upsetting him, although she couldn't help noting that she was the only one who seemed upset. "I'm heading back home and to work. I'll see you later."

His hands were already back on the newspaper. "Goodbye, Sugar," he said distractedly.

Casey burst into tears as she reached the car. She felt such a rush of guilt, sadness, disappointment, and regret. She cried them out as best she could and then let pure anger fuel her drive back to Pleasant Valley. Her father was trying to manipulate her, and it wasn't fair.

She was relieved to return home, where she could ground herself back in her life, her flowers, her animals. This was where she belonged, not in the corner office and the conference room. Her father would never see it, though. Now she had her answer to the questions that had been cycling through her mind since his heart attack. No, there was no second chance for them, no possibility to overcome the past and forge a new and better relationship. She would simply stay here in her happy world and continue to have a distant relationship with her parents, centered on infrequent holiday visits and charity fundraisers.

She stayed home for the rest of the day, not wanting to be around people and answer questions about her father's health. She wasn't due back to the clinic until the following morning anyway. Unfortunately, that morning was a Saturday morning, meaning that she would have to see Will. She had no idea what she would say to him, but she did know this: it was over between them. She could not risk developing even more feelings for a man who was so obviously cut from the same cloth as her father.

***

Will was at an adoption event with another volunteer the following morning, so she didn't have to face him right away. There were so few animals left in the shelter. Will and Howard had taken four cats and two dogs with them

Chapter 10

in Howard's old van, and there were only three others left at the shelter: the longsuffering tortie Daisy, a kitten that had already been claimed by a family who would pick her up after they returned from vacation, and the dog Buddy, who was too old to be taken out to events. Of course, the African grey was still here, as were a handful of hamsters, and there was now an iguana who needed a home. But they were quickly clearing out. She let herself feel some pride about how well things were going, given the circumstances, as an antidote to how childish and dependent her father had tried to make her feel.

When her first appointment arrived at 9:00, she and Jakob got to work. He was uncharacteristically subdued, probably trying to be respectful of the emotional week she had had. They worked efficiently and were able to get through everything lined up for that morning, including several extra appointments rescheduled from earlier in the week. It felt good to back in the familiar routine of work and too busy to think much about her father or Will.

As Casey, Bethany, and Jakob were finishing up their lunch, Jakob got a text. "Howard and Will are back," he said and went to help them unload the animals. He came back a few minutes later. "They did well today! Adoption applications for Pickles, Shaggy, and two of the hoarding rescue cats." Casey smiled. Will had worked his charm once again.

"By the way, this came in." Jakob handed her an application. "It's for Daisy." She glanced at it and saw Will's name on the application. A yellow sticky note was attached to the front: "Don't say a word!" She laughed, and Jakob did, too, after surmising from her expression that it was safe to do so. Casey had been teasing Will about his growing connection with Daisy, who always seemed to be curled up in his lap when he was working at the shelter desk. She was pleased for both their sakes.

Will found her as she exited an exam room a few minutes later. "How are you? How's your dad?" he asked, placing his hand on her arm.

She enjoyed taking in the sight of him, as always. But she felt differently this time. Certain there was no future for her and Will, she was determined to convey that to him through her words and body language. She was resolved not to indulge in long looks and bantering situations—and certainly no kissing—with him.

She stepped back. "Thanks for asking. I think he's going to be fine, and the good news is he's seriously considering backing off from work a bit."

"Great, I'm so glad. And how are you?"

"I'm fine. Just tired, ready to spend some time at home. How are you?" she asked this in what she hoped was a basic small-talk tone, warding off any further intimate conversations about how she was doing.

"Great, thanks." He resisted her new demeanor by moving back toward her, invading the space she was trying to establish around herself.

"I see you want to adopt Daisy, and I won't say anything except okay, great!" she said, attempting a breezy tone. She stepped to the side to reestablish some distance between them. "You can take her home today if you like. Just grab one of the carriers and bring it back next week."

"Okay," he said slowly, staring at her.

"Um, thank you for taking her; I'm sure you'll give her a wonderful home."

"Okay," he repeated. He leaned back and crossed his arms over his chest, his eyes narrowing as he studied her face.

"Sorry to cut the conversation short, but I've got a lot to catch up on here." She took two more steps to the side, turned, and scurried over to the front desk as quickly as possible. She bent over Bethany, who was seated behind the desk, quickly inventing a reason to talk to her.

Casey couldn't help feeling disappointed when she heard Will walk away and close the door behind him without another word. She willed herself to concentrate on the tasks ahead of her. The day passed quickly, and she made plans for an early departure, hoping to sneak out without having to see Will again. She owed him an explanation for her coldness and an end to any hopes he might have for their relationship, but she was feeling too cowardly to face him. His physical presence was overwhelming. Would it be horrible to tell him over the phone?

She asked Jakob to close up the shelter for her and scooted out the door, calling a quick goodbye to Bethany.

Will was standing by her car, and her heart sank. No quick getaway after

Chapter 10

all.

"Casey, can I talk to you?" he asked.

"Um, okay," she said, wondering how he had known that she would try to leave early. It hurt to think that he knew what a coward she was.

"What's wrong?" he continued. "You seem strange. I'm worried about you."

She tried to seem reassuring. "Oh, no, I'm fine. No need to worry about me. I'm just tired." She smiled nonchalantly. "It's hard for me to be away from home and out of my routine. I just need to get home." She looked at him meaningfully, but he didn't appear ready to give way just yet.

"You seem strange with *me*. Have I done or said something to offend you?"

She looked at him, willing him to let this go, to let her go. He stared steadily back at her.

"No, you've done nothing." How could she tell him what she had decided that week, and why?

"Something has changed. Tell me, please." His tone was demanding rather than pleading.

He put his hands on her shoulders, and she stepped away from him, leaning against the back of her car. He looked surprised. He couldn't know how desperately she needed to avoid his touch in order to maintain her resolve.

"It's been a hard week, that's all," she said. "It's made me think about a lot of things."

"What kinds of things?"

"Things about who I am, about my life, about my future."

He stepped toward her but didn't touch her. "Does that future include me at all?"

"What do you mean?"

He answered her immediately by bending his head and covering her mouth with his own. The force of his emotions felt so good, as did his lips against hers, surprisingly soft at the same time that they were firm and demanding. Her body couldn't help but respond as she realized once again that, even after everything that had passed between them, she was in love with him. It was more than that, in fact: she loved him. It would be so easy to give in, to tell him that she wanted him in her future, to let him continue to kiss her. But she wouldn't like the end point of all of that, so she had no business continuing down the path toward it.

She finally found the strength to break the embrace. "No, I can't do this."

"Why not? I thought we were starting to get somewhere. What has changed?" He sounded genuinely confused and hurt.

"I don't think we're right for each other," she finally declared, looking down and away from him.

He laughed loudly with what seemed to be genuine amusement. "Are you kidding? We're made for each other."

She looked up at him in surprise. What a statement!

He laughed again and repeated himself. "We're made for each other. I've known it since the first moment I met you. Even when I've been angry with you—or fending off your anger at me—I've known that eventually we would find our way to each other." He looked at her, still smiling, but then he grew serious. "Casey, I love you."

She was shocked. She knew he was attracted to her, that he enjoyed bantering with her and teasing her, that he had been willing to devote a great deal of time to her. But she had never considered that his feelings may have turned into love, even though hers had. It felt so good to hear the words; they shook her to the very soles of her feet.

"I wanted to tell you this the other night, after dinner, but the timing didn't seem right," he continued. He laughed, but without amusement. "I guess the timing isn't much better now. But I had to tell you." He looked at her searchingly, trying to determine her reaction.

His declaration made her even more determined to end things. She couldn't let this situation between them continue any further, and she regretted that she had allowed it to come this far.

"Will, you can't love me," she said, her somber tone matching the deep sadness she felt. "We're not right for each other. I'm sorry that I've allowed my attraction to you to let you think there could be something between us. But we have different definitions of love, different expectations of life. We're not compatible."

Chapter 10

He reached his hand out and smoothed her hair back from her face, an intimate gesture that was surprising given what she was trying to communicate to him. He was like her father: not listening to her and taking her seriously at all, instead just patting her on the head. She felt her anger flare.

He noted her reaction and pulled his hand away immediately. "What is your definition of love?" he demanded. "And why do you think it's so different from mine?"

How could she explain? "You want to love me—if that's really what this is— by taking care of me, helping me, doing things for me. You want to treat me like a child, in other words."

"What is your evidence for that? I mean, you're right: I want to take care of you, help you, and do things for you. But how does that mean I'm treating you like a child?"

"This whole shelter situation! Instead of working with me on my terms to ensure the future of this shelter, you have been telling me what to do, showing me the 'right' way to solve the problem, helping me the way you want to help me, but always with this attitude that you know best and you need to help me realize it."

"That's love, Casey! I love what you love, I want what you want. I want to spend my time helping you get what you want. How is that the wrong kind of love?"

She felt her eyes tear up. "It's the way my father has always supposedly loved me. And the message it communicates is: you're wrong, everything you do is wrong, and you'll only be worthy of my time and love when you do things *my* way!"

This wasn't how she wanted this to go at all. She wanted to be strong, purposeful, clear. But now the floodgates were open, and her despair was rushing out, beyond her control. She felt the tears fall down her cheeks.

"You're just like him, Will. You live through your work, you care more about contracts than relationships, you manage people through money. And then you decide that you love me and want to 'help' me—how I despise that term!—by trying to change me. And I can see what our future would be

Shelter

together: the same life that my mother and I have had with my father. Who now almost died and left us because he's worked too hard for too long!"

She saw sympathy in his eyes but also the beginning of anger. "You are projecting a lot of feelings about your father onto me, Casey. I've done none of those things, and I'm nothing like him. Let me explain my point of view—will you listen to it?"

She nodded reluctantly. She supposed he deserved the right to speak his mind.

"I met you and loved you immediately, really." He smiled at her, but she didn't smile back. She was working too hard to stifle any further tears. "And then we found out about all this other stuff, and you asked me to do something for you that I could never and would never do: you asked me to go back on my word, to deny my own sense of integrity." She looked at him in surprise. "You did. And for a cause that was already lost."

She scoffed at that and looked away. He placed his hand on her cheek and gently turned her face so that she was looking at him. "It was," he said as he looked into her eyes. "Ramsey was determined to sell. He was looking for buyers. If it hadn't been me, it would have been someone else."

She forced herself to acknowledge—to herself, not to Will—that this was probably true.

Will dropped his hand and continued. "And then I decided to help with the shelter. Okay, support," he hurriedly stated as she rolled her eyes at his word choice. "There were two paths before me. I could donate money. In fact, I was ready to have the company make some kind of deal with you, such as a property exchange where we put you on another piece of land to set up shop. We've made those kinds of deals before when our plans affected someone else already using that land. It's part of our community relations strategy." She flinched at that word. Of course he would consider relationships a matter of strategy.

"Or I considered giving the shelter a personal donation," he continued. "I've given money to animal-related causes before. But I realized either of those would confirm what you thought of me: that I was all about the deal, managed people through money, as you just said."

Chapter 10

She looked down. When he put it like that, it seemed like such a narrow way to categorize a man capable of such great kindness and understanding.

"So I asked myself: what else can I give? There were really only two other options: time and expertise. Time was tricky. I have worked every Saturday since I was 14 years old and started mowing yards. But I decided I could clear out Saturdays, spend them with you, be another pair of boots on the ground. Win win all around: I help you, I get to spend time with you, and I get to practice living as if there are more important things than work.

"Second, I had expertise: I'm good with money, I'm good at raising money, I have enough emotional distance from the situation that perhaps I could provide some advice. And so that's what I did. It was not to force my will on you or show you that you weren't good enough. It was honestly to help a cause and a person that I believe in. You don't need me—I know that. You can save lives, for crying out loud!"

She managed a half smile, grateful for his acknowledgement, which was more than her father had ever given her.

But his ego was bruised, and he had to defend himself further, so he kept going and quickly unraveled her goodwill. "And let's face it: you did need some 'support.' It's okay to need other people, isn't it? You were too close to the situation. You couldn't see that the shelter was in jeopardy because it was on land that was yours temporarily, out of kindness, rather than permanently through a legal contract. You were working and worrying yourself to death, which was not sustainable. You were going to have to work even harder to save the shelter and couldn't see that it might be better if you closed the shelter and took some time to reorganize. But I could see those things because of my distance from the situation, and because, *unfortunately*, my heart is not as big as yours and doesn't get in the way of my head. So that's another way I could help. Isn't that good? Shouldn't we complement each other instead of replicating each other?"

He was simply repeating her father's words: she was impractical, she was incapable of making money, she thought with her heart instead of money-making logic. She had heard it that morning, and she had heard it her whole life, and she simply couldn't hear it anymore.

"Please, Will, no more. I don't need to be told of my deficiencies; I've been hearing about them my entire life, and I already got a nice earful about them this morning." She glared at him. "If you want to help me now, then let me get in my car and go home. I don't need or want your kind of love!"

Something clicked in her head, and she remembered her father saying something about Will Ingalls having his way. She looked back at him, eyes narrowed, now on the offensive. "And, by the way, my father said something about how, if you had your way, he would donate money to the shelter. What was he talking about?"

Will hesitated and then sighed. "I did something that I now know was the wrong thing to do."

She raised her eyebrows and stared at him, waiting.

"When your parents were in the shelter that afternoon and I had some time to talk to them, I mentioned that I knew they had been giving you money through that made-up foundation and asked if they would make a very large donation toward building another shelter in the future. I wanted—"

"Wait a minute," she interrupted. "How did you know about this foundation?"

"I saw the name when I was looking at past donors and thinking about how we could contact them about donating again. I didn't recognize the name, and was surprised that an entity pretty much unknown in animal charity circles would be donating so much to you. So I kind of put two and two together and did some research to confirm it."

She felt like an idiot. If it had been so obvious to Will, why had it not been equally obvious to her? Perhaps she hadn't wanted to look that particular gift horse too closely in the mouth. Perhaps she hadn't been as determined to maintain her independence and lofty morals about "ill-gotten gains" as she liked to think.

As always, anger at herself made her even angrier with Will. "How dare you?" she asked. "You had no right to approach my father about my personal business. I can't believe you would interfere in that way!"

To his credit, he took her anger and remained calm. "You're right. I didn't realize what a serious mistake it was until I learned more about your

Chapter 10

relationship with your parents at dinner the other night. I'm sorry, Casey. I truly am."

She balked. "Knowing more about my relationship with my father is just the icing on the cake. Even before that, *even before that*, you chose to go behind my back and solicit my father for funding. See what I mean?" She was beginning to yell, and she made a concerted effort to lower her voice. "You 'help' how you want to help, rather than consulting me about how I want to be helped. I guess because you think I'm not capable of helping myself. And that's what I cannot bear."

"Casey, I just—."

"And again I say to you: if you want to help me, then let me get in my car and go home." She pushed away from him and turned to open the car door. The tears came to her eyes again, unbidden, as she added, "And stay away from me. I never want to see you again!"

Will looked stunned. He backed away from her and just stood there, silently watching as she climbed in her car and drove away.

Chapter 11

"Casey Worthington Young, I would like to request your company tomorrow so that we can talk about what you did to your father yesterday," her mother said on the phone later that night. Casey wished she had listened to her instinct not to answer the phone. When Katherine used her full name, which included Katherine's own illustrious family name and therefore held near-sacred status, Casey knew she was in for it.

"What's going on, Mom?" Casey asked, not bothering to mask the exhaustion in her voice.

"Your father told me about your conversation this afternoon, which was very hard on him."

"It was hard on me, too."

"Well, you're 32 years old and have a healthy heart, so pardon me if I don't feel the same level of sympathy for you, dear." The endearment at the end softened her words a bit, but Casey knew she was angry. "I'd like to talk to you about it. Would you please come and have lunch with me tomorrow, just the two of us, at the club?"

Casey wanted to retort that she was tired, that the week had been hard on her, too, that she had a million things to do in order to catch up at work and at home. She couldn't explain that she was also an emotional mess because Will had told her he loved her and she had told him to get lost, but those two

Chapter 11

facts were in the mix as well. Her mother wanted to see her, so she would have to go.

"Yes, Mother. I can meet you there at 1:00."

"Perfect, I'll see you then."

Casey moped around the house and yard the next morning, trying to comfort herself with animal care and garden work. It was a beautiful, sunny day, not too humid, the kind of perfect summer day that normally made her rejoice about life. But that day her heart was too heavy even for the weather to cheer her. Her emotions about Will ran the gamut: from anger and certainty that she had done the right thing, to longing and regret that she would never see him again.

The part of her that cared so much about him wondered how he was. He had had so little love in his life. If he truly loved her, and now she had rejected him, how did that make him feel? She wanted to reach out to him, comfort him, but of course she couldn't do that. Then again, maybe he was he fine, simply going about his day as normal, thinking about work, taking Barney for a walk, planning his week, simmering in anger against her, and feeling glad that he had dodged the bullet of another bad relationship with someone who had daddy issues. She couldn't stand to think about that possibility either.

When she arrived at the country club, she found her mother already seated at their usual table. Casey bent down to kiss her mother's cheek, and Katherine smiled faintly at her. They made a minimum of polite small talk and ordered their food—salads for both of them because neither was there to enjoy a big meal. Of course, ordering a salad made Casey think of Will. Would he forever haunt every moment of her life?

That thought must have made her look unhappy because her mother asked, "What's wrong, Casey?"

Casey smiled at her. "Nothing. I just want to hear what you have to say."

Katherine took a slow breath and then began. "I was angry when I called you last night. But what I am now is concerned. Not just about your father and his health but also about you, dear. I am trying to understand your feelings about your father, which I can only assume include me as well. So really I'm here today to listen to you. Please tell me what you feel about your father, about our parenting, and why you seem to be so at odds about our role in your life."

Casey hadn't expected this. She had planned to play a defensive role in today's conversation, not an offensive one. "I don't know where to begin, Mom," she finally said.

"I'll ask a question, then. When your father asks you about joining the firm, you fly into a rage. Why is that?"

That was a concrete question Casey could dig into. She explained to her mother everything that had been in her head on this topic during her last conversation with her father. "I have a good life, Mom," she concluded. "I've accomplished a lot, and I'm happy. I don't know why you both can't see and respect that. I feel sometimes that you would rather I live here and work for the family and be miserable because that's what would make *you* happy."

To her credit, Katherine did indeed listen carefully. The food had come in the midst of all of this, and their salads had sat untouched. Now Katherine took a small bite and chewed in her slow, meticulous way, apparently thinking about how to respond.

Finally, she said, "Casey, there has always been a lot of pressure on you. You're an only child, and the only child in your father's direct line. He has always had hopes and expectations that perhaps we have both placed too firmly on you. But let me explain something about him."

Casey chewed her own bite of salad and waited.

"Charles was born to a family that imposed a lot of hopes and expectations on him as well. That wasn't easy on him when he was a child. The family was wealthy, spoiled, profligate. His mother judged him on his attractiveness and manners rather than on the core of who he was. His father was, for all intents and purposes, an alcoholic and gambling addict. Charles wanted to prove that he could do something great on his own, not because of the money and status he had been born into. That's hard to do in Nashville, where as you know the aristocracy of the Old South continues in many ways as it has for centuries. So he put everything into this business. It's who he is to a large extent."

Chapter 11

"Well, there's a lot there that I take issue with, Mom. First of all, if he understands so well what it's like to live under burdensome family expectations, then why did he do the same thing to me?"

"He didn't do the same thing to you. He has supported every aspect of who you have become, Casey. We would fight like cats and dogs when you were growing up. I wanted you to take ballet lessons and learn to play the piano. He would say, 'Leave her be, Katherine. She wants to be in the Science Club.' I wanted you to do cotillion, and he would say, 'Don't force all that manners and status nonsense on her.' He wanted you to be your own person in the mold of who he thought he was: someone who worked for what he had, someone who built skills and expertise rather than eating teacakes at a silly party."

Casey didn't know about any of that, and it raised questions about her mother's motivation. Katherine read her mind and added, "I came around to his point of view for the most part. But my emphasis was on connections. I thought that you would better be able to do anything you wanted in life if you had the connections to help you. Because that's another part of life in Nashville: success and opportunity sometimes depend on who you know more than what your abilities are. I didn't want you to be left out of anything. But we compromised and, I think, mostly left you to become whom you wanted to be."

Casey thought this over quietly, and Katherine interceded again, smiling as she mused over her memories. "You know his parents cut him off, finally. We were so poor when we were first married. My parents disliked him because they felt he had taken me away from my birthright, although over time they grudgingly came to admire him. He worked so hard, and he saved so much. We had a set budget. If we made money over that, then we could go out to dinner or see a show or have fun. Otherwise we went to free museums, dollar movies, stayed at home and watched TV on our little television set that we had bought used from a friend."

Casey had heard these basics before but had never noticed the dreamy smile on her mother's face as she retold them. "Those were good days, Casey. It was just us; our families no longer mattered."

Casey smiled at her, imagining her parents young and, in their own way, roughing it.

"Then his business took off by leaps and bounds, and we started to live well again. And now you see where we are. The takeaway point here is that your father identifies with his business and wants to give it to you because it is what allowed him to be his own person in the world. It gave him freedom from his family. And that has meant more to him than anything."

"But I want to be my own person in the world."

"We understand that, of course. But Casey, your life is a bit too ragtag. It's wonderful that you're an accomplished veterinarian and you have your own clinic, but it's barely enough to support you and those two employees. And they are employees who take advantage of you. Your house is in constant need of repairs and work, and you always seem to be juggling money to pay for them. We see you living in continual stress. You're 32 years old and have not yet found someone to marry and give you the most important thing in life: a child." Her mother stretched her arm across the table and held Casey's hand, looking at her with a maternal tenderness that Casey had not seen since she was a little girl. "It's hard for parents to see all that; it makes them want to help."

Casey was lost in this tenderness for a moment because it felt so good, until it began to remind her of her father patting her hair the day before, and then Will smoothing her hair after that. Sometimes tenderness masked a patronizing attitude.

"Mother, you're looking at me as if I'm a child because you're talking about me as if I'm a child. You and dad think I can't take care of myself. But I'm doing fine. I love animals and I love providing services to a community. I'm enmeshed in relationships in Pleasant Valley that are about social transactions rather than financial ones." At least until Coach Lifestyle Solutions showed up, she thought bitterly. "I have more than enough money, I love my crazy house in the country, and I will meet the right person when I'm ready. But you and dad talk to me as if I'm living in the midst of deficiencies that can only be fixed by my working for your company. That work and life would make me miserable, Mom, can't you see that?"

"Yes, of course. And this might be hard for you to understand, but your father doesn't ever actually expect that you will change your mind and join him. He says it to you not as a critique of you but because it is how he fulfills his fatherly duty. He wants you to be safe and secure and well cared for, and he simply wants to remind you that those possibilities are yours for the asking. So would it be possible for you to stop saying, 'My parents are trying to control my life because they think it's deficient' and instead say, 'My parents are trying to show me they love me by steering me toward a life that they know by personal experience can be a wonderful one'?"

"Maybe I could if they would let me explain my life to them, if they ever even seemed interested in it."

Katherine shook her head. "That is not fair. I have seen your father try to ask you questions, but you get angry immediately and shut him down!"

"That's because he's not there to listen; he's there to 'help'! I start telling him about an interesting patient I have, and his next sentence begins with, 'Well, why don't you …?' He's always trying to fix things for me, make them better, tell me what I should do instead of letting me tell him what I am doing."

Katherine smiled. "That's what men do, dear. Women—wives and daughters and otherwise—have been complaining about this since time immemorial. They show us they love us by fixing our problems for us. He doesn't mean any harm!"

Katherine looked at her with eyebrows raised. "I think it wouldn't bother you so much if you changed your frame of mind, dear. You are trying to prove yourself to him. If everything is so wonderful in your life, then why do you need to do that? Why can't you just let your life speak for itself? Why do you always change the subject or just say you're leaving? Instead, talk to us. Tell us what you're doing. Ignore us when we seem to criticize and keep talking."

Casey had no idea what to say to that one. It didn't seem like a fair critique, but was it? It was essentially what Will had told her the other night at dinner. Why did she feel so defensive when her father or Will suggested that she could do something to improve her situation? Were they speaking to some insecurity or deficiency she felt within herself? She would have to think about that some more.

Katherine continued. "I think it's time you take what your father is offering you at face value and stop getting so upset and defensive about it. It really hurts him, especially when you start talking about what an awful industry real estate is and how you don't want to live the life he has lived. Why do you get so angry with him, Casey? Does it have to do with what you said the other day about him not being there for you?"

Casey felt relieved. She could leave a complex topic that would require some soul-searching and move into something much more straightforward: that her father had chosen work over her during so many moments in his life, despite the fact that he was a wealthy, successful businessman who could afford, financially and otherwise, to put his daughter above his work.

Casey passionately defended this complaint to her mother and gave several examples of the most painful absences during her childhood. Again her mother listened carefully. Then she said, "Relationships are always a push and pull between how one loves and how the other wants to be loved. I understand what you're saying because I felt it at times over the years, too."

Casey was surprised by this. She pushed her half-full plate aside and leaned forward to show her mother that she was all ears.

"In those early days, your father worked all the time. We were living without much money, and he was at work instead of with me, and I began to wonder exactly how I had benefited from this marriage. So I left him and went home to my parents! We were separated for six months."

Casey was shocked. She had never heard this before. Of course, her parents would not be eager to admit such a failure to her or anyone else.

"What happened, Mom? How did you get back together?"

"Well, we had to work out this balance between how he wanted to love me and how I wanted to be loved. He explained that he was loving me *through* his work. He had married a rich girl and taken it all away from her, and he wouldn't feel that he had done right by me until he restored me to my former glory. Money to him came to equate taking care of his family, just as it does for many men. I tried to encourage him to see that I had married *him*,

Chapter 11

not his financial prospects, and that I needed time with him in the midst of all that work. So we worked at it and found our compromise."

Casey nodded, but then said, "Well, you call it a compromise, Mom, but I think you really lost out. He worked all the time when I was growing up, even after he had more than enough money to keep us all in style. He bought you presents instead of being there with you. He did the same with me, too."

"I know it seems that way on the surface, Casey, but that's because you're looking at it through a particular lens: yourself. You didn't see or chose not to see other examples. When it came to me, for example, your father always made it home for dinner at a certain time, unless he was out of town. He got up and into the office early so that he wouldn't have to stay late. That was his promise to me, and he kept it. And I liked presents! He knew that was the way I liked for him to show me he was thinking of me: even in the midst of a deal that was occupying all his time and attention, he made time to think of a silly little gift or an extravagant one that would please me. He would remember everything I had ever said about what I wanted and find a way to give it to me.

"Once I told him of a schoolmate I had had whose family was from Hungary and that one day she brought to class a delicious kind of Hungarian pastry that I had now forgotten. Twenty years after I told him that, Casey—twenty years!—for my birthday he flew in a top Hungarian pastry chef to present me with every Hungarian pastry ever known to man in hopes that I could rediscover that one that I had loved. So he wasn't just giving me a diamond necklace that his secretary picked out so I wouldn't be angry that he missed a golf game we had planned at the club. It wasn't like that at all. And we worked it out. I have never felt deprived of his time and attention. And if I had, I know that I could have told him and he would have fixed it—because that's what men do. They fix things.

"As for you, Casey, he was there more than you think. He was there behind the scenes, insisting that we support any hobby or interest you had. He was arranging things, pulling strings, making contacts on your behalf: internships, shadowing experiences, whatever they might be. I know you will hate to hear this, but when you were on the waiting list for that summer

Science Camp in high school, he made a $50,000 donation to the camp on the condition that they let you in."

"Wait a minute. I thought he was all about making our own way in life, not just paying our way."

Katherine smiled. "With a few exceptions. You were heartbroken that you might not get to go to that camp, and he felt that you had worked hard enough to earn it and deserved a chance. Once he was in Knoxville and running late for your band concert, and he drove to the Knoxville air field and found someone to fly him to Nashville. Left his car there and everything!" She laughed. "And when he couldn't be there, he was on the phone, asking about every moment of what you had done or how you had performed and how loudly the audience had clapped or laughed. He wanted to know every moment of it. You have no idea how many things he rearranged so that he could be there as much as he could. He once lost out on an important deal because he wasn't willing to miss Christmas Eve with you. He didn't put you first every single time, but he put your first a lot. But all you choose to see are the times he wasn't there."

Casey listened and nodded, adding all of this new information and perspective to the list of things she would have to think more about.

Katherine obviously sensed victory because she bulldozed forward. "And now, Casey, honestly I'm ashamed of you sometimes. Your father asks you about things and you won't even tell him. He offers to drive down and visit your clinic and take you to lunch, and you tell him it's not a good time. He tries, and you rebuff him, and then you make these highhanded claims that he's not interested in your life. And then you get mad and run away to your little town and your little house and congratulate yourself for having escaped from us."

It was uncanny how her mother had pegged her. And all these years Casey thought she hadn't been paying attention!

"You're the problem, dear," Katherine continued. "I wish you could see it. You're his only child—his only child, Casey—and you rebuff him again and again."

This made Casey angry, probably because it also made her feel guilty. "I

Chapter 11

can admit that that's partly true, Mom, but I don't think you're being fair to my point of view. He also 'rebuffs' me, as you call it. The way he asks me about my life is not the way I want to be asked, and the way we talk about it is not the way I want to talk about it."

Katherine was not going to give in. "Yes, but you're younger than he is and more flexible. A man of his generation is not able to rethink the way he talks to his daughter. This is where you have to be a bit more willing to take what he offers. He's never going to be your buddy who calls for long conversations about all the interesting patients you had that day, who laughs at the antics of Jakob and the eccentric old lady who brings her poodle in. He's going to be your father and make judgments and make suggestions. *You can adjust, however.*"

She grabbed Casey's hand again, but this time in a firm rather than a tender grip. She looked her daughter hard in the eyes. "And you will have to adjust, Casey. Your father could have died, and he will be in danger for the rest of his life. His relationship with you is a major source of stress in his life. For you it's an irritation, an occasional concern that you escape from by living in Pleasant Valley. By contrast, it *wears* on him. And I will not have him upset by any more of these little conversations like the one you had yesterday. Do you hear me?"

Now Casey did feel like a child, dressed down by her mother over something she had done wrong. But this time Casey felt that she might just deserve it. Maybe she had been acting like a child. A hurt child with some actual grievances, perhaps, but a child nonetheless. She muttered, "Yes, ma'am," and hoped that Katherine was finished.

They finished up their meal in small talk about her father's recovery and made no return to these deeper issues. Casey was relieved when she was finally able to, in Katherine's words, escape to Pleasant Valley.

For the rest of the day, Casey went over her mother's words again and again. She tried to be less angry and more sympathetic to her parents'—and especially her father's—point of view. While a week before her mind had only been able to focus on the painful memories, now her mischievous little memory could only recall the happy ones. She remembered her father winning the biggest teddy bear at the county fair for her, teaching her to ride a bicycle even though she was too scared to try, letting a long-haired stray cat shed all over the living room furniture despite Katherine's objections because Casey was worried the cat would be scared outside during a thunderstorm. He had gone over her homework, helped her with science projects, taken her along on runs when she developed an interest in track and field during college. She added to all of this her newfound knowledge that he had been there other times, too, behind the scenes. He still wasn't exactly the father she had wanted, but hadn't he been good enough?

She also mused over her mother's question: why was she defensive about her life if it was perfect? And wasn't she missing the most important things: love and children? Those thoughts naturally led her to Will. Just before nightfall, she went out to the barn and saw the bag of feed that he had carried from the car for her. That prompted her to remember every nice, helpful thing he had done for her. It was difficult for her to recall the selfish, arrogant, imposing monster she had built him up to be in her mind.

These thoughts plagued her in the following days. She called her parents a couple of times to check on her father. She made no moves to resolve anything because she wasn't sure how to do so, other than to move forward and try to reestablish their relationship.

And what to do about Will? As it turned out, Henry Carruthers helped her decide. On Thursday night he called to catch up with her and let her know his latest exciting news: he was buying a condo. He was telling her about the neighborhood, its nice restaurants and bars, and how he looked forward to the little bit of a social scene he might be able to enjoy there.

And then he said, "I'm also seeing someone now. I just thought you should know."

Her immediate reaction was to feel thrilled for him, and she told him so. She asked the expected questions about his new love interest, and he gave her the basics about the woman, who was also a resident at the hospital.

He said, "I'm sorry that nothing ever worked out between you and me, but I always had the feeling your mind was on something else. Or maybe someone else. Anyway, I hope you're not offended by my telling you about

Chapter 11

Ashley."

And in that moment, in the face of such thoughtfulness, Casey realized that she loved Will so deeply and wholeheartedly that it was impossible for her to consider anyone else, even someone as wonderful as Henry. She had to be with Will. All of their problems were nothing more than ridiculous obstacles she had allowed to come between them. She laughed to think of their first-date joke about her daddy issues. She hadn't known the truth of those words at the time! How could she have made the mistake of projecting those issues onto that wonderful man, simply because she had not gotten her way with regard to the shelter?

But she was finished with all of that. When she saw him on Saturday, she would apologize and confess that she loved him, too.

It was the longest week of her life before Saturday finally arrived. She left early for the clinic, eager to be there and ready when he finally arrived. After she had opened the place and made a cup of coffee, she pulled up her e-mail to find a message waiting from him. He had sent it at 4:00 that morning.

Dear Casey,

I appreciated finding out what you really think of me in such a public forum. I see now that I will never be anything more than a greedy real estate developer in your mind.

In any case, something has come up that will consume all of my time and attention for the next few weeks. Unfortunately, I must take a leave of absence from work as well as other commitments, including the animal shelter. The timing seems right, as things are wrapping up there in the next week or so. And, as you made so clear, you have no wish ever to see me again.

Take care of yourself,
  Will

She had gone immediately to the e-mail from him, but now she noticed a series of e-mails in her inbox from members of Save Wild Tennessee. A few of them had the headline "Down with Coach!" She opened the first and saw an e-mail from Shay:

Hey everyone,

Check out the new ad campaign against Coach. I think it turned out just like we wanted it. Hopefully this will get some coverage for our new campaign.

S.

Casey clicked on the link to the Save Wild Tennessee website and watched in horror as a video aired accusing Coach Lifestyle Solutions, and Will Ingalls personally, of a variety of ethical violations against patients as well as the environment. Casey's own face and words from the interview she had done with the newspaper reporter at the protest were interspersed with sensationalist images of mistreated elderly people and environmental destruction.

Even if she had agreed that Coach committed such violations, she would have found the video tasteless and over the top. But to think that her name, face, and words were taken out of context as supporting this crass slander against Will and his company! No wonder he was so angry with her.

She immediately called Shay.

"What were you thinking?" Casey yelled into the phone, her anger with herself intertwining easily with her anger at her fellow board members.

"Whoa, back off, Casey. What's your problem?"

"That video is my problem! What is that? You make these ridiculous, overstated accusations, with those tasteless photos—all that is bad enough. But then you put my name, face, and words on top of it? Without even asking me?"

"First of all," Shay replied, the tone of her voice indicating that her level of anger now matched Casey's own, "it's a great video. We all worked hard on it. Second of all, you were busy with your father and we didn't want to disturb you. Since you obviously don't recall, let me remind you: when I informed you in an e-mail last week that we were putting together a new video for the website, you wrote, 'Okay, I trust you!' So we did it all ourselves, not wanting to bother you. And this video is just like other ones we've put up. What's your problem all of a sudden?"

Casey forced herself to breathe deeply a couple of times. Shay was right. They had done similar things in the past, but she hadn't noticed how potentially harmful they were because those had all been faceless corporations, faceless real estate developers whom she had automatically assumed to be evil and deserving of their ire. She had seen her father in all of them.

But this was Will. She might not agree with the industry he had chosen, and she might wish that he had a different sensibility and set of policies regarding the environment. But she knew he didn't deserve this level of accusation and negative publicity. He had been willing to listen to her and potentially work with her. And now there was no chance he would continue listening and take her concerns about development and the environment seriously.

Shay was also right that Casey, too distracted by what was happening with her father, had given the executive board *carte blanche*. She had forgotten her sense of unease at the previous meeting, when she had worried that they were latching too quickly onto the idea that Coach had had some ethical violations in the past. She should have paid more attention, especially since Will's corporation was one of the ones they were targeting.

She swallowed her pride. "You're right, Shay. You're right."

"What's really going on?"

"I think we have wrongly portrayed this company. I've gotten to know the head of it, Will Ingalls. He's been volunteering at my shelter to make up for buying the land, and he's not the monster we've made him out to be. In fact, I think we might have been able to work with him. And now there's no chance of that."

Shay grunted. "Uh, it would have been nice to have that information before, Casey."

"You're right."

Shay relented a bit. "I know you've had other things on your mind, though. Anyway, being a nice guy isn't enough, you know; Coach really is tearing up acre after acre. I still think the ad campaign is a good idea. It will attract more radical people to our campaign. That's what we were talking about as we worked on this. We're all a bunch of aging professionals. We need to get some crazy young people involved in SWT, broaden our horizons a little bit. So we decided to go edgy on this one. I'm truly sorry that you don't like the end product."

She said this, but she didn't sound terribly sorry. Casey had been feeling for a while that Shay, Richard, and Latasha were going in one direction, while she and Sallie were going in another. Perhaps Casey's reaction to this video was a sign that the gulf was becoming too wide to be crossed.

"Well, thanks for hearing me out," Casey said.

"No problem," Shay said. "Gotta run now. Talk to you later."

Casey hung up the phone and then got on the internet. She could see a long response to the video from Mandy Tremaine, Coach's counsel, in the comments. She skimmed them to find a more detailed restatement of what Mandy had said at the town council meeting. She also looked on Coach's website to find, on the home page, a link to a "Response to the Save Wild Tennessee Video," with much more detailed information.

Surely that would be the end of it. It wasn't likely that a small feud between an unknown environmental organization and a real estate corporation would draw anyone's attention.

She reread Will's email at least 100 times and wondered what he was going through that would require him to leave work for a few weeks. She told herself that it was clearly none of her business; he had taken her at her word and intended never to be seen by her again. Now she would have to face not only a world without Will but the realization that she was completely at fault for his absence in her life. She had run him off, not realizing how much she loved him, and now she had publicly accused him of what he hated most: being a bad person. She thought back to their dinner conversation and what he had told her about his lifelong attempt to recover from his youth, and she understood how badly she had hurt him.

Chapter 12

As August turned into September, summer seemed hotter and more humid than it had ever been. Casey's air conditioning was out at the house for a few days before she could find someone who was available to fix it, and the poor plants in her gardens were droopy no matter how much she watered them. Even the chickens didn't want to venture out into the yard, preferring the cool of the barn. When it finally rained after what seemed like weeks, it was a hot rain that made the atmosphere even more humid and produced clouds of gnats and mosquitoes that plagued Casey every time she went outside.

The misery of the weather reflected the misery she felt inside. She hadn't heard from Will for days, obviously, and she had been nursing a broken heart and a mind full of regrets. She had been going over and over her mother's words and not knowing how to act on them. Both situations left her feeling terrible about herself and how childish she had been toward those closest to her.

Sadness collects sadness, so each day seemed to bring additional disappointing news. She lost a couple of long-term patients to old age. It was always hard to put a beloved animal down and share the grief of its humans, but it was even harder now, when her emotions were so on edge. And she received a startling call from Miss Peggy, proud companion of the chihuahuas Bonnie and Clyde.

"Casey, honey, I have some news for you and a request for help," Miss Peggy said.

Immediately Casey felt a sense of dread. "Yes, Miss Peggy?"

"My children have decided that it's time for me to move into a home! You see, I had a bad fall last week, and the kids want me all locked up in a home where I can't hurt myself."

Casey felt tears come to her eyes. That was another problem these days: she was continually weepy. "Well, I'm sure your children want what's best for you, and it's probably hard for them to find a balance between keeping you safe and giving you your freedom. But does that mean you'll be moving away from town? I know that would be hard on you."

"No, they booked me a room in that new home that's coming in back behind your clinic. I have to move in just as soon as it's built." She sounded truly mournful, especially when she dropped the next bit of news. "And of course that means I have to give up my sweet boy and girl! I need your help to find them a good home, Casey!" She began crying hysterically.

Casey tried to reassure the woman that she would help.

"They have to go together, you know. They've always been together with each other and with me. If they can't have me anymore, they have to at least have each other." Miss Peggy went on to detail all the other requirements: whoever adopted them had to be kind, hopefully not with a lot of other pets or, heaven forbid, children who would pull the dogs' ears and accidentally step on them, and willing to dote on them for most of the day. The dogs were very particular about their food, when and where they went potty, and what time of day they had their snacks.

Oh dear, Casey thought. Older people often spoiled their pets with more time and attention than younger, busier people, which made it more difficult to find them a new home. And Bonnie and Clyde were on the older side themselves, living their lives in a well-worn groove of habits. They wouldn't take easily to a different environment. Still, Casey would have to try.

She finished up the call with many reassurances that things would turn out just fine. The good news was they had several months to figure this out, she reminded Miss Peggy, so she should just relax and enjoy her remaining time

Chapter 12

with the dogs and not worry too much. Casey would keep her up-to-date on any progress she made finding them a nice, new home.

As they hung up, Jakob tossed a newspaper down in front of her. "Check this out!" he said, sounding concerned rather than gossipy.

She saw a picture of Will and the headline "Ethical Concerns Surround Retirement Home Firm." Immediately her cheeks began to feel hot. She read of the Save Wild Tennessee accusations against him and his company. But there was much more to the story than that. His brother, Tom Ray, was on trial for embezzlement and fraud related to work he had done for Coach Lifestyle Solutions. There was a picture of Will on the following page next to a photo of a man in handcuffs, his face turned away from the camera.

Tom had worked for the company two years ago, in Missouri. Will had not told her that Tom had come back into his life. The article stated that, after a long estrangement and a prison sentence for Tom, the two had restarted their relationship and Will had brought his brother into the company. A series of fraud and embezzlement charges had ensued, and Tom had been on the run ever since. Now he would face the music, and, if prosecutors had their way, Will might just be next.

The article ended: "The case goes to trial in one week, and then time will tell whether William Ingalls is an innocent man and his company upholds the high ethical standards that he claims."

Casey was aghast. She turned to Jakob and saw that he was, too.

"Poor Will!" they both cried out at the same time.

Casey's mind ran back through everything Will had told her about his brother. She had sensed that there was more to tell, so why hadn't he kept talking? Because he had seen her face and realized that he had already laid enough heavy information on her. "There's so much more I want to say to you," he had told her later that night.

She felt even more ashamed that her words had been used to accuse him publicly of something for which he and his company were innocent. That might be a small slight, easily explained and forgiven, except for the fact that it had coincided with this bigger, much more serious problem. Will's ethics—his ability to prove himself as the good man that Coach knew he could be—were being called into serious, now legal question. How he must be hurting!

Casey had no idea what to do. Would he welcome her apology? Would it make things worse? As she thought about the situation the rest of the day, she felt paralyzed, just as she did about the situation with her parents.

The next day brought another big blow: Jakob announced his resignation as vet tech. He was taking a job as manager of an HVAC company owned by a distant cousin of his.

"Doc, I'm sorry to leave you!" he said, and Casey felt the now-familiar prick of tears forming in her eyes.

Casey could see true regret in his face. They had worked so closely for almost three years now, and she realized how much she had come to depend on him over the years, as a vet tech and shelter volunteer, and even more as a friend.

"Well, you have to do what you have to do, Jakob. But why the change? You love working with animals."

Jakob answered here in an uncharacteristically sober tone. "I really love Katie, Doc, and I'm ready to marry her. I know how you all see me: I'm flighty and can't be serious about anything, and I goof around too much. I realize it's time I start growing up and being a man, or Katie's never going to marry me. She hasn't said as much, but I know it's true."

Casey wanted to reassure him that he was fine just the way he was, but she understood the reality of the situation, too. Jakob *did* need to grow up. Katie had been through a lot of upheaval and was now very mature herself; she would never trust her life to someone in whom she didn't have complete confidence.

"The manager job pays great," he said, "and I'll get to work with my cousins. They're going to train me, and I may eventually get to go in with them as partners. So it's a good future. Katie's pretty happy."

"Are you happy, Jakob? Can you enjoy this kind of work?"

"Yeah, I think so. I like the business side of things. And I'm still going to volunteer with you at whatever shelter you build in the future, although

Chapter 12

I might not be able to volunteer quite so much time." He looked at her apologetically, and she smiled to let him know it was okay. "But I need a job that's going to go somewhere, you know? And I'd never be good enough to get into vet school and become a vet, so there's nowhere else I can go here. I can't just be a vet tech forever."

Casey nodded and gave Jakob a big hug. "I'm happy for you, Jake-O, I really am," she said, meaning it. "I'll miss you like crazy, though. I can't tell you what your work here has meant to me."

Jakob turned down his lips and said, "Aw," making a caricature of her teary-eyed sad face. She couldn't help laughing, and fortunately that brightened up the tone of the conversation a little bit.

"Actually, I think I need to do some growing up, too," Casey said. "My parents basically said it, Will said it—so wish me luck, too!"

He looked sly. "What did you do to run Will off, by the way?"

She turned away from him so he wouldn't see the expression on her face and know how hard this question was on her. "I don't know. He probably just has his mind on this trial."

"Oh, B.S.! He's so in love with you. All you need to do is call him up and tell him that you're in love with him, too, and everything will be fine. Or I can do it for you." He picked up the phone. "Puh-leeze let me do it for you!"

She laughed and grabbed the phone from him, then hung it up. "It was just a little crush. It's over." It hurt her even to say the words.

Jakob grunted and took the file folders she handed him. Time to get back to work. Casey simply couldn't bear to continue talking about Will and everything she had lost.

That night she sat on the back deck and drank a cup of hot tea even though it was sweltering outside. It was time for an assessment session. She pulled out a legal pad and her favorite list-making fountain pen and went to work. "All the Ways I Need to Grow Up" she wrote at the top of a clean page.

First of all, she needed to stop thinking of escape. Her mother was right: instead of facing things with her parents, she had simply built a life away from them, where she could go and pretend everything was okay. And Will was right: she had also been escaping from a world of greed and other bad things, thinking that life in a small town would be simple and idyllic. "STOP TRYING TO ESCAPE FROM PROBLEMS!" she wrote in large letters, triple underlined.

Second, she needed to set the tone for a new relationship with her parents. This one was going to take some thought and effort, but for now she noted what her mother had said, which she had been thinking about over and over again in the last few days. "BE YOURSELF! ACCEPT YOUR FATHER AS HIMSELF!" she wrote, adding four underlines this time. Bold letters, exclamation points, and lots of underlines: that was the way to ensure big life changes.

Third, she needed to tell Will that she loved him and thought he was a good man. She knew it wouldn't get her anywhere with him; she accepted that there was too much water under the bridge now and she had lost him forever. But she had to swallow her pride and let him know. She owed him that after weeks of questioning his motives and character in such obvious ways, culminating in the Save Wild Tennessee video. The question was whether a word from her would add insult to injury when he was already going through so much. Should she act now or wait? "FIGURE SOMETHING OUT!" she wrote this time, since she had no idea what to do.

Next, she had to take her business in hand. The shelter was just about emptied out, and she would literally have to be out of it the following week. And then she would have to make serious strides towards building a new shelter. She would have to find a replacement for Jakob and develop higher expectations for that future employee and for Bethany. She would have to write down some plans and stick with them. This was the easiest area of change on her list, so she spent about an hour making detailed notes about how and when she would act on specific points to improve her clinic.

She went to sleep feeling satisfied that she was moving forward. Her biggest realization of the day was that she had been too passive about life in recent years, allowing it to act on her rather than acting upon it. She had delayed decisions, put off dealing with problems, and depended on others to help her out even as she had gone on and on about how independent she was. She was an escape artist, really, and now she had to turn herself into someone who was proactive and went after what she wanted. As distressed as she was about the problems mounting in her life, she felt flashes of excitement. These problems had brought self-awareness, and self-awareness would bring improvement. She couldn't wait to get started.

***

That night she dreamed of Miss Peggy's little chihuahuas visiting her at the retirement home. She woke up with a crazy thought: why not have an animal shelter *at* the retirement home?

She got up, fed Meow, fixed a cup of coffee, and sat down on the back porch to enjoy the first cool morning they had had in a while and make some notes. Within an hour, she was so excited that she took a step she wouldn't have dreamed of taking just the day before: she looked up the number of Brad Anderson, community relations liaison for Coach Lifestyle Solutions, and left a message asking him to call her.

Two days later, after a couple of conversations on the phone with Brad, she was at the luxurious office of Coach Lifestyle Solutions in downtown Nashville, sitting on a couch outside the office of the Vice President of Facilities. Brad was at her side. She had put a lot of time into her appearance in hopes of projecting a professional air that would be taken seriously by all the people she had to meet with today. She also did so on the off chance that she ran into Will, although Brad had assured her that Will had taken a complete leave of absence and would not be in the office again for some time.

She was relieved that he would not be there to hear her idea. She wanted it to go through without his approval or disapproval and succeed—or not—on its own merits. She wanted to honor his help and advice to her by implementing a plan that was practical, sustainable, and sound. And then she would use that to make a public apology to him for her role in the Save Wild Tennessee video. After much thought, she had realized that her words of love and apology would mean little; she had to prove them through her actions.

Brad was excited. "I think they're going to love this!" he said. Every sentence he spoke came with an implied exclamation point at the end. He reminded her of Jakob in that way, so she now found him endearing rather than irritating, as she had at the town council meeting so many weeks before.

The door opened and a man came out and introduced himself as Ed Washington. He was tall and thin, with deep black skin that showed off the whitened edges of the hair that framed his face. He seemed friendly enough, and Casey tried to feel at ease. As she entered, however, she was discomfited to see that Mandy the lawyer was seated in the office as well. Mandy didn't rise to greet Casey, but she put out her hand for a handshake and smiled noncommittally.

After a bit of small talk, Casey presented her idea to them. It was simple: the retirement home would have an animal shelter attached. Residents could move their pets into that shelter when they entered the facility, and there would be visiting areas where they could spend time with them, or areas on the property where they could take them for walks.

The shelter would also continue its mission of taking in animals that had no home or were losing their home, and residents could take part in the care for them. It would be therapeutic for someone suffering from illness or depression to bottle-feed kittens, help socialize new dogs, or walk animals in the woods. It would be good for the animals to have so many eager sets of hands to pet and brush them or give them snacks.

There would be a director on site who would manage the shelter and oversee resident interactions with the animals, and there would be staff members dedicated to the business of running the shelter itself. She proposed that Jakob be considered as director, as he had the experience and networks in the community to ensure that the venture succeeded. Not to mention it would give him the kind of professional position he sought in order to impress Katie, while still allowing him to work with animals.

The venture, Casey explained, would also provide a wonderful interface between the retirement home and the community, which she knew Coach Lifestyle Solutions highly valued. As she spoke, she shared articles she had presented with scientific findings that backed her claims about the

Chapter 12

therapeutic value of pets for the elderly and ill.

She finished, her face flaming. She felt it was a wonderful idea, and so did Brad. But the other two had their poker faces on as they listened.

After a few moments, Ed's face broke into a slow smile. "I like it," he said simply.

Mandy was not so supportive. "Yes, it's a great idea until a dog bites a resident, or another one gets cat scratch fever because she's bottle feeding a feral baby cat, or someone falls and breaks a hip because the dog he's walking runs too far, too fast. And then there are those people from all over the community coming into the home, seeing all the nice things, thinking about how they can come back and rob it. This is a highly problematic proposal. Well, it's not a proposal yet. It's still at the crazy idea stage."

Mandy flung her long hair back and smoothed down her blouse. "But that's not to say that we won't think more about it." She looked at Casey with a slight, close-lipped smile.

Casey felt a surge of happiness and satisfaction. They would think about it! Now they could take her crazy idea and figure out the details, look into insurance, design the setup. Casey could walk away from Will's territory, safely, without facing him, and leave everything in their hands. And hopefully this would lead to the continuation of a shelter in Pleasant Valley, a safe home for so many animals, a nice facility that could properly house them, and the happiness of women like Miss Peggy, who wouldn't have to leave their precious pets behind during one of the most vulnerable periods of their lives.

Ed asked, "Would you be willing to consult with us on design and basic needs for the animals, if it comes to that?"

Here Mandy intervened. "No way, Ed. We will go by industry standards through expert recommendations. Plus let's remember that Dr. Young here has been no friend to our little outfit." She stared at Casey with eyebrows raise, challenging her to deny the claim.

Casey blushed. "You're right. And that brings me to the second point I would like to discuss with you. My words about your little outfit were recorded before I knew you personally and then taken completely out of context."

Mandy grunted and then smirked at her. Ed smiled at Casey sympathetically.

"So," Casey continued, "I would like to make it right somehow. I thought that, if this idea proceeds, we could do some kind of press release about it, and I could make a statement about how Coach turned my problem into a solution and saved the lives of countless animals, and so forth and so on. And we could include in that statement that I'm an executive board member of Save Wild Tennessee, with me making a further statement about how we have to find ways to work with corporations rather than simply accuse them in the press. Will that do?"

Mandy shrugged and half nodded her head. "We'll see. Anyway, I think that's it for now, right, Ed?"

He walked toward Casey and extended his hand. "Yes, we'll work on this idea and let you know how it pans out. Thank you so much for your time."

She smiled at him and said, "Thank you, nice to meet you." She glanced over at Mandy, who simply gave her a brief, two-fingered wave.

Casey left the building in high spirits and drove over to her parents' house to join them for lunch. It felt indulgent to take another whole day away from the clinic and shelter, but it also felt good to do so. She wanted to savor the first feeling of accomplishment and celebration that she had experienced since Will had departed, and the feeling that she had done something *for* him, even if it was too late. And she wanted to attempt to share that accomplishment with her parents, in line with her newfound desire both to be herself and to accept them as they were.

Her father was now free to move about the house, so she found them both sitting at the kitchen table, waiting for her arrival. He was reading the newspaper, Casey noted, and Katherine was allowing it to happen.

They greeted her warmly, and Imogen brought out the food as Casey sat down: grilled chicken, wild rice, and salad with a bland dressing. Heart patient food, Casey thought with a laugh as she saw the dismayed look on her father's face.

They made their way through the usual pleasantries. Casey thought

Chapter 12

Katherine seemed a little wary, but her father engaged with her as he normally did.

"So what was your meeting in town about?" Charles finally asked.

"I went in to present a proposal to Will's company that they build an animal shelter into their new campus in Pleasant Valley."

Charles grunted. "Why would they want to do a thing like that?"

Casey ran through the list of benefits that she had just presented to Ed and Mandy.

Charles grunted again. "They're in the business of building retirement homes, not saving animals. In their shoes, I wouldn't even consider it."

"Well, I know it's easy to jump to that conclusion," Casey began, keeping her voice neutral. Actually, it was easy to keep it neutral. She was feeling so good about the meeting—and about her step toward being proactive about the shelter situation rather than waiting for things to happen—that even her father's disapproval could not bring her down. "But Will's always looking to brand his company as an option for people who want their lives to go on much as before. For example, they site their campuses in downtown areas so that people will feel that they still live in a community outside of the property itself. This proposal would make them unique: giving retirees a chance to keep access to their animals, even once they enter an assisted living situation. I think the idea might fly."

She took a bite of salad and glanced at her mother, who nodded at her and smiled gratefully. "That sounds like a good idea, dear," she replied.

Charles grunted again. "We'll see."

He took a bite of chicken and grimaced, no doubt at its flavorlessness. He must be missing the rich, spicy foods that he favored. "Who's going to run this shelter—you?" he asked Casey.

"No, but I am recommending that Jakob become the director. That's another benefit of this proposal for me. I will no longer be running a shelter, which means I can devote more time and attention to my business and other things." She smiled at him. Surely this would meet his approval; it was one of the changes he had suggested in their last argument.

"Now *that* I'd like to see," he said, but in a sarcastic rather than approving tone.

"Well, I think it shows good thinking on Casey's part, Charles," Katherine chimed in. "She's trying to take control of this shelter situation, which has been on her mind for quite some time, as you know."

Charles nodded, willing to concede to Katherine if not Casey. Normally Casey would pick at him, asking why he couldn't just support her rather than being so negative about her idea. But this new, more grown-up Casey again realized that she didn't much care what he thought about the proposal. She only cared what Ed and Mandy would think and whether or not they would allow the proposal to come to fruition. And, of course, she cared what Will would think one day when he heard about the proposal, whether he would understand that it was one way she hoped to apologize to him and thank him for all the support and guidance he had given her over the previous few weeks.

So, instead of getting upset as she might have in the past, Casey simply changed the subject. "I saw the Thompsons' house is for sale. Don't tell me they're planning to retire and move to Panama at last, after all these years of talking about it."

"Why, no," Katherine replied. "They've decided to move to Croatia instead! Apparently Croatia is the new Panama."

As Casey left her parents' house an hour later, she was smiling. She had made it through an entire hour of pleasant conversation with her parents. She still felt good about herself, and she felt better than she had in a while about her parents. Charles had even said, as she was getting ready to leave, "Keep us up to date on how your proposal works out." That was big progress for him, for their future relationship.

Maybe this growing up thing won't turn out to be so bad after all, Casey thought as she backed her car out of her parents' driveway and headed back to Pleasant Valley.

If only she could share her triumph with Will. She longed to sit on his couch again, sharing her thoughts while he listened and reached over occasionally to touch her hand or arm. And then she would listen to him, too, and finally hear those others things he had wanted to say to her.

Chapter 12

She banished the thoughts. There was no point in spinning daydreams about Will. She did wonder how he was faring in terms of his brother's situation, however. She knew the bare facts because she had been reading everything she could find online about the situation. The trial was set for the following Monday, and Will was working closely with his brother's lawyers.

Will's own fate still looked to be at risk, as the prosecutor had developed a theory of the crime that had Will taking advantage of his brother's criminal background to deflect the blame from himself. Casey hated to read these things because she knew how easy it was for a reputation to be ruined by such hints and theories in the press. She wondered how Will was handling it all.

As she was pulling into the driveway, her cell phone rang.

"I'll be at your house in two hours," Samantha said without even greeting her first. "You're going out for a night on the town with me and the girls."

"What are you talking about?" Casey asked.

"I shared the tale of your little screw-up with Jami and Jen, and we're taking you out tonight so you can forget your troubles."

"I love how you remind me that I screwed up and then pledge to help me forget it. Nice work, Sam."

Samantha quoted Walt Whitman: "Do I contradict myself? Very well, then, I contradict myself. I am large and contain multitudes."

"Wow, I'm impressed."

Samantha chuckled. "Dress slutty, and I'll see you in a couple of hours."

"I don't really—"

"Yeah, I know," Samantha interrupted in her harshest voice. "You have to feed the this and the that, and you're kind of down these days, and you'd rather wait and do it another time. Right?"

"Something like that." Casey sighed, realizing she was not going to be able to get out of this. She really didn't want to go out on the town and fake smile while her friends—well, two of them at least—drank too much and got stupid.

"But here's what you don't know," Samantha continued. "I've spent the last two weeks dealing with hand-foot-and-mouth disease. All five children, one by one. So I need this night out, even if you don't. If you three don't go out with me, I can't be held responsible for the kinds of poor choices I might make while looking for an alternative form of entertainment."

As always, Sam secured Casey's acquiescence by making her laugh.

"Whatever," Casey said, trying to sound sulky even though she was still giggling. "Just don't give me hand-foot-and-mouth disease."

"See you at 5:00," Sam said and hung up.

***

"No one gorgeous is going to fall in love with someone who is either wearing a lab coat or jeans and hiking boots all of her life," Jamila explained after they had all been seated as Lazlo's, a trendy new restaurant in Nashville's The District neighborhood.

Her three glamorous friends had been admiring the short length and plunging neckline of Casey's dress, which Samantha had forced her to change into upon arriving at her house. Casey had been dressed in what she thought was a nice pair of cropped black pants, a floral silk tank top, and black high heels. But Samantha had insisted: Casey needed something much sluttier than that. She needed to think of herself as on the prowl at one of the hottest new venues in Nashville, not as a cat-lady dressing up nice to go out to dinner with her aging friends. Samantha had anticipated Casey's sartorial preferences and brought along a selection of dresses from her own wardrobe.

"These are my 'I swear' dresses," she had explained. "As in 'I swear I will be able to fit into them again someday!'"

Now Casey scoffed at Jamila's comment. "What if I want to attract an animal lover and avid hiker?"

Jamila rolled her eyes. "Even *that* guy wants to see these"—she indicated Casey's boobs—"rather than the coat and boots."

Casey tried to change the subject. "How's Anton?"

Jamila proceeded to explain that Anton was always working, worrying about their future after she gave up her job, but very tender towards her and

Chapter 12

the growing baby. "He loves to keep his hand on my belly all the time in case the baby starts kicking."

"You still don't know the sex?" Jen asked.

"No. So much of this process has been *planned*, with all these schedules and shots and pregnancy tests at the clinic, that now we're enjoying as many surprises as possible." She rolled her eyes and added, "But my grandmother keeps saying she can tell by the way I'm carrying it that it's a boy."

Samantha laughed. "That's what my mother-in-law said about all three of my girls! Wishful thinking on that old bat's part, I guess." She sighed. "Oh, it feels good to be out and away from the kids for the night. They are monsters, all of them."

It was true. They were remarkably willful children. Samantha was of the contemporary mindset that mothers should never fuss at their children, and they walked all over her. She looked at the expressions on her friends' faces. "I know what you're thinking: I made them that way!" They all nodded. "But you'll see I was right when they turn out to be the most secure, mature, well-behaved children on earth."

Samantha sighed again. "In the meantime, I need alcohol." She signaled to the waiter to bring her a second mojito. Casey could foresee that she would be driving home that night, so she made a point to sip her own drink more slowly.

They laughed about motherhood, and Jamila and Samantha went back and forth about their different parenting philosophies. Just as in college, the two often bumped heads, but it was part of their friendship chemistry. As their argument went on, Jamila's accent got more Jamaican as she shared "Mama Mary's" parenting advice. And Samantha's voice got higher pitched and more hysterical as she dished out real world examples from her own experience that illustrated the potential limits of Mama Mary's wisdom. Jen and Casey just listened, laughed, and occasionally noted that one or the other had scored more points in the contest for who was right. Casey soaked it up, feeling as worry free as she had in months. Maybe it had been a good idea to come out tonight after all.

They decided to move on to one of their favorite dive bars from college, going from glam to down-to-earth as they spilled out of the cab and into the bar. There was live music, some low-key rock and folk by what appeared to be a college band. This was a place for beer rather than mojitos, but Casey opted for seltzer instead.

Jen shared with them her frustration with her job. She had always wanted to be an engineer and loved the work, but her manager and team were giving her trouble. "It's tough in a man's world," Jamila commiserated. "I'm sure they see your cute little blonde self and think you can't possibly know as much as they do."

"Actually, my manager is a woman," Jen said, and they mocked Jamila about her reliance on gender stereotypes.

"And you were the Women's Studies major?" Casey teased her.

"Minor only, my friend. And if her female manager is acting that way, it's because she has been forced by the patriarchy to behave like a man instead of in solidarity with her sister comrades." She smiled winningly. "Now aren't you impressed?"

That led to a long conversation about their struggles at work, how life hadn't turned out exactly as they'd hoped in terms of finding a calling, and whether or not they should try something else. As Jen and Samantha continued drinking, they got more and more maudlin.

"Of course, we can't all love our jobs as much as you do, Casey," Samantha said, "although I really do feel your pain lately."

"Yeah, me, too," Jen added. "I'm sorry about the shelter."

Casey shrugged. "I should have joined that sorority at Vanderbilt and then I'd have wealthy friends who could donate tons of money to my cause instead of you losers."

Jen shook her head. "Has Mama Katherine ever forgiven you yet for that?" she asked, referring to Katherine's insistence all four years that Casey join her own beloved sorority.

"No, she still brings it up a dozen times a year at least. At one of her recent fundraisers she introduced me to Carrie Ann Overton—remember her?"

"Homecoming queen, president of the sorority, perfect body, quarterback boyfriend, perfect body," Sam recited. "Did I say perfect body?" She looked

Chapter 12

down her own pudgy body and grimaced.

"Yep. After we met, Mother told me how much Carrie Ann's husband is worth and then said, 'That could have been you!'"

"Well, Carrie Ann was after the MRS degree, sorority or no sorority," Jamila said.

This led them to a conversation about parents and their expectations, money, and other serious subjects that had continued in their lives since college. They all came from upper middle-class backgrounds but had tried to go their own way in life, which had made a somewhat bumpy path for each of them. Jen's parents didn't think a woman should be an engineer. Jamila's parents thought she should be a wife and mother instead of a public defender. At least they were finally getting their wish! Samantha's parents had planned her marriage to a family friend since her birth and weren't thrilled with her choice of Charlie, who was a bit too much of a redneck for their tastes.

"Geez, this night has gotten sad!" Samantha cried out. "What's wrong with us? We're too late for a quarter-life crisis and too early for a mid-life crisis, so we'd better just get over it!" She suggested they get away from the slow-paced rock and take a cab back to the bar of the restaurant where they had started. "We'll be back with our cars there," she announced. "And there were lots of hot guys there. I say we don't go home until we've forced Casey to pick one of them up!"

Everyone but Casey agreed that was a fine plan, and back they went.

Their choice of prey had the misfortune of looking over at Casey one too many times during their first half hour back at the bar. He was a very good-looking man, and probably quite a bit younger than she was. Casey hoped her friends would forget about him and not do anything embarrassing.

Casey made the mistake of mentioning that she was still sad about Will and not in the mood to meet anyone else. It was a mistake because then they decided to berate her for the whole situation.

"Casey, you messed up," Jamila said. "You were too hard on him."

"Okay, wait a second," Casey began in an attempt to defend herself. "It was complicated!"

"This guy spent weeks feeding kittens he didn't want, doing research on grant opportunities, and spending every Saturday and sometimes Sunday volunteering at your shelter," Jen added. "And you ran him off? Please—you're an idiot."

"Doesn't he sound exactly like George, though? A little too good to be true?" Casey didn't believe those words even as she said them; she had no doubt now that Will's efforts had been sincere.

"Fair point," Jen chimed in, taking another sip of whatever fluorescent green drink she was quickly emptying.

Samantha shook her head. "I think you should call him and apologize, but I know you're too stubborn to do it. So time to move on." The others murmured their agreement.

"And by 'move on,' of course we mean meet a new guy," Jamila said. "And I think we have bachelor #1 sitting right over there." They all looked at the man, who noticed and smiled hesitantly.

Samantha rose from her seat.

"No, Sam, please, no," Casey begged. She stood up and put her hand on her friend's arm. "Not tonight."

Samantha saw the tears welling in Casey's eyes and smiled sympathetically. "On one condition," she said.

Casey looked at her in dismay. The condition was probably going to be even worse. "What?"

"That you go up and get us the next round of drinks," she said gently, patting Casey on the back.

Casey looked at her in surprise. "You're letting me off the hook that easily?"

"You had the same look on your face my kids have when it's time for a shot," Samantha complained. "Took the fun out of the whole thing."

Jen started chanting, "Drinks! Drinks! Drinks!", and then she and Samantha laughed uproariously. Casey and Jamila exchanged knowing looks before Casey began weaving her way through the crowd toward the bar.

While she was waiting to get the attention of one of the very busy bartenders, she looked around at the crowd. Everyone seemed so young

Chapter 12

and so happy. She, by contrast, felt old and unhappy. Somehow the day's achievements no longer felt so fantastic; instead it felt as if they had come way too late. She was old, unhappy, and bad at relationships, which suggested that she might remain unhappy for quite some time.

A movement a few feet away from her caught her eye, and she looked over to see Will trying to swallow the face of a tall, auburn-haired woman whose dress length barely covered her butt cheeks. As Casey watched, in shock, Will pulled the woman toward him and started to lead her out of the bar, patting her on the butt as he did so. It was clear enough why he was in such a hurry to get her somewhere else, presumably the apartment where he had so recently tried to swallow Casey's face.

Casey felt her face grow hot and the tears begin to roll down her cheeks. He was already involved with another woman! She wasn't surprised to find him with such a gorgeous one; she could easily imagine that woman as the dessert-avoidant kind Will had mentioned during their first date. But she hadn't thought he was the kind of guy to be in a bar like this, making out like that, with a woman like her, before leading her back to his apartment.

Was this a sign of his current state of mind? Had the trial and public doubts about his ethics made him go off the deep end, behave recklessly, return to some of the wilder days of the past? That was hard to reconcile with the hardworking, church-attending, Daisy-adopting, thriller-reading, cheesecake-joking businessman persona that he had presented to her. But then again, she reminded herself, she did not really know him all that well. A couple of deep conversations and a long car ride or two should not give her the false sense that she knew his character and could predict his behavior.

In any case, the situation made clear that he was over whatever they had once shared. She had known this already, but seeing it in action broke her heart completely.

The bartender looked at her face and smiled kindly before taking her card. "Don't worry, I'll bring the drinks," he said, gesturing to her to return to her table and friends.

She returned and told them what she had seen, and then the night's theme changed to Will-bashing as the bartender approached with their drinks.

"He's the idiot!" Jen declared.

"Who needs him?" Jamila added.

"I never did think he was good enough for you," Samantha finished up, hiccupping. She started looking around again for Bachelor #1, but fortunately for Casey he and his friends appeared to have left the bar.

Casey could only take a few minutes of talking about Will before she started to feel desperate to return home. Fortunately, the other three understood, and a few minutes later they were parting ways. Samantha immediately passed out once she was tucked into the passenger seat of her own SUV, and Casey drove home in silence, replaying her whole short relationship with Will over and over again in her mind. She came to the heartbreaking conclusion that she couldn't have meant all that much to him if he was able to get over her so thoroughly and so quickly.

"Well, Meow, looks like it's just you and me for the long haul," Casey said as she turned out the lamp beside her bed that night and the cat took his usual position along the length of her chest. She had worn a t-shirt that said "Cat Lady By Choice" to bed, hyper aware of the complete and utter lack of irony in those words. Meow purred into her as Casey willed herself to stop crying and fall asleep.

Chapter 13

Today was the day: the shelter was to close.

Casey felt proud in a way: they had miraculously found homes for all but three of the animals: the old dog Buddy, the old cat Randall, and the African Grey parrot Jackie. She was reconciled to the probability of keeping all of them herself. Jackie the parrot could be the practice's mascot and then come home with Casey on weekends, and she could make room for the dog and cat in her rambling house and yard. Good thing Meow was so easygoing. She hoped Buddy and Randall would be, too. The situation wasn't ideal for any of them, but it was the best option, and she felt certain they could make it work.

Otherwise, she felt sad. The building would be demolished the following week and thus would end an important chapter in her life. She tried to remember that the end of one chapter meant the beginning of another, but it was hard not to focus on regretting the past and all the steps and decisions that had led to this moment.

She turned to Jakob and forced herself to smile. "Thanks for being here with me for this."

He put his arm around her shoulders and smiled at her comfortingly. "It's how it had to be, Doc. But don't worry: you'll open another shelter again someday soon. And I'll be your most favoritest volunteer."

Casey hadn't told him about her proposal to Coach nor her idea that Jakob be the shelter's first director. She hadn't wanted to get his hopes up or do anything to mess up his opportunity to work at his cousin's HVAC business.

"I certainly hope so." She pulled back and tried to assume a brisk and businesslike air. "All right, that's it for the day. See you Saturday night?"

"You bet. We'll be there with bells on. Katie said she's looking forward to a meal that someone besides me cooks."

Casey laughed. "Well, it's nice to hear you're trying. But I do plan on putting you to shame. I'm making my specialty: mushroom risotto. After all, this is your goodbye dinner. It has to be a good one."

Jakob looked at her in horror. "You didn't pick the mushrooms yourself, did you?" Her mind flashed back to his refusal, a couple of years earlier, to sample some of the morel mushrooms she had found growing in the woods behind her house. "Then it really might be my goodbye dinner!"

"I guess you'll have to find out the hard way, won't you?" she said.

***

For the next few days, Casey checked the internet daily to read the latest on Will's brother's trial. Finally, the following Thursday, it was over. Tom Ray had been found guilty of multiple counts of fraud and embezzlement and sentenced to 18 years in prison.

"In a surprising twist," the article read, "although Ingalls testified against his brother, he was called by the defense to give a statement in the sentencing phase requesting that Ray be granted leniency in where and how long he was incarcerated. Ingalls cited a long history of mental health issues and called for Ray to be taken to a facility where he could receive adequate treatment. In his sentencing decision, however, Judge Keaton discounted those concerns."

Casey marveled at Will's desire to help a brother who had taken advantage of him in criminal ways. She thought back to the boy who had had to choose between himself and his brother, at Coach Ingalls' insistence, and who had no doubt lived with the guilt of that choice ever since. And now he must also suffer the guilt of having testified against his brother. Despite her hurt that Will had moved on so quickly with another woman, her heart was full

Chapter 13

of pity for him.

A few paragraphs down, she read, "Prosecutors have ruled out pressing criminal charges against Ingalls as well, citing new evidence that Ray lied about his brother's involvement in the fraud and embezzlement schemes. Ingalls, a well-respected member of the business and philanthropy community, has made no public comment. His lawyer released a statement on his behalf, however, claiming certainty of his own innocence and faith in the justice system's ability to distinguish between fact and fiction. The statement included no comment on his brother's conviction or sentencing."

Casey gasped in relief: Will would not have to worry about a trial. There had been so little mention in the press of his potential involvement, and such a focus on Tom's evil past and how he had taken advantage of Will's kindness, that hopefully the gossipmongers would not wag their tongues with claims of Will's dishonesty and guilt. She hoped in some small way that her own statement, which she had prepared carefully and submitted to Mandy's office in case the proposal was approved, would help clear up any confusion about other accusations against his ethics and character.

After she treated her last patient in the clinic the following evening, her heart was so heavy with worry and sadness and a longing to see Will that she made a crazy decision: to hop in her car and go see him. A few minutes later, she was flying down the interstate into Nashville. Fortunately, she was going against the end-of-the-workday traffic, which was slowed down for miles.

As she drove, she tried to figure out what she would say, but her thoughts were too jumbled.

Pulling into a guest parking spot outside his apartment building, she decided that she would simply say, "Will, I'm sorry!" and take it from there. She accepted the possibility that he would end the conversation there and tell her to get lost, not wishing to hear any more from her. If he let her continue, she would proceed through all of her regrets. Hopefully her spontaneity would underline her sincerity.

She entered the building and was greeted by the doorman.

"Hello! Will Ingalls, please."

He frowned. "He came home from the office and then left again, just a couple of hours ago. I don't believe he's returned, but I'll buzz him."

The man called Will but received no answer. "It appears he is not home."

"Do you have any idea when he'll return? Should I wait?"

"I'm sorry; I have no idea what to tell you."

"Thanks."

Casey returned to her car and sat for a few minutes. It seemed ridiculous to wait when he might not be home for hours. What if he had returned to the office to catch up on work and ended up staying late? What if he had gone out for another date with the supermodel and stayed out all night or, worse, returned with her and made Casey watch them enter the building together? But then again, what if she left and he had just run out to buy some groceries?

After a while, she decided to leave. It had been weeks since she had seen or talked to him. What was the hurry now? She would return home, call and leave a message with a few words of apology, and then explain more if he ever called her back. Then that would be the end of it.

Now she was caught in the backed-up traffic, and her slow progress made her feel even more defeated. She realized she was getting tired and hungry and needed a break, so she pulled off at the next exit to find a gas station, use the restroom, and get a coffee and snack.

As she returned to her car afterward, she couldn't believe her eyes: Will was leaning against the driver's door, smiling at her mischievously. "I just went to Pleasant Valley to see you, and here you are!"

"What? Seriously?"

"Yes, seriously."

"I just went to Nashville to see you, and here *you* are!" Casey replied, amazed.

"What?"

"Seriously!"

On impulse, she lunged toward him, wanting desperately to hug him. He opened his arms wide, and she fit snugly against his body. His arms pulled her into him for a few moments, and she took in the smell and feel of his body

Chapter 13

that she had missed so much over the past few weeks. His hand caressed her hair, and he kissed her on top of her head. Then he gently nudged her away from him and looked down at her.

"I've missed you," he said, stroking her cheek with his thumb.

All of a sudden, an image of him in the bar with his lips all over the hot red-head flashed through Casey's mind. "Well, you seemed to be doing just fine without me the other night!"

He looked confused. "What are you talking about?"

"I saw you in the bar last weekend with your face and hands all over that, that ... floozy!"

He barked out another one of his trademark guffaws. "Did you just use the word 'floozy'?"

She glared at him.

"And you were at a *bar*?" he continued, still laughing.

Casey could not imagine what was so amusing.

"And now you're mad?" He laughed triumphantly and then hugged her again. "You know, you've given yourself away now. You can't pretend that you don't like me just a little bit when you're so obviously jealous."

Casey pulled back again and put her hands on her hips. "This has nothing to do with being jealous or mad. I simply pointed out an inaccuracy: it can't be true that you missed me when you were finding other entertainment just fine."

He laughed again. "Okay, but let me remind you of one pertinent fact here: I have an identical twin brother who was in town but out on bail for the last couple of weeks and who *loves* to go to bars and get handsy with floozies!"

Embarrassment washed over Casey, and she felt her own trademark blush moving into her face. "You never told me he was your identical twin," she said meekly.

He nodded and looked intently at her, still smiling. "You were jealous!" he teased.

"A little bit," she admitted, smiling.

"Well, then, why did you bother to come see me today?" he asked more seriously.

She swallowed, as her temporary embarrassment turned to much deeper shame. Now she had to find the words she had been unable to find for the last hour or so.

"I was coming to apologize to you—well, really, to make several apologies to you. And to tell you that, no matter what the media said or no matter what that stupid Save Wild Tennessee video implied, I think you're a good, kind, honest man who has never done anything but try to be my friend and support me." She felt tears prick her eyes.

There, that wasn't bad, she thought. There was so much more to explain, but she had covered the basics.

There was tenderness in his eyes as he continued to gaze at her. "I appreciate that. But you said one thing wrong: I never wanted to be your friend."

He sighed heavily as he looked around the parking lot. "Let's get out of here. There's so much to talk about." He reached down and grabbed her hand, squeezing it gently. "We're closer to my place. Would it be okay to go back there?"

She nodded.

"I still have to get gas." He pointed to his car at the pump. "I just saw your car and came right over to wait for you."

She had so many questions, including why he had gone to Pleasant Valley. But they could wait. She knew he would have a lot of questions, too. She let the fact that he was happy to see her sink in. It wasn't over between them after all. There was still a chance that all could be made right, that she could find out whether he still loved her and show him that she loved him, too.

"I'll just meet you there," she said and got in her car.

The doorman smiled at her quizzically when she reentered the building with Will right behind her. "Ah, you found him."

"Hi, Larry," Will said. "Have a good evening."

They took the elevator up and entered his apartment, which had the same unlived-in look that she remembered.

"Would you like something to drink?" he asked.

"Just some water, I guess."

Chapter 13

"There is nothing here to eat; it's even worse than usual. Should I order a pizza or something?"

"I'm really not hungry," Casey said. "There's so much I want to say to you."

He smiled and nodded. "Okay, talk first, eat later. I'll get your water."

He met her in the living room with a glass of water and a beer for himself, and they sat down.

"So you came here to see me?" he asked.

She nodded.

"To apologize?"

"I've been sitting on it because I saw in the papers that you were caught up in the trial, and I didn't want to disturb you. But then I read last night that it was all over, and I kept thinking about it today, and I just felt I would burst if I didn't come over and say what was on my mind."

"Even though you might have caught me at home with the floozy?" he asked, grinning.

"Even if. I mean, you deserved that apology no matter what." She couldn't help adding, "But I'm really glad I didn't catch you at home with the floozy."

"Well, I accept your apology. I have to say I was really mad at you when I saw that video, but Mandy explained everything to me today, and I understand. But you seem to keep thinking I'm a bad guy," he said. "I don't get it! All that stuff about how I treat you like a child and force my way onto you. I really can't understand it, Casey." He looked at her. "I try, but I can't understand it."

She didn't realize she was cracking her knuckles until he looked down at her hands in surprise. She giggled. "Guess I'm a little nervous."

He reached over and held her hand.

"Yes, that's another apology for me to make," she said. "Remember how I told you I had daddy issues? Well, guess what? It turns out I really do have daddy issues."

She laughed and was relieved when he laughed in return.

"Every time you said something about helping me, I heard his voice. The last time I spoke with you, we had just had a huge fight, and I kept hearing him instead of you as you talked to me. I've been taking all of that out on you from the moment that I found out about the deal you made with Mr. Ramsey, and it wasn't fair. I'm really sorry, Will. No wonder you gave up on me."

"Hmmm," he said. "Daddy issues. Well, you did warn me."

"Yes, that's true! So it's all your fault, really. I withdraw my apology."

He laughed. "Fair enough." He jumped up. "I really am hungry. I'm ordering a pizza. And then we have to talk business."

While he went to grab his phone and make a call, Casey stood to look out the window over the view of the river and downtown. Another beautiful sunset was in the making, which lit up the city in spectacular color.

Will returned and stood beside her. "One of the proposals that went up through the channels while I was away and was waiting for my final approval this morning was this." He handed her a binder about two inches thick with papers. "Pleasant Valley Campus: Final Plan Draft II" it read on the cover.

"Okay. What about it?"

"Turn to the marked page."

She did. It took her a moment for the import of what she was seeing to register. This was a description of the animal shelter that would be attached to the facility—her idea brought to life in images and words!

"What does this mean?" she asked. "Are you going ahead with this plan?"

"Of course we are," he said. "It's brilliant. Absolutely brilliant. We'll have the facility there, residents can participate in the care of the animals, residents can keep their own pets there and visit them, and the pets that don't belong to residents can be adopted out. It benefits everyone."

She actually jumped up and down for a second, feeling months of worry wash out of her body and be replaced with pure joy. "And you approved it?"

"Kind of. It was in the stack of things that were basically approved while I was gone. I just had veto power. Everyone knew I would like this idea so they went ahead with it. My only problem with it is that I didn't think of it myself." He grinned again. "So how did this happen? How did you come up with the idea?"

She explained about Miss Peggy, her words tumbling out in her excitement. Will watched her in amusement.

Chapter 13

"It's still not a perfect solution," Casey said. "They won't be living with her in her room, and they'll have to be around other animals all the time. But she'll get to spend a lot of time with them, and they'll have time with other people as well. So it's a good second choice."

He nodded, and she decided to throw him a bone. "Also, it's practical. It's realistic. It's sustainable. It's good business."

"That's why I'm disappointed in myself for not thinking of it." He took the binder, put it down on a table, and then put his arms around her waist and drew her close. "Really, it's a good plan. And it will be an excellent selling point."

"Business is business, right?" she teased.

"Exactly." He kissed the tip of her nose and looked at her with those deep, rich, warm eyes. She felt they were the kindest eyes on earth, but she also liked that they could burn with desire for her, as they did now.

"That was part of the apology, you know. I wanted to show you that I understood the things you have been trying to tell me over the last few weeks, and that I could act on those things for myself. Thank you for approving the idea."

"You really have nothing to thank me for. You came up with a good idea and sold it to the right people. I haven't done anything. You didn't need my 'help' with this one." He smiled gently.

"Good. I wanted this to work as a good business idea, not as a favor you or anyone else did for me. It really does feel more sustainable."

"We can make this a model for future projects."

"It will be good for your brand."

He laughed. "Thank you for putting so much thought into these apologies. They are all accepted." He kissed the tip of her nose again. "And I think everything has been in service of a good end: we know each other better now."

She took a deep breath and decided to tell him the one last thing she still had to tell him.

"There's one thing about me you still don't know, Will. And it's another thing that I'm truly sorry I didn't tell you before."

"Uh oh, you sound serious," he said, looking sideways at her, concerned.

"I *am* serious. It's that I love you."

His eyes searched hers, as if he wasn't quite sure he believed her. They asked questions: really? for how long? what does this mean?

She decided to go for it. She reached up and grabbed the back of his head with her hand and pulled him toward her for a kiss. "I love you," she said again and then kissed him again. "I've loved you since the first moment I met you. What I regret is that it took me so long to see it."

He kissed her back, gently, as if amazed. He pulled her back and looked at her with so much love it overwhelmed her. She felt the tears come into her eyes.

"God, it's good to hear you say that," he said at last. "I love you, too, Casey."

Her cheeks grew hot, but in a good way this time, the result of having the man of her dreams tell her he loved her and then look at her with such certainty, such a sense of possession.

"There's one more thing to show you." He picked up the binder from the table and said, "Look at the next marked section in the binder."

She did so and examined the text and some of the photos for a few moments. The updated design called for keeping the vast majority of the woodlot and building a nature trail through it. It would be a wheelchair-accessible plank path with side rails and places to stop, sit, and look out into the woods. There would be interpretive signs that explained some of the wildlife to be found there. The next section explained the addition of a 20-acre pollinator and grassland bird meadow with native grasses and perennials, also with a well-built path for nature watching. These would not be pristine natural places by any means, with humans still having access to the interiors of these little ecosystems. But they represented a wonderful compromise, far beyond her wildest hopes for the property.

She looked up at him in wonder, and he said, "I have things to apologize for, too."

"Well, apology accepted! This is amazing."

"No, what's amazing is that I've taught you to think like a greedy real estate developer, and you've turned me into a nature freak."

Chapter 13

He bent down and placed his lips on hers tentatively. Then he looked her in the eyes again as if searching for something. He seemed to find it, and then he began to kiss her again and again, each kiss deepening in its passion and in its insistence. She dropped the binder and ran her arms up his back, tasting his mouth with her tongue. He ran his tongue across her bottom lip and then began planting a trail of kisses down her neck as his hands explored more of her body. She pulled herself even tighter against the length of his body, wishing she could merge with him. This was the kind of love she had dreamed of, that she had desperately hoped existed out there, somewhere, for her.

"I really thought you had given up on me," Casey said much later in the evening. They were on the couch and had continued talking—and sometimes kissing—well into the night. They had talked about their weeks together, his business, her clinic, Casey's daddy issues, and the events that had led to Tom's trial and sentencing.

"No, I just needed to go off and sulk for a while and then deal with my brother's trial. I was going to come back. I told you: I like to win."

"Well, guess what?" she teased. "You did. You outcompeted all the nonexistent men in Pleasant Valley who were vying for my hand."

"Wow," he said, the mock-arrogant look that she had liked so much back on his face once again. "I amaze even myself!"

Epilogue

Fourteen months later, they were standing on the front lawn of the Pleasant Valley Retirement Home and Assisted Living campus, having just cut the ribbon and posed for their picture in the local paper, surrounded by town council members, Chamber of Commerce employees, and Jakob, the new shelter director, with his wife Katie. It was a beautiful place, especially because of its natural setting, in Casey's opinion. It was fall now, and the leaf color in the woodlot was particularly spectacular. There wasn't much to the meadow just yet, but the grass and flower seeds had been sown, and next spring it would begin to grow into a wondrous display of life and color.

Now Will pulled her off to the side so they could survey the property together, his arm resting lightly across her back. "Happy with it?" he asked.

"Yep," she replied.

They stood there in silence, and she thought of all that had happened over the last months.

One of Will's first projects had been to "help" repair Casey's relationship with her father. On their first Saturday night date as a new couple, she was telling him a bit more about her relationship with her parents and some of the lessons she had been learning over the previous few weeks.

"What do you think they're doing right now?" he asked.

"Probably eating dinner, getting ready to watch a movie. If I were there

Epilogue

for the night, we'd play some cards."

"I love cards! Let's go visit them."

"What?" She looked at him in surprise.

"Let's go visit them. Right now."

"Why would we do that?"

"Let's get the ball rolling on your new relationship with your father. Tell him about all these new things: me, the acceptance of your proposal to build a shelter within the retirement home. Give him a chance to be part of it all."

Casey suddenly remembered that Will was operating from a very different perspective from hers: that of someone who knew what it was like not to have a family. You have one, he seemed to be telling Casey; let's not take it for granted.

So that's what they had done. She would never forget the look on her mother's face when Casey walked in and introduced Will as her boyfriend. Katherine had spent the entire night looking over to make sure Will was still there and not just a dream. Charles had had to be discouraged from talking nothing but shop with such a well-known, up-and-coming real estate magnate, seemingly certain that he was in the presence of a man after his own heart.

They had chatted for a while over decaf coffee and low-fat lemon pound cake, then played hearts well into the night. Casey told her parents of the retirement home shelter, and Will joined her in answering their questions and convincing Charles that it was a viable business idea.

"Maybe the two of you could convince me to try a few new things over at CY Properties," Charles finally said. "If Katherine ever lets me go back to work there, that is," he added gruffly.

Casey felt the old resentment rising. Of course, Charles would only take her ideas seriously when they had been legitimized by Will's acceptance. She was opening her mouth with a sharp response when she caught a warning look from her mother out of the corner of her eye. Instead she smiled and said, "That would be great, Dad."

Will winked at her from across the table.

Months later, it had been a very different conversation when they showed up so that Will could make the old-fashioned request of their permission to marry Casey. That part of the conversation had been easy and full of joy. But then Casey had informed her parents that they wanted a small wedding, just the four of them, at a small mountain cabin near Pleasant Valley.

Katherine had been dismayed. "You cannot ask me to have a small, out of the way wedding for my only daughter." Casey had looked at her significantly and then later told her mother in private that she didn't want Will, who had no family, overwhelmed by a wedding with Casey's large extended family in attendance and hundreds upon hundreds of family "friends" to boot. Katherine graciously accepted that explanation in exchange for Casey's promise that she could throw the party of the year afterward to formally present her new son-in-law to their social world.

Casey wanted neither a big wedding nor a big party, but it was a good compromise, her way of acknowledging her parents' needs as well as her own. In that moment, she truly felt that her relationship with her parents was growing into something new and better.

The party was fun. Jamila and Samantha were in attendance with their husbands and kids, Jamila obviously in love with their new baby. Jen was alone, but Casey noted with interest that she was often in deep conversation with Dr. Henry Carruthers, whose relationship with Ashley had just come to an end. Her friends had already met Will and approved wholeheartedly, but only after they were informed it was Will's twin brother who was making out with that woman at Lazlo's. They insisted on dancing with him again and again, or forcing him to dance with Samantha's little daughters, and Casey had never seen him loosen up and have so much fun.

The other special guests were Coach Ingalls' sons, Will's adopted brothers. They hadn't grown up together, and they weren't close by any means, but the two men had nevertheless made the effort to attend in order to show their support of Will and his new life. Casey liked them immediately and hoped that they might play more of a role in Will's life in the future. After all, they were the only people in the world who could share Will's memories of Coach Ingalls, and that might be enough to produce a lifelong bond. She said something about getting together the following Christmas, and they seemed to like the idea, too.

As for Tom, Will had written to tell him of the marriage but not heard anything back, and he seemed reconciled to the possibility that his brother might have cut himself off from Will entirely. Casey didn't know if she hoped that Tom would come into Will's life again or stay away forever—she wasn't sure which would be best for Will—but she knew they would handle whatever happened together.

Now they were married, with Will settled into her house in the country. They had Meow, Daisy, and the old cat Randall, Barney the German Shepherd, Buddy the old mutt, and Jackie the African Grey parrot living with them.

"I never thought I'd be a guy with three cats," Will said one day, shaking his head. "What's next? A bunny rabbit? A bedroom full of guinea pigs? One of those little fluffy dogs that I carry around with me in a pink purse?"

"Or a chicken coop in the living room?" Casey suggested.

He rolled his eyes. "You could probably even talk me into that."

She knew he was happy, though. He had gone from a lonely existence to a house full of animals and love. And just one month before, they had discovered Casey was pregnant. He had the family he had always wanted, and he expressed his amazement and gratitude to Casey on just about a daily basis. She never tired of hearing it since she was feeling pretty amazed and grateful, too.

Announcing the pregnancy had turned Charles and Katherine to one of their favorite refrains: the possibility that Will would join Charles's company and allow Charles to step back into semi-retirement. Charles always called the venture "Charles Young and Son," to which Will would reply, "William Ingalls and Father." When they told her parents that she was pregnant, Charles immediately said, "Charles Young and *Sons*."

Casey wasn't sure what would come of this conversation, especially since Will was showing more of an interest in green building and permaculture, which she doubted would meld well with Charles's vision. Casey had found a new direction for herself and Sallie within Save Wild Tennessee: working closely and cooperatively with developers to help them see how they could meet their goals in a more environmentally sustainable way. She had an appointment with her father and some of his executives the following week. Casey laughed to think they were closer to "Charles Young and Daughter" than they had ever been before.

Casey's thoughts returned to the scene before her: the retirement home, the natural setting, her wonderful husband at her side. She put her arm around his back and shifted her position so that Will was facing her. She still enjoyed drinking in the sight of him, although she decided she would have to convince him to grow his hair out a little longer again. He was much too clean cut now, and not nearly as dangerous looking.

"You know, this is the beginning of a beautiful partnership," he said, lifting his hand to indicate the facility. "We can do this again and again and again, all over this great nation of ours."

She said, "Just think of all the money we can make!" at the same time that he said, "Just think of all the animals we can save!" They looked at each other and burst into laughter, thinking of all that they had come through and all the happy times ahead

Please review this book on Amazon! That way other readers can find it as well. And keep reading to find out more about my other books and how we can stay in touch.

Thank you! - Eliza Harwell

About the Author

Eliza Harwell is a romance reader turned romance author. She's an Arkansas girl who lives in Maryland with her husband, her garden, and not nearly enough pets. Eliza grew up reading Jane Austen, Victoria Holt, and Nora Roberts, and has since explored all sub-genres of romantic fiction. She likes to write about smart women and challenging men who come together and—spoiler alert!—find true love despite their differences. She also likes to keep her writing sweet. After all, romance is exciting enough!

Please follow her on her website, www.elizaharwell.com, where you can sign up for her monthly newsletter, free downloads (including an excerpt from her current work in progress), and lots of extra insights into her books and characters.

Also by Eliza Harwell

Read more books in the Bridging Divides Series: A smart woman. A challenging man. Different worldviews. Can they find a way to bridge the divide?

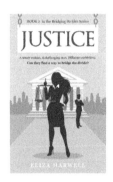

Justice (Book 2 in the Bridging Divides Series)
Tori Quinlan is a prosecutor who takes the pursuit of justice personally. When her former boss and lover Sam Stone comes back to town in hopes of overturning one of her most satisfying convictions, Tori's whole world starts to fall apart. She vows to fight Sam in the courtroom, but can she fight him in her heart?

Land (Book 3 in the Bridging Divides Series)
Abby Smith has a new job as landman for Far West Energy Company. When landowner T.T. Baldwin invites her to spend a week on his ranch, she jumps at the opportunity to convince him and his family to let her acquire their mineral rights. But first she must outcompete her rival, handsome Ty Pennington, and navigate the hostility of Billy Baldwin, T.T.'s nephew and heir apparent. Can she win her first lease without losing her heart? (Coming September 2020.)

Made in the USA
Monee, IL
10 September 2020